The Dragon Knight's Curse

By D.C. Clemens

Table of Contents

Chapter One

I regained consciousness long enough to see the fuzzy stone of the basement ceiling before passing out again. There were flashes of outer awareness afterwards, but my sight could never pierce beyond the darkness my shut eyelids created. The only images I experienced were colorful hallucinations with no rhyme or reason, except perhaps some ghoulish reformations of Clarissa's face. Within these brief bouts of perceptiveness was the upsetting notion that my insides were baking and that the remote voices I heard were responsible for the cooking. This internal roasting forced out every drop of water from inside me, which soaked every inch of my shivering body…

A calmness permeated me the next time I recovered the strength to lift my leaden eyelids, both within and without. My naked body, still moist from fresh sweat, was under a thick wool blanket. My skin itched, but I didn't move to relieve myself. For a while, all I did was fill my lungs with cool air and stare dumbly at the ceiling. Then, like an innocuous solar eclipse, Marcela's inverted head entered my field of view, her black hair prickling my forehead.

"Finally awake, eh? Can you talk?"

I tried speaking, but I coughed instead, convincing her to remove her face. When I finished expelling the buildup of dried drool in my throat, I tried to sit up, but a jarring pain quivered the left side of my chest. I winced and let my body settle back on the bed.

"Whoa there," said Marcela. "Rathmore says moving would be bad for you right now."

"Where is Doctor Obvious?" I asked with a sore voice.

"He and Clarissa went out hunting. He's interested in seeing her feed or something."

"How long was I out?"

"Uhhh, six or seven days? I don't know *exactly* how long. Time is hard to keep down here, and Clarissa and I weren't around at first. Oh! Wait here!" Her bare feet scuttled off somewhere before the scurrying girl returned a moment later. She suspended a small vial filled with a greenish liquid over my head. "Rathmore says to give you this in case you woke up. You're supposed to drink it all up."

"What is it?"

"A bunch of plants put together. Let's see, glemlock, sprite root, black wh-"

"Okay. 'Health potion' would've sufficed."

"Geez, you would think you'd be less grumpy after surviving death."

"Was I that sick?"

"I meant from the fight with Vey and the other guy. By the way, thanks for killing her."

"It had to be done, nothing more."

"Yeah, whatever. I'm glad she's dead. Here, take your medicine." The fourteen year old placed the unexpectedly cold vial in my right hand. "Drink every drop. It tastes like your swallowing pee, but it always makes me feel better."

I uncorked the container and dumped the entirety of its contents down my throat. Despite her proclamation, I actually enjoyed the spicy flavor and wished I hadn't consumed it so quickly.

She giggled. "Did you know I saw your thingy? It was kinda cute, but Ghevont says they get bigger. Is that true?"

"Ask again in a few years. Where's Ara-, I mean, where's my sword?"

"Ara? Does your sword have a name? Or were you thinking of something else?"

"Where is it?"

2

"Under the bed."

"Can you hand it over?"

"Uhh, no."

"Why not?"

"It's too scary."

I sighed. "You tried handling it? Didn't Clarissa tell you not to touch it?"

"Maybe, but I just wanted to see it. How can you hold that thing?"

"We have an arrangement."

"Why can Clarissa hold it?"

"I trust her. You can handle it this time if the instant you touch it you say, 'Mercer wants you.'"

"Um, okay."

The girl crouched to act on the request. She yelled the words at the sword. A second later and the metal hilt clanked against the stone as she dragged it. She lugged up the weapon and laid it next to me. Aranath's warm energy flowed back into me when my fingers clasped the leather encased scabbard.

From inside my head, the dragon said, "I see your strength is returning. I'll make certain not to remove your corruption so abruptly if you suffer a wound as deep as the one you've received. Its natural healing power should lessen the resulting misery. Regardless, I have a clearer idea of how to employ your corruption during combat should the need arise in the future. Still, I can sense your prana has recuperated. It won't be long before you can move around again."

Aranath's diagnosis didn't differ from Ghevont's, who returned with the vampire half an hour later.

Clarissa gave me a cup of water and sat on a chair next to my bed, to which Marcela said, "She's been watching over you since we came back here. I

3

hope you appreciate her, Mercer, because we had lots of time to talk and it doesn't sound to me like you do."

"I said nothing of the kind, Marcela! Don't heed her, Mercer."

"I've yet to. Ghevont, what were you saying?"

The scholar fumbled with an empty potion vial. "Oh, yes. Combined with your corruption, my singular concoction should aid your recovery nicely. I suspect you'll be out and about within three days, though you certainly shouldn't lift anything heavy with your left arm for at least another week."

"So I'll be able to travel in a week?"

"Travel? I recommend two weeks of recovery time before going anywhere."

"Do we *have* to go anywhere at all?" asked Marcela.

"*You* can stay right here," I replied.

"If Rathmore's going, I have to go, too."

"First of all, no you don't. Secondly, I haven't even agreed to bring Ghevont with me."

"But you must," said Ghevont.

"Well then, that settles everything."

"Oh, good. I was expecting more of a discussion."

"Ever heard of sarcasm, scholar?"

After a quick rumination, he said, "That's what that was? Ahh, that makes more sense."

"We'll talk about this later. Someone just get me more water."

'Later' came after two more days of rest and thinking. During that time, Aranath released a dash of my corruption every so often, using its soul-defiling power to aid my physical body's recovery. In spite of Ghevont's healing potions and my corruption, I knew the five inch long gash running down my chest would leave a scar for life, however long that ended up being. Once I became accustomed to the irritating sting that spawned every time a muscle in my chest contracted or extended itself, I was able to get out of bed and stretch my legs. Feeling sick while remaining stationary reminded me too much of my first memories, so getting up and moving around even a little helped my mental state immensely.

As I ate a steaming bowl of watery vegetable soup, I saw the girls climbing out of the basement to gather more food from the little garden near the little lake. This gave me the opening I wanted. I called Ghevont over, who was, as usual, looking over some tome. He rambled over with the book still in hand and sat down on the chair Clarissa normally occupied.

"What is it, Mercer? Ah, you have a gleam of seriousness in your expression."

"Do I ever not have it?"

"Well, I suppose it would be more precise to say your aura of seriousness has grown. What do you need of me?"

"You still wish to join me, yes?"

"Recent events have compelled me to seek out truths beyond what I can find in my hovel here. I'm also very intrigued to see how you progress as a-"

"Ghevont."

"Oh, you wanted a shorter answer, didn't you? Yes, I would like to join you."

"Then I need you to look for the map's location."

"The map of the god's grave?"

"Yes. If we can find its grave, then we'll find more of these Advent cultists. Whatever book or scroll your father used to find the map must still be here or in one of your other hideouts. I doubt he took it with him when he left the forest."

"Yes, that's probably true. Actually, ever since learning what father was after, I've been linking some threads on that front already. Since you

5

appear well enough, I would like to go to the other hideaways and gather the volumes I believe will benefit in the search. Are you planning on looking for my sister's assistant as well?"

"What you find will determine the order of my other goals, but my first aim will remain the same. I would like you to take me to Gwen Prothoro."

"Why is that? I told you, she was a simple woman whose only gift was looking attractive to Riskel. I'm sure by now that beauty has faded considerably."

"Yet your father trusted her to watch over his children when he left north. It occurs to me that he might have trusted her with more than that, even if she didn't know it."

Ghevont thought things over before saying, "A possibility we can't ignore. At any rate, it will be pleasant to see her again… if she's alive."

"Do you think she'll do you a favor and watch over Marcela?"

"Oh my, I don't think Marcela will enjoy that very much."

"What she would enjoy is not my concern. I can live with you tagging along, but gods help me if I have to worry about a child getting involved in my business, a business that will see her dead if she stays with us. You've seen a hint of our enemy, I can't imagine you'd be fine with her joining us."

"No, I suppose I wouldn't, but she'll put up a splendid fight."

"If I have to, I'll get you to place a deep sleeping spell on her so we could make our getaway."

"That seems harsh, no?"

"Says someone who takes corpses from their resting place, but I doubt it'll get to that point. I'll talk to Clarissa about what to do with the girl. Spending some weeks with her should have given her a bit of insight on the matter."

Before Ghevont could stand fully erect, he reset himself back on the chair. "By the way, in case the sickness has made you forget, my sister is still waiting for her burial by dragon flame. Can we see to that tonight?"

"You haven't buried her yet?"

"She's in a hole, but I've yet to fill it. I've prevented her body from decomposing with my coldest spell, so no worries about her looking or smelling too unsightly."

"And Corbin's body?"

"He's also being preserved, but I'm planning on dissecting him later and testing the effects of several spells on his corpse."

"That reminds me of another favor."

"Yes?"

"If you have access to my body after I die, don't cut me open or perform any of your experiments."

"But you'll be dead, you won't feel anything."

"Nevertheless. I guess this goes for Clarissa and Marcela as well."

"But a vampire will make a wonderful specimen! And Clarissa has been nothing but cordial with me."

"She won't be if she knows what you would do to her corpse."

"You're certain?"

"You really do need to get out more."

We went to Vey's grave site before dawn would make its way to us. Both girls were sleeping, making giving an excuse unnecessary. Vey's body was located about five hundred feet west of the fort, where she was resting in a rectangular hole five feet deep. The corpse was overlaid with tree branches and leaves, though I knew dragon flame would not need the aid of the tinder to burn it to ash. The ball of light Ghevont used to light our way exposed Vey's bluish face, which came from the icy spell preserving her form.

"Did you tell the girls anything about this?" I asked Ghevont.

7

"I knew you wouldn't want me to talk about dragon fire to them, so I lied and told them I had already buried her."

"Good."

I summoned dragon stones and began dropping them randomly in the grave.

"How fast will this be?" asked Ghevont.

"Pretty fast."

"I've read that burning bodies with dragon fire typically comes with ceremonies."

"Typically, but my sword tells me that this circumstance will not require them."

"What circumstances would?"

"For one, I'm not yet a true Veknu Milaris. Not only can't I summon a dragon, but dragon fire is still beyond my control, control that would be needed in a real ceremony. You also don't usually burn an enemy who's handled corrupted souls. Dragon fire is reserved for heroes of armies, leaders of nations, and other Veknu Milaris. Despite my amateur status, this is still an honor for your sister, and my dragon is somewhat begrudged by this."

"Fascinating. I wonder if your own corruption will affect your progression into Veknu Milaris? Very well, you may activate the dragon stones."

The stones ignited their runes. Within seconds the entire pit was swathed in a bright blaze as white as a howling blizzard. It was as though a tiny star had budded beneath the ground. This intense light lasted half a minute longer before losing its intensity. It died away quite quickly after that. The burning ended a couple of minutes later. Ghevont cast his light spell again, revealing that the pit was filled with nothing more than a light sprinkle of ashen dust.

"Incredible," whispered Ghevont. "Nothing but ash now."

8

The scholar waved his hands over the grave, casting a spell that crumbled the dirt walls until it filled the unmarked grave.

Chapter Two

It was evening when Clarissa came out to the fort's old courtyard to see me practicing my stances with Aranath in hand. I took the cup of water she handed me and leaned the sword by the large tree we sat against.

"Glad to see you're mending quickly."

"There's a few perks to being corrupted. Speaking of volatile things, I've been meaning to talk to you about Marcela."

"Yes, I've been thinking about her, too. I know you wouldn't allow her to travel with us."

"You two appear to have gotten close these past few weeks, so do you think there's a chance we can reunite her with her family?"

"I still haven't gotten much information on them, but I doubt it. She's too headstrong to admit she might have made a mistake leaving her family. Poor thing, she was must have been only seven or eight when she ran away. I don't think she even remembers why she left in the first place. She keeps changing the story."

"Then do you know of the least irksome way to be rid of her?"

"I think so, but she would have to travel with us for the first part of the journey. You see, there's no way she'll live in a domestic setting, but say we entice her with a more stimulating environment where she can learn to fight and still be watched by people we trust."

"Ah, the guild house in Ecrin."

"Yes. I'm certain Silver will get the siblings to train her and she can act a kind of apprentice to them. Besides, you can also update the old guild master with what happened here."

I groaned. "I didn't want to travel all that much with her, but that is a good solution. She'll probably see training herself as the key to staying long-term with Rathmore and jump at the opportunity."

Clarissa smiled. "Glad you liked the idea. It's all I had."

The lone idea was presented to Marcela the next day. She was torn by the notions of leaving Ghevont and of bettering herself through training, particularly in a city as cultured and stirring as Ecrin. Her official answer was to say she would mull it over on the way there, but her glittery eyes told me she wouldn't pass up the prospect when it arrived, so I walked away satisfied.

As for the journey itself, I felt I would be sufficiently mended to leave Gremly after another week. It might take another month to be my full self, but since I doubted the start of the expedition would not have us fighting anyone strong enough to challenge our group, I decided it would be judicious to schedule the trip in the midst of my recuperation. There was also the likelihood that the Advent would realize Corbin and Vey had been gone far too long for something not to have happened to them, leading to an ambiguous fate for Vey's assistant.

The possibilities were twofold. If he was seen by the Advent as a true believer of their cause, then he could be reassigned to aid another project, making him harder to find. Then again, if they concluded he was only loyal to Vey, they would kill him. I had to learn what Magnus knew before any of that happened.

Meanwhile, I was interested in knowing what Ghevont would turn up in his search for the grave map's location. He had headed to the other hideouts to gather his father's old research. It required a few trips for him and his helper girls to acquire all the volumes and scrolls he believed could prove useful. Once he had all he needed, he speedily began skimming over everything. His time in Gremly had him already read just about everything available, so it was a simple matter of looking for any key words that stood out and tying the threads he discovered.

Ghevont shook me awake three days after he began his printed rummaging.

As I groggily awoke from what was too short a slumber, he said, with barely suppressed excitement, "I'm starting to see it, Mercer! Listen to this." He cleared his dry throat and unraveled some of the scroll he held. "'And so the heavens were heavy with woe and discord-'"

"Ghevont."

"Hmm?"

"What are you reading?"

"The opening passage of Alder Beerling's *Summertide*."

"The epic poem?"

"Yes… You want me to summarize my thoughts, don't you?"

"That would be best, yes."

"Forgive me, Marcela never stops me from elucidating to my heart's content. Okay, let's see… Oh, do you already know the story of *Summertide*?"

"I haven't read anything myself, but it's about the fall of Old Voreen, right?"

"Essentially. Making up a prevalent portion of the poem is the story of Jages Mar, who was an influential young general of that old kingdom. He was living in a time when the country was in a severe state of decline and regularly beset by barbarian hordes and swelling sands on every side. Desperate for a way to strengthen his country, the general set out to find various items of lore."

"And the grave was one of them?"

"No, the poem never explicitly states that he sought the fallen god's grave, but my father's notes in this section suggests a kind of breakthrough on that front. If only I had known what he was looking for earlier! It would have been easier for me to research his research. In any event, I remembered another volume my father had with him. I was confused when I first read its contents years ago, but now I know how it's related."

"What volume?"

The scholar dashed out of the chair and grabbed a thick tome off a nearby table. He laid the hardcover beside me and opened it. "It's a comprehensive collection of numerous literature titles and their probable authors and known editions. I discovered my father had made notes in the section regarding the genesis of *Summertide*." A pale, thin finger pointed at the piece of the page he spoke of. "Notice anything?"

"It says there are three known versions of this poem."

"Right, and I can only find two in the hideouts. The newest version contained too many changes for my father's liking, and Beerling's, while presumably translated from the original work, also contains too many contemporary allusions to make it useful."

"Then you think your father was searching for the original."

"I think that's what lured him out of Gremly. My sister said Corbin betrayed father, right? Corbin must have lured him with the idea that he found the original work. Or perhaps they really found the item, and thinking he no longer needed him, helped snare him on behalf of the Advent."

"Possibly, but why do you think this poem interested Riskel so much in the first place?"

"Look at this…" He flipped the book over, showing me a faded crest of a giant sea serpent wrapped around a ship. "The insignia of modern Voreen. My father took this with him when he left the country, meaning he was on this scent years before coming here. Something or someone in Voreen peeked his interest, I'm sure. Whatever that was, we need to find the original *Summertide* story to progress any further."

"If any are left. I imagine the Advent go out of their way to find every copy they can to destroy them…"

I didn't realize how long I was quiet until Ghevont said, "Uh, are you okay, Mercer?"

"Aye. I was just thinking."

"About what?"

"I was wondering whether I should try and use an Alslana connection to find the original work, but that could end up being too risky. The attack in Qutrios suggests somebody with authority is aiding the Advent from within the kingdom. If this theory is correct, then the Advent could hear someone is on to them and panic."

"Isn't panic in your enemy a good thing?"

"When the blade is already up against their throat, but if they see it being unsheathed from a hundred feet away, then they have time to counter it, perhaps devastatingly so. No, we'll keep this between ourselves until I ponder some things over. Did your father keep anything on the Advent?"

"Very little. What I did find only explains why he had so few records on them. They are an old cult, first appearing nineteen hundred years ago in the continent of Efios. I don't know their history, but I imagine a cult wouldn't have a wide reach beyond their home territory, making accounts of them in Iazali or Niatrios scarce."

"Their reach appears to have grown, then. Anything about this god of theirs?"

"I'm afraid not. Many cultures sometimes speak of a lost god. Depending on the account, this god could have been the fifth god of strife or a benign seventh god of balance. It's most often the former. For instance, one of the many theories explaining Degosal's destruction states that a failed attempt to summon a deity caused the empire's downfall. Whether this god is related to the Advent's version or any other in Orda, well, there's simply not enough information to say one way or the other."

"I suspect we won't know for certain unless this god is raised, and I have a feeling that would be a very bad thing. Keep looking for anything else of note." He stood up and began to leave. A fizzing sensation in my stomach made me realize this would be a good time to be more affable. I opened my mouth the minimum amount it required words to exit and said, "Oh, and Ghevont. Good work."

The scholar's own lack of social graces had him hesitate on saying the natural response to that statement. He did eventually turn all the way to face me and replied, "That is, yes, I mean, thank you."

Ghevont informed me of a handful of other noteworthy details over the next few days, such as that the original *Summertide* would be written in the language of Old Voreen. Thanks to various scrolls and his educated father, the scholar said he had a basic understanding of several languages, including the one used in the original poem, but he would go ahead and sharpen his knowledge of it. It was just as well, since Aranath told me that while he might roughly understand the spoken language, there was little chance he could read it. In fact, the dragon wouldn't be useful reading any language other than his own.

I took it upon myself to read the epic poem. According to the tale, Jages Mar searched the world's ruins and wastelands for two decades in search of an item or spell that could restore his country. He found a few mythical objects, love, lovers, children, betrayal, and experienced the death of many of his friends, but he inevitably came home empty-handed. The end of Niatrios' first empire happened shortly after he died.

Whether this man existed, conjured from an imagination, or a composite of both real and fake people was a puzzle left to historians who cared about particulars. My only concern was wondering how the parent Rathmore viewed this saga. I hoped meeting with Gwen would clear this and other matters up.

It wasn't long before I urged everyone to get ready to move out. The last place Ghevont knew her to be was a town hugging the border of southeastern Gremly called Omauwend. It was to be a journey of five hundred miles, or about two weeks away with a steady walking pace. To drastically cut

15

the chance of being slowed by other people's problems, I planned to travel most of the way within Gremly itself. This would also cut the chance of finding food to eat. The forest didn't seem to have animals any heavier than a squirrel and the most nutritious vegetation came from tree roots. To discourage starvation, Clarissa agreed to carry most of our food in a knapsack to help keep the rest of us burdened with other items.

Ghevont, for instance, brought a satchel chock-full of scrolls and books, which still wasn't all he wanted to bring, so he had Marcela carry bindings of her own in her little satchel. I had to remind him that continual traveling would tire the pre-woman and it was best to lessen her load. Ghevont spent a few hours reevaluating which books to leave behind. He wanted me to lug around another bag full of literature, but the best I did was put two small scrolls in my inner cloak pocket. Even in my less than ideal state, I expected to throw myself into any fight that befell us, so I didn't want to be laden by tens of thousands of words.

Before we left, Ghevont etched several runes in and around the fort. I assumed they were defenses or warning systems, but I didn't ask any clarifying questions. Marcela had the expected mixture of excitement and trepidation at leaving Gremly and its people-repelling power for a good long while. In the time Clarissa and the adolescent were in town, the vampire had bought better fitting clothing for Marcela to wear. While the child gladly sported the cleaner attire, she refused to put on any kind of footwear.

Clarissa's preparation involved draining the blood of rodents in vials so she had emergency blood to drink. She could go four or five days without ingesting the vital liquid, but doing so would weaken her far too much to move during the day.

With everyone being as ready as they could be, we set off.

Chapter Three

With Aranath adjusting my prana accordingly, and Ghevont's spell doing the same for him and the girls, the peculiar hex over the forest lost its mind bending influence. With little in the way of predators, human dwellers, and bad weather, our southward excursion went at a quick pace. I expected the encumbered Ghevont to slow us down at times, but he was fitter than his scrawny frame suggested. Marcela had all the energy youth offered and often had to be reined in by Clarissa or risk getting lost the old-fashioned way. The only reason I cared if she went missing was knowing the others would waste time looking for her.

At any rate, walking through the misty, gloom-filled forest had me feeling as though we were the only people left alive in the entire world.

Fighting against the silent void imbued in Gremly were the ongoing conversations between the girls and the scholar. All Clarissa had to do was ask Ghevont a simple question and the scholar would rant on for an hour or two in his reply, which often jumped from subject to subject and which would sometimes not answer the primary question. As long as they didn't try involving me, I too enjoyed hearing an impassioned, if erratic, Ghevont tell his theories on why some people had no talent for spell casting, or ramble on about how maddening it was that ancient humans did not write down more of their exploits.

A week into our journey, as everyone strolled a few yards behind me, Ghevont was explaining to Clarissa ways to improve her water spell.

"Oh, that's a good idea," said Clarissa. "Trying to put out Mercer's fire spell will definitely help strengthen my own. Have you seen it in action? It's hot enough to melt the stones after just a few seconds."

"That's to be expected from dragon fire. Legends say-"

"Wait, what did you say?"

"Oh dear. No, what I meant to say-"

"Mercer!"

I stopped walking and hung my head before turning to face the scholar. He removed his satchel and handed it to Marcela, telling her, "Look after these for me, will you? I would like my body to be donated to an academic institution."

"Huh? What's going on?" asked Marcela, who could not hold on to the heavy sack of books and dropped it. "I want to hear about dragons."

"That's up to Mercer now."

I rolled my eyes. "Shut up, Ghevont."

"But I need to, well, okay."

Clarissa, with arms crossed, glared at me a moment. I kept my staunch eyes on hers, letting us speak without having to use words.

When she decided to converse vocally, she said, "This does explain a few things. So, it's true, then?"

"Yes."

"Why didn't you tell me?"

"If it ever became important, I would have."

"I think your definition of 'important' is different than mine."

"I'm a long way from controlling his flame much less summoning Aranath himself, so I didn't want to put any grandiose ideas about me in your head."

"Who's Aranath?" asked Marcela.

"Aranath?" said Ghevont. "As in Aranath the Sky Lord? One of Kyloth's foremost-"

A glance from me stopped him in his uttered tracks.

Marcela stamped her foot. "What's going on?! Why won't you let him talk? All he said was that your fire was like a drag- Ooooh! I get it! But then that means… Oh… But that's not possible, right? Ghevont?" He shrugged. She cocked her head and stared at me. "Nah, I don't believe it."

"Good," I said, turning back around. "Let's keep moving."

"Wait! Are you being serious or not?! C-Clarissa, he isn't serious, right?"

"Well," began Clarissa, "ask yourself this, when have you known Mercer to joke around?"

Since I didn't hear our youngest member say anything, I assumed her to be in contemplative silence. I had to make sure later that Marcela would keep her knowledge of my power a secret before we reached Ecrin. A few minutes after we resumed our stroll, the youth began asking Ghevont questions about dragons. Knowing I had a direct link to such answers, I paid little attention to the scholar's accounts. Of course, that didn't mean a lack of curiosity.

The next time I found myself watching over three sleeping travelers, I strode just out of earshot and sat against a tree.

"Who's Kyloth?"

"You would know if you ever read more about the War of Dragon Fire," replied my sword.

"I guess I was afraid you might see me as presumptuous if I looked into your past."

"You think me delicate, boy? That old war does not define me. Kyloth was the elder dragon I served."

"The one who began the war?"

"I would not say he 'began' it, but he did lead it."

"And what's with 'Aranath the Sky Lord' thing?"

"A human habit," he grumbled. "Though I confess it was something of an honor to be designated as such, as only the most fearsome dragons were given titles."

19

"Yeah, but why 'Sky Lord'?"

"You'll see for yourself if you ever summon me."

"Which human gave you the title?"

"The last Veknu Milaris I partnered with."

I paused my questioning when I realized Aranath had likely been comparing me to his previous partners during our time together. I didn't only have the experience of a dragon on my side, but that of several ancient warriors. "What was he like?"

"*She* was a brutal warrior. Her prana was as fierce as your released corruption, but with far greater control. Her name was Irene Renauld."

"A Renauld? Then she was related to Morris Renauld?"

"Now Morris I would say really instigated the war. She was his youngest grandchild."

"Was she also the one to seal you?"

"She had already passed by that time. Kyloth sealed me away, which he did shortly before the battle that buried Nimbria."

"I see. So what's it like in your realm? What did you do for five hundred years?"

"I still reside in my home realm, a land that cycles between fire and water. Most dragons sleep through the times of volcanic fire and scarcity. We awaken when the seas swell with rainwater again. As I am being punished for war crimes, the elders have not attempted to remove the barrier separating me from the rest of my kin. With little other choice, I've passed most of the time by hibernating for long stretches."

"The history book I read said that all rebel dragons were hunted down and killed. If the elder dragons know about you, then why haven't they attempted to carry out that sentence?"

"I believe your tome stated that all dragons in *Orda*. I am not in Orda."

"But still."

A wordless minute passed, though I could still pick up a low rumble that came from deep within his throat. The best I could equate the noise to was a cat's purr, but it certainly didn't come from satisfaction.

When he spoke again, he said, "Sometimes I wonder if the elders will someday break down the barrier and carry out their justice. It is a formidable barrier, but without Kyloth to reinforce it, it will fall with focused effort. The war occurred at a time when I would be considered young and at my most aggressive. Perhaps the elders have given me that justification. The main reason the elders even allowed some of my kind to be bound by a summoning spell was that sharing power with a human helps mitigate a young dragon's brashness."

"So because you were young you were spared?"

"Or perhaps they simply do not wish to kill any dragons they do not have to. I'm certain our numbers have not yet completely recuperated even after five hundred years. As the barrier prevents any contact with my kind, I can only speculate on their reasons for leaving me alive and alone."

"It must be a difficult life."

"Indeed."

"What was even the point of sealing you?"

"I was not the only one to be sealed away. The plan was for Kyloth and the rest of my winged comrades to join me. The war was going against us, so we were going to retreat and recoup our strength, but the other elders must have discovered our intent. I do not know what happened after the battle of Nimbria. The enchantment on the sword was supposed to be a way for us to remain in contact with this realm, but if no one is alive to take advantage of the capacity, then the incantation is moot. It was only when you read that history tome did I learn that the war came to an end with Kyloth's death a few months later."

"You don't think the dragon elders will stop me from becoming Veknu Milaris, do you?"

"They might if they discover us before the connection is forged, but that is unlikely with our realms still severed. As I'm certain my presence is being watched, however, then a summoning will alert them of our link. I can already hear their stipulations if we reach such a height, though I sense you're getting ahead of yourself."

"How far am I from summoning you?"

"You are progressing, but it will require another year of dedicated training to have the prana necessary for the act. Even then you will not be able to summon me for long. Most humans at your stage will need another decade to summon a dragon for more than a few moments. A decade more to become true masters. Still, if you gain some measure of control over your corruption, then perhaps the time required will be less. We shall see."

The rest of our trip within Gremly went by smoothly enough. I felt my left side regain its strength to the point I could practice two-handed sword stances without a sting gushing outward with every sharp motion. My overall health steadily returned as well. It used to be that I would tire before even Marcela felt like stopping, but my hard-earned endurance soon displayed itself in our shorter rest periods.

Wanting to make sure our visit with Gwen stayed as brief as possible, I told Ghevont to not tell his former guardian about the death of his sister. Ghevont agreed, likely because he wouldn't want to be in the position of consoling anyone. Perhaps he was also afraid that seeing someone grieving for Vey's death might make her passing more of a reality, though I doubt anyone outside his unsocialized mind would know if he was ever in mourning. In the same vein, I told Marcela to begin referring to Ghevont by his first name instead of his last. When she asked why, I let her know that if anyone learned

22

he was Rathmore's son, it would trigger an inquisition on her friend. She assented, but she needed some time to self-adjust.

There came a point when it was necessary to exit the forest and find a road that led to Omauwend. It was a little surreal when I stepped out of Gremly's dreary domain for the first time in weeks. The fresher air, brighter sunlight, and resonances of nature made it seem as though I were no longer exceptional, but merely another living being among a trillion others. The first town we encountered informed us we were still a full day's journey from our destination. With everyone well rested enough, I pushed us to make the trip in half that time.

We approached Omauwend in the late afternoon. Ghevont noted how the town was noticeably larger than when he last left it. Some of Gremly had been cut down to make room for it, though tendrils of its mist still creeped out. With a light rain falling, we traversed the peripheries of the town and looked for the scholar's former home. When we wandered into the western outskirts of town, Ghevont pointed at a rundown house. It looked like a straw hut, but it turned out to be mostly made of frayed wood.

On reaching the derelict shelter, Ghevont said, "I'm positive this is it."

"And I'm positive she doesn't live here anymore," said Marcela.

I told Clarissa to go inquire with the nearest neighbors while the rest of us examined the home more closely. Looking through a glassless window showed the inside to be bare except for a degraded straw bed and curtains of spider webs dangling from the cracked ceiling.

Clarissa came back and said, "Gwen still lives in town, just on the east side of it. She's apparently married to a blacksmith and has two kids."

"Interesting," said Ghevont. "I was not expecting her to recover from my father's death. She was quite devastated when she heard the news."

"It's hard, but people can move on from tragedy," said Clarissa, looking at me as she did so. "Especially if they find someone else to help them through it."

"Yes, my studies, combined with my personal experiences, appear to reliably imply that sentient beings, while initially rendered incapacitated by a loved one's passing, do gradually recover their emotional stability over time. I wonder if time alone can heal these jarring impacts to the soul? They are both in the realms of the immaterial. In all probability-"

"Ghevont," I said. "Keep it in your head when we're in public."

"Right, of course. Sometimes it's difficult to separate my mind's thoughts from my speech."

The short trip to the opposite side of town ended when we recognized the cadenced clanging of hammer on metal on anvil. The origin of the clatter came from a smithy, whose door was open to allow the heat of the forge to pour out onto the little grassy hill the property was perched on. I assumed the home nearest it, a wide one-story brick home sitting twenty-five yards away, belonged to Gwen and her husband. A sign at the bottom of the slope read 'No job requests at this time.'

As we made our way up to the worn footpath, a figure became outlined by the red glow of the workshop's entrance. The hammering stopped and a broader figure stepped behind the first. They each made their way down to us.

As expected from anyone in his profession, the older man was a well-built fellow, if a little stout. Despite the combustible danger it presented, a thick black beard concealed his lower face. The younger man, who also wore the blacksmith's apron over his burly physique, looked to be about Marcela's age. The girl child's unblinking gawking of the young man told me that not so childish feelings were stirring within her.

"Sorry folks," said the parched voice of the more mature blacksmith. "I'm not taking any requests right now. Maybe next week."

Mistaking him for our leader, his words were directed at the oldest member of our group, but it was I who said, "Your sign works well enough, sir. We're here to see Gwen Prothoro."

"She hasn't used that name in seventeen years. It would be Gwen Droland now. What's this about?"

"Old acquaintances. If you please, can you inform her that Ghevont is here?"

"Ghevont? Vey's brother?"

"You know Vey?" asked Ghevont.

"Aye. She visited a few years ago."

"She actually visited?"

"You Ghevont?"

"Yes, uh, mister, sir."

"Well, well, then this has been a long time coming! Peter, close down the forge for me… Did you hear me, boy?" The young man took his eyes off Marcela and ran back up the hill. "Now, if you'll follow me, we can join Gwen and my daughter preparing our feast for the evening. My name is Cecil Droland. No need to introduce yourselves just yet. We'll do that when everyone is gathered."

"How is Gwen doing?" asked Ghevont.

"She's the epitome of stalwart health and vibrant spirit. What about you? Your sister hardly mentions your state."

"Oh, I'm well indeed. I merely lack some sun and musculature, things you've appeared to have gotten plenty of. Tell me, was your own father a strapping man?"

Clarissa chuckled. "Don't mind his oddness too much, sir. He's a scholar interested in many aspects of life, both small and large, but this has led to a lack of social poise."

"I see."

A dozen strides away from the house had us sniffing the boiling whiffs of chicken, sweet spices, and baking potatoes. Cecil opening the door had an almost solid cloud of this cooking wash over our faces. My stomach growled with the promise of a real meal.

"Gwen! Come meet our guests!"

From an unseen room, a high-pitched voice replied, "Guests? Is it the Warrens?"

"See for yourself!"

Hurrying out from a room to our right was a smiling woman with short brunette hair. The fine wrinkles on her fair face said she was closer to fifty than not, but besides being a little plumper than Ghevont described, she wasn't too far off from that description. I lamented that I couldn't see the body and face of her twenty year old self.

Her amber eyes swept over us until they spotted something familiar. She covered her open mouth with both hands, only to drop them at once. "Ghevont!?"

For the first time since knowing him, Ghevont initiated human contact. He walked up to her with spreading arms. She moved in and they met in a warm embrace.

"I knew you couldn't stay away forever!" Gwen said in a sniveling voice. "What took you so long to come back?"

"Nothing, I suppose. Nothing but my own passiveness. I'm sorry."

"No apology needed. Look how you've grown!"

Fulfilling my desire to see a younger Gwen, her daughter entered the room. She inherited some of her father's features, such as her pronounced chin and broad shoulders, but she was otherwise a fledging version of her mother. Even the length of hair matched.

"Mother? What's going on?"

"Melea! This is Ghevont!"

"Oh, Vey's brother?"

"Do we have enough food to offer our guests?" Cecil asked his daughter.

She counted us and answered, "We should, as long as everyone doesn't eat like you, Dad. Dinner will be ready in a few minutes."

"Excellent, then let's move this gathering to the table."

The rest of us introduced ourselves when Gwen's son came in a few moments later. We next told them of the invented way we knew each other—namely, that the girls were Ghevont's apprentices and I was their bodyguard.

"Bodyguard, eh?" said the blacksmith. "Where did you learn to fight?"

"Everywhere I've had to."

"May I see your sword?"

"No sword play in the house!" remonstrated his wife.

"I only want to see its craftsmanship, dear."

"I would wait until after dinner, Mercer. My husband is just a giant child and is bound to knock something off a shelf. Now, Ghevont, I'm glad you're finally visiting, but is there something in particular that led you here? Are you in trouble? Is it your sister?"

I espied Ghevont from my corner seat, who briefly did the same to me.

"N-no, nothing in particular. Spending time with my companions here simply reminded me of past company."

The conversation while we ate our chicken and soup was largely anecdotal. It seemed Gwen's family believed Ghevont and Vey were related to her by way of a cousin I was sure didn't exist. This imaginary cousin had died and so Gwen reared her children for several years before another imaginary relative took them north. Shortly after that and the children had gone their separate ways.

I kept quiet when possible, of course, but that didn't stop Melea from taking glimpses in my direction. I conceitedly thought she was mimicking her

27

brother's interest in Marcela, but when I made eye contact with her, she didn't smile or look away sheepishly. I soon realized she was smarter than the rest of her family—she was suspicious of us.

The crisscrossing dialogue went on well after dinner. At least the meal turned out to be good. The talking died down when everyone noticed a dozing Marcela. Arrangements were then made for everyone to find places to sleep. Marcela was given the lone guest room, which she would share with Clarissa. It was next agreed that Ghevont would take Peter's room, while Peter moved in with his sister. My plan was to take the bed after Ghevont woke up, but for now, only Marcela went to sleep.

It took a half hour more for the other youths to follow her lead, so I just needed for the blacksmith to take his leave. Luckily, his arduous day of work soon wore on him.

After he could not stifle a yawn, Cecil said, "Well, there's much to do tomorrow. I'll have to bid you all a good night. How long will you be staying with us?"

"Not too long, I'm afraid," said Ghevont. "A couple of days?"

"At least another night," I said.

"If it isn't too much trouble," added Clarissa.

"Of course not!" said Gwen. "I wouldn't mind if you all stayed the rest of my life."

"I would," I muttered below anyone's hearing range.

The loud rabble of the house dropped significantly after Cecil left us alone with his wife. Going by the occasional twitch in her eyes and hands, she had figured out somewhere in the middle of the reunion that we must have known of Ghevont's infamous last name. Still, I don't think she was worried as much as she was trying to figure out the real reason for our visit.

Clarissa and I scooched closer to Gwen's end of the table. With no one else taking the initiative, I said, "We know the real link between you and Ghevont."

"I had a feeling. So you're not a bodyguard, are you?"

"I'll be whatever I need to be to find what I'm after."

"Which is?"

"Did Riskel leave anything with you other than his children?"

"Like what?"

"Literally anything. A document? Information?"

After a half second of reminiscence, she said, "Oh! He did leave me a journal of his poetry."

"What do you mean 'his poetry'?"

"Just give me a moment and I'll show you." She left the room, returning in the promised moment. She handed me a little leather-bound book. "The only nonliving keepsake he gave me."

Opening the journal, I asked, "He didn't say anything about it?"

"No, only that it was something to hold me over until he came back."

"Do you remember why he left? What he was after?"

She pressed a chubby finger on her chin. "He mentioned something about picking up an important book from somebody."

"From Corbin Tolosa?"

"He never gave me a name."

"Do you mind if I look over it?"

She glanced curiously at Ghevont, who nodded. "Sure, I guess."

I was reading Riskel's poem book a third time, so I was dangerously close to nodding off under the torchlight just outside the house. With the middle of the night being her domain, I wasn't surprised to see Clarissa walk up and sit beside me.

"Find anything yet?"

"I've found that Riskel was quite sappy. He was also a terrible poet."

"Really? So you don't think there's some kind of secret code you need to break? Maybe there's a hidden rune or something."

"No, Aranath couldn't feel a trace of prana on any page, and while I'm uncertain of my decoding abilities, I know the staleness of these words alone would be enough to deter most from probing too deeply."

"But doesn't it sound strange that a man as smart as Riskel wrote so badly?"

"A little, but he could've been writing down to Gwen's level."

"So you're saying a man known to have killed dozens of people for the sake of horrific experiments was a romantic? I don't know if I find that funny or scary."

"I would define 'romance' as a scary amount of feeling."

"True. Hmm, I wonder whether I would have been smitten with Riskel? He seems to have been very charismatic for such a malicious man."

"His goals were malicious, but I suppose the man himself couldn't have been much different from Ghevont."

"Uh, Ghevont isn't exactly charming."

"I don't mean his personality, just the fact that most people don't look like their true persona. If Riskel actually bore a likeness to the depraved caster many portray him as, then he would have been hanged years before he left Voreen. I'm sure most of his friends, colleagues, and strangers he passed on the street never knew what went on in his head."

She leaned back in her chair and looked up at the sky. "Kinda like how I never saw Trevon's true nature."

"That's different. You saw it, you just chose not to acknowledge it."

"You're right, they are different. Choosing to be blind is worse than having a real reason. If I only-"

"Stop."

"Stop what?"

"Going over your mistakes. I know them, you know them, so there's nothing left to do but move on. I made a mistake coming here, but I won't waste time regretting it. We move on, that's all."

"I don't think it was a mistake coming here. Ghevont and Gwen are obviously very happy they got the chance to reunite after all this time. Knowing Ghevont, he would have probably realized too late that he wanted to catch up with family."

"I guess she would count as his last living family member."

"Not really. Isn't Marcela like family to him by now?"

"An odd family, but yeah, I suppose so."

Smiling, she said, "We're all rather odd, I guess."

I didn't like what she was forcing me to think about.

We persisted in silence as I pretended to read the poem book for another few minutes, but I couldn't help ultimately saying what I was thinking. "You should really stop following me."

"What? Why?"

"Because you might die, and that possibility is bothering me more and more."

She blinked at me for a moment, judging my disposition and thinking of a response. When she came up with one, she said, "I don't want you to die either. It's why I *have* to keep watch over you. If you don't want me to follow you headlong into danger, then *you* shouldn't head right for it, but you will, so there's no getting rid of me just yet."

I think she expected for me to respond with some conviction-filled declarations, but I was too tired to keep talking. I shrugged and closed the book. Standing up, I said, "I'm going to sleep. Keep watch over the place."

"Oh, uh, sure thing."

31

Chapter Four

Ghevont and Gwen spent most of the next day together. Marcela, interested in the blacksmith's work for more than one reason, disbursed her time between watching Peter at work and being with Ghevont. Clarissa stayed glued to her bed for the early part of the day, but came out when the damp weather weakened the sunlight to the point even a starving vampire wouldn't be troubled by it.

I was left to my own devices, which included showing Cecil my blade. The experienced blacksmith was quick to comment on the steel's masterful craftsmanship. By looking down its edge and flicking it with his finger he concluded that the steel had likely been forged using a lengthy antique process that required the precise involvement of a skilled caster.

"Where did you obtain such a fine blade?" he asked me while cutting the weapon through the air outside his smithy. The sword sang with every swing, though my own evaluation told me he only had a basic understanding of swordsmanship.

"I found it in an old ruin."

"Really? Which ruin still carries treasures like this one?"

"A forgotten one. I only accidentally fell upon it, and that blade is the only reason I stand here today."

He put the sword back in its sheath and said, "If I could forge a sword like this, I would be working for kings. Keep it close."

"I intend to."

That was actually the second conversation I had with Gwen's family that day. The first occurred after I awoke to alleviate Clarissa from her night watch duty. I wandered the premises thinking I was the only person now stirring, but when I ambled to the back of the home, I saw Melea feeding grain to about fifteen chickens. I would have preferred to avoid her, but I was doing nothing to muffle my walk, so she heard my approach and turned around.

"Good morning, Mercer," she stated with a drowsy voice she failed to hide. Some light drizzle fell from the gray skies, but nothing that could bother a butterfly in its flight, so I doubt it did much to stir her.

"It sounds as though you could have slept more of it away, Ms. Droland. I apologize if our presence has disturbed a restful night."

"All your presence has done is made me have to sleep in the same room as my brother, something I haven't done in ten years. That is far more disturbing than any stranger's presence."

"If that remains your biggest disturbance in life, then you can say you've lived a good one."

"Or one that has been far too quiet… But do you think looking for the best of what life has to offer also means inevitably seeing a few disturbing things as well?"

"I believe the best and worst can come right to your door, whether one seeks them out or not."

"I imagine being a bodyguard means having disturbing things come at you more often than not."

"Sure."

She went back to feeding her clucking chickens. I read this as my cue to leave, but before I took a step a full step back, she asked, with rather abrupt conviction," Are you really a bodyguard?"

"That's the story I'm sticking with."

Facing me again, she said, "So you aren't one?"

"Not officially, but I act like one sometimes."

"Then who are you? And why the lies?"

I remained silent, my eyes boring into her own.

When she finally flinched, she said, "What are you doing?"

33

"You've been wary of us since learning Ghevont was Vey's brother, yet you aren't afraid of me. I can even guess you haven't told your brother anything of your suspicions, have you?"

"Why does that matter?"

"Because it tells me you're upset with your mother, not worried about danger. Do you believe Ghevont and Vey are your half-siblings?"

Forgetting herself, she said her "No!" louder than she wanted to. She collected herself, smoothed her apron, and continued by saying, "You presume too much."

I shrugged. "Perhaps. I can only assure you that Ghevont is not a long lost sibling. If you want to be eased further, I can also tell you that you no longer have to worry about Vey ever returning."

"You mean Vey is-"

"I wouldn't tell this to Gwen. Despite the woman Vey turned out to be, your mother would only remember her as a loving child she helped raise."

"I did not want more secrets, Mr. Bodyguard."

"Sometimes we're lucky if that's all we get. I wouldn't concern myself with your mother's past. It appears she has largely moved on from it."

"All the more reason to share it with me or father."

"That's what deathbeds are for."

"Is it really as bad as that?"

"No, but it might make you think less of your mother, something a mother might wish to avoid."

"All you're doing is increasing my need for answers."

"So speak with your mother about it. I'm only saying it would be unnecessary. It's certainly something that can't wait until I'm days away from here. Besides, I have no doubt you'll someday have your own secrets to keep from your parents and children."

"Did you get whatever secret you were looking for?"

34

I bowed. "I'll keep that to myself."

The ultimate goal of Dranall was over three thousand miles away, so I was eager to restart my journey. I set that restart time for noon the next day. Everyone appeared sadder at the impending separation, which I expected between Gwen and Ghevont, but for even Marcela to display genuine regret surprised me. It reminded me that I was just as ignorant about the formation of human connections as the scholar was.

I expended much of my time looking over maps, making sure we traveled on routes clear of human congestion. My group enjoyed another supper and breakfast with the family before getting ready to leave. Gwen, using the soggy weather as her excuse, wanted us to stay longer, but I assured her that only a tempest would dampen my purpose. Not long after they supplied us with good foodstuff and wishes of luck, we were off.

The loquacious scholar kept in contemplative silence for the rest of the day, but his usual mood returned after our first night's rest in the wilderness. For my part, the words that came out of me were often related to battle preparation—whether that came in the form of Advent, trolls, an army of drunk pirates, or a petulant child. I specifically needed Ghevont to use his variety of spells with a warrior's fortitude and instinct, especially in ambush situations. More than anything, I wanted him and Clarissa to work well together.

The basic plan was to always have Ghevont fight defensively with his array of ward spells and distractive techniques while Clarissa made certain no one reached him or Marcela, who was to always stay right behind her friend. I would, of course, act as the main offensive pawn, moving about as I saw fit in a fluctuating battlefield.

In addition to practicing strategy, there was practicing our individual casting ability. Clarissa focused on strengthening her water spell. She accomplished this by trying to douse my dragon fire as quickly as possible, which I manipulated to last as long as possible. With Ghevont's guidance, the vampire was also training to turn her water into ice and steam. In anticipation of living with the Warriors Guild, Marcela also joined our training regimens. She did not yet have the endurance to train for extended periods, so much of her time was spent getting her stamina up with the fundamentals. Ghevont and the girls mostly trained among themselves, but I occasionally provided input when I saw something not to my liking.

With a pair of people not acclimated to lengthy travel, combined with tiring combat drills, I was more inclined to pay for a carriage ride. It was on one of these rides that the chance to test our battle capacity presented itself one muggy evening. My quiet quartet was on a small cart being pulled by a large horse and its gaunt, dark-skinned rider. The bumpy road we traversed was a solitary one, with tall trees making it darker than it already was.

The first sign that something was not so tranquil about this leg of the journey was the far off neighing of several stressed horses, neighing that closed in from behind us. Stamping hooves and excited shouts from humans followed an instant later. All this sounded quite familiar to me.

We were at the bottom of a hill, so I hoped we could avoid what was coming by remaining incognito. "Get us into the forest as soon as you can," I told the rider.

"Why?" asked Marcela. "What's going on?"

"Sounds like incoming bandits, but they'll hopefully pass us by if we hide well enough."

"Hide? Shouldn't a mighty dra-" My hand covered her mouth and I used the other to point at the stranger in our midst. She pushed my hand away and said, "Whatever! Be a coward."

The cart found cover behind some bristly bushes just before the first pair of centaur-like figures appeared over the hill. Behind them was a thundering stagecoach pulled by four horses. The overwrought beasts were being whipped to their limit by their human director. The top of the stagecoach

36

also held two archers, who did their best to keep the bandits at bay with a flurry of arrows. One arrow found its mark in a brigand, knocking him off his horse, but his companion nearly knocked an archer off the carriage when a fireball exploded at the carriage's roof.

Three more hollering horsemen arose behind the stagecoach.

"Mercer," whispered Clarissa, though we were still far away enough to speak normally without the aggressors hearing us. "Shouldn't we help them?"

"An unnecessary risk. We'll let them pass and go around wherever they end up."

Clarissa's eyes narrowed to the point I believed she was capable of acting out her vampiric nature on me. In lieu of piercing my skin with her fangs, she leapt out of the cart. I groaned as I followed after her. I firmly ordered Marcela to stay with the cart and motioned for Ghevont to trail Clarissa. The stagecoach had reached the hill's nethermost by the time my squad reached the edge of the road, meaning the vampire's targets were less than forty yards away. I held back Clarissa's impromptu body with an arm and pulled out my distractions.

"Just knock them off their horses," I ordered Clarissa. "I'll handle the rest. Keep any spell from hitting her, scholar."

When the inbound party was a second closer, I stepped out from the forest and stood in the center of the road. Before anyone of them reacted to my presence, I chucked three explosive stones over the head of the nearest bandit. The flash-bang made the bandit's horse rear up high enough to drop its passenger. The stagecoach horses responded by swerving sharply away from the unpleasant effect. Their panicked hooves trampled over the fallen bandit and shoved their fellow beast aside before slowing to a stop at the road's edge.

At the same second the stagecoach horses were stomping his comrade to death, the second bandit saw one of two versions of me rushing at him. This fleeting illusionary diversion was all that was needed for Clarissa to propel the grunting second bandit off his steed by a jet of water. The archers, seeing whose side we were on, trained their few remaining projectiles on the three other attackers. The bandit Clarissa swatted to the ground had no time to get his bearings before Aranath introduced himself to his neck. Both archers displayed the same amount of mercy.

With the odds flipped against them, sword, spell, and arrow made short work of the now reticent robbers. The last bandit almost galloped behind the shelter of the trees, his glassy ward spell strong enough to deflect the bitter bolts, but the gray haired archer nocked his arrow and told his younger compatriot to "Wait until he's on the ground." His keen eyes trailed the escaping horsemen for a moment before letting his arrow fly. The projectile struck the horse's foreleg, making it tumble. An arrow from the younger archer flew next, an electrical light enveloping its broadhead.

"I got him."

"Go make certain, and end the horse's misery as well."

They each hopped off the stagecoach to inspect the damage. As it turned out, the only passenger was an old man, an old man who believed the newcomers were just as apt to rob and murder him as the bandits. The rider and archers were more grateful for the aid, but offered no material thanks beyond a few spare coins. Clarissa only took the coin so she could give it to our own driver.

"I hope you're not angry with me," said Clarissa when we were back on our moving cart.

"I'm not angry."

"Really?"

"Well, I'm annoyed, but you still have some leeway with me, especially after I didn't tell you about Aranath. Just be aware that this flexibility can only stretch so far. Choose wisely which fights you throw us in."

"I don't *want* to throw us in any fights, but I can't just let bad things happen right in front of me."

"Bad things are sometimes done by good people. Yes, the bandits we helped execute would have killed those on the stagecoach, but do you know who those on the carriage were?"

"Just some rich old guy and his bodyguards."

"Why would a rich old man be on a lonely road with only a pair of archers defending him?"

"That does sound odd," said Marcela. "You'd think he'd hire more guys."

Concurring with her, I said, "You can also imagine an ordinary old man unused to danger would be more appreciative of our efforts. No, the real owner of that stagecoach would have been surrounded by a large escort on a road such as this. A well-to-do merchant or sariff farmer would also never wear the leather armor I saw under his cloak. Most people with coin never admit to themselves that attackers could reach them and so don't wear protective gear."

"So you're saying that carriage was stolen?"

"Most likely, or at least bought for much less than its worth. That old man was probably a bandit higher-up with a dwindling support system."

"I see," said a dejected Clarissa. She perked up again. "But you didn't know any of that before. There might've been a family in there for all we knew."

"We would have heard their screaming. Anyway, I'm not chastising you, I'm just saying you have to be more selective where you point my sword, for both our sakes."

"What about our sakes?" asked Marcela for Ghevont and herself.

"I care less for those."

"Mercer!" chastised the vampire.

Chapter Five

The rest of the journey to Oclor's coast was only hampered by more mundane affairs, which largely involved a few late summer downpours. One powerful thunderstorm in particular compelled us to find shelter in a large town. We were slowed further when Ghevont ended up separating from us inside the deluge.

We scoured the town for an hour before finding the scholar in a brothel. He was speaking to a group of, at best, scantily clad women about the best natural tonics to take to treat the most common ailments related to their precarious profession. I noted that Marcela's wide eyes carried the same spark of attentiveness as when staring at Gwen's son.

While in a town big enough to have one, I went over to a courier office to write a message to the Warriors Guild in Ecrin, informing Braden to expect us to arrive in two weeks. I paid extra to use carrier birds, since I didn't think there would be a point sending a missive by horseback and have us arrive only a few days later. It wasn't until after the transaction had concluded did I realize this was the first time I spent coin on such a trivial discrepancy. The younger me wouldn't have bothered sending a missive at all, much less care when it arrived. Was I changing? Or was I filling out the barren personality of my lost self? I ultimately concluded the only thing I could—I was thinking way too hard about it.

On finally reaching a random port town, little time was wasted buying passage to Ecrin. Less time was wasted before learning that Ghevont and Marcela were prone to seasickness. In turn, seeing their queasiness made me experience some woozy spells, though I never gave up my food to the sea. The vampire was never bothered by the rocking ship and the results of nausea. In fact, she got the most training done.

She implemented the plentiful water around us to practice her spell, trying to use it to help push the ship forward. I doubt she actually helped the ship along, but I was convinced the hefty resistance training would prove effective. When his stomach wasn't too unsettled, Ghevont merged his wind spell with that of the crewmen, who used it to propel more air into the square sails.

The density of ships increased the nearer we came to the wealthy Alslana nation, drawing Marcela's astonished eyes. The huge patrolling warships staggered her when they floated past us. They were at least three hundred feet long and frequently neared four hundred feet. These gleaming brutes were often plated with metal sheets, protecting them against the more powerful fire spells. While one could assume this metal armor would slow a ship to a snail's speed, the dozens of navel casters onboard could offset the effect by applying water and air enchantments when necessary. In addition, advanced runes and spells existed that lowered the weight of objects they were cast on to. These weight-shedding runes would usually be placed on the metal sheets themselves.

Our refreshed feet touched Eastern Ecrin's steady land beneath a new moon. Serving to supplant the moonlight were the temple's six lighted spires over ten miles away. Marcela didn't believe at first that these massive stone towers were built by humans, not until we walked closer to them and could clearly see their smooth surfaces and the purposeful placement of black and white stones.

"Can we climb to the top?" she asked me.

"You'll have plenty of time to explore once you're settled here."

This remark reminded the girl that she was soon to be living with strangers in the middle of a bustling city, urging her to seek comfort in her intellectual friend. She grabbed his hand with both of hers, startling him. He looked down at the nervous child. To my surprise, Ghevont responded well. He said nothing and clutched her hands tighter.

Our final walk as a group ended when we reached the guild house in Central Ecrin. In spite of the time of night, the guild remained active. A few armored warriors were speaking outside the long building, and the nearby stables kept busy with incoming and outgoing riders. Due to their current low availability of warriors, a sign outside their front doors encouraged all job offers to be "grave in nature." Nonetheless, the major headquarters always had people on staff, thus allowing the public to freely enter the building to make their requests.

A few minutes after we told the front counter our business with Braden Silver, we were told he would see us in his second floor office. Entering the small room showed us the one armed man dressed in a white nightgown, which he covered with a flimsy blue mantle when he sat behind his desk.

"Ah, Mercer, Clarissa, I was glad to hear you made it out of Gremly safely."

"Me too," said Clarissa. "We apologize for disturbing your rest."

"It's nothing. Having only one arm stops me from being as physically active as I once was, so sleep is less important. Now, Mercer, your note didn't really explain who your new friends are."

"The girl is Marcela," I answered. "I would like for her to stay here with Cat and Ethan."

"Are they here now?" Clarissa asked.

"They've been busy running errands throughout the city. I'm not throwing them into the fire just yet, so I suppose giving them an assistant wouldn't hurt."

"I want to be more than an assistant!" said Marcela. "I want them to train me. I can already use a couple of spells."

42

"Frankly," I continued, "I have nowhere else to put her, but she's spirited and I wouldn't have brought her here if I believed her unable to cope with the training."

"Say no more, Mercer," said Braden. "We were undermanned even before this valkrean business. If someone vouched by you can help, I'll accept it. In fact, I wouldn't mind hearing that your other friend here wants to join as well."

"He's more scholar than warrior, I'm afraid. Nonetheless, his aid in Gremly has proven useful in our mission."

"You were in Gremly, scholar?"

"Lived in it for some time, former guild, err, I mean, current guild master. Hmm, that's not right either, is it?"

Turning to a more succinct speaker, Braden asked me, "What happened when you crossed into Gremly?"

"I learned that an ancient spell is cast over that place, one that is subtle and looks to disorient the mind. Once that was subverted, I was able to find an old fort and this man in its basement. Braden Silver, meet Ghevont Rathmore."

"Hullo," said Ghevont cheerily, blissfully unaware that the sharpening eyes and straightening back from Braden meant he was ready to cut him down at a moment's notice.

"Riskel's son?"

"Correct, but I assure you that I have not inherited my father's partiality toward unscrupulous experimentation on living entities. However, I will say I inherited his insatiable thirst for knowledge. Indeed, few men will be able to claim-"

I cleared my throat, getting him to stop. "As I was saying, Ghevont has demonstrated his desire to not be confused with the rest of his bloodline. He helped me trap Vey Rathmore, his sister, who was following in her father's footsteps. She was killed in combat with us, along with one of her masters."

43

"Her masters?"

"Yes. This one in particular funded projects and supplied her research with victims. He was a former Voreen ambassador turned business man named Corbin Tolosa. Recognize the name?"

"Can't say that I do."

"Do you know the name 'Advent'?"

His eyes went to the ceiling as he pulled out a hidden memory. "They are an old cult, are they not?"

"Yes, and Corbin and Vey belonged to it. Vey only joined to get revenge, since it was apparently they who lured Riskel into a trap all those years ago. The Advent seem to want to resurrect a dead god, and that old business was to find a map leading to its grave. According to Vey, they succeeded in finding it, but they now need a great deal of power to accomplish their ultimate goal. The way they're choosing to acquire that power is to steal it from eidolons."

"Wait, you're saying the Advent are responsible for the valkrean abductions?"

"It fits everything I've experienced so far."

"The fit is one-sided, it seems."

"What do you mean?" asked Clarissa.

Braden stood up and looked out his little window. "The last few weeks have brought word of eidolon summoners being abducted beyond Iazali, and much of our intel points the finger at the Sisterhood."

"I'll claim ignorance on that group," I said.

"The latest leadership of Vlaukris, the southernmost nation in Kozuth. They aren't all women, mind you, but every major general is. They led a coup about fifteen years back and haven't given up power since."

"And how are they connected with the valkrean incidents?"

"For one, no valkrean has been attacked within their country, and I know our guild there has encountered resistance to our investigation. More than that, we learned the Dracera Empire was able to extract information out of a captured enemy warrior before he killed himself, though exactly who he was and what he said hasn't been revealed. In fact, little of what I'm saying is official."

"We understand, guild master. We won't spread this in taverns."

"Yes, I know, but if what you say is true…"

"So you think the Sisterhood is using the Advent?" wondered Clarissa in the guild master's pause.

"Or the other way around," inputted Ghevont. "Hmm, but then why didn't Vey mention them to us?"

"She admitted herself that she wasn't a high-ranking member," I reminded him. "Still, you'd think she'd notice the Advent weren't working alone."

"Whatever information I'm getting behind my desk," began Braden, "I'll assume that people encountering real opposition in the field have the best information. I can at least guess the Advent are acting as stealthy foot soldiers in this. Although, I find it concerning that their name has not come to our attention yet, even if it simply means our investigation isn't being as thorough as it should be."

"But you should prepare for the worst case implication."

"Aye, it's how I've lived this long, young swordsman."

"Uh, what's the worse implication?" Marcela asked.

"They're worried someone is giving everyone bad information," replied Clarissa. "Right?"

"There's already signs Alslana has someone abetting the Advent," I explained. "The cult appears well-organized, and the Riskel matter suggests they've been active for at least a few decades. Who's to say they haven't

45

infiltrated a major information organization here and there? Bad information is always worse than none at all."

"Untrue," said Braden. "*Reacting* to bad information is worse than having none to respond to. We all have to tread carefully." He used his mantle to wipe beads of sweat off his brow. "It'd be best that this cult remains believing that we're on another track, so I'll refrain from spreading official word of them, but duty will oblige me to bring them up if our other leads continue hitting dead ends. What's your next step?"

"Dranall. Vey informed us that more information can be found there, so I'm going."

"Ah, our only permanent guild house in Etoc is in Dranall. Last I heard, Malcolm Greer heads that chapter. Kind of a bastard, but an honorable man and will assist you if you mention the help you're giving me. I'll even send a message to let him know you might be visiting. However, I would keep Clarissa away from him, as he'll recognize a vampire as easily as I can." The vampire shifted her feet and narrowed her eyes in alarm. "You have no worries from me, miss. I've concluded that Mercer is not the type to have a trail of bodies following him, so I can guess you don't feed on people, but Malcolm won't take that into consideration. His parents were killed by one, you see. His entire purpose is now to be rid of your race."

"That's been the purpose of many people, I fear," said Clarissa. "Thank you for the warning."

Braden nodded. "Now then, anything more you need to tell me?"

"No," I answered, pulling out a sealed letter from my pocket, "but can you make sure this gets to the proper person?"

He took it, read the name on the front, and said, "It'll be done." He then stared at me a moment before saying, "You know, I left the arena in Qutrios confused about something. Our lone enemy was outnumbered by my men and the city guards, but he sliced and burned through us with only one

46

limp arm to show for it. Then you show up. You don't even cross blades with him before he decides to retreat. I'm beginning to see what he saw in you."

Marcela, who had not let go of Ghevont's hand, turned her confused expression from me to the former guild master. "What? He's not that great. He'd rather run from a fight."

"Then let that be your first lesson, little miss," said Braden. "Not every battle should be fought. The guild's job is to support citizens, not nations in conflict, even if it's supposedly obvious when one party is in the wrong. The most difficult decision a warrior can make is when not to fight. I'm sure Mercer has his reasons to not want to draw a blade, just as I have mine. You'll have your own as well. Now, I'm assuming all of you would like to rest up before morning arrives."

We all agreed.

As we headed for a room full of beds, Clarissa asked, "What was that letter you gave him?"

"A note to a noble."

"Wait, you mean Odet?" she whispered, making certain no guild member who passed overheard.

I nodded. "I've updated her on what we found, but I also told her to keep an eye out for any original copies of *Summertide*."

"And why not tell Braden about it?"

"I trust him, but I can't trust his comrades if they're the ones to find it. Besides, after thinking it over, I believe Odet is clever enough to look without drawing as much notice as the guild would."

"But you could still be getting her into danger."

"Royals are always in danger."

"Did you at least send my regards or something?"

"Uh, sure."

"Liar."

47

We had to wait a day and a half for Ethan and Catherine to return from whatever they were doing. I never bothered to ask. Ethan wanted to spar, but I used my mending wound as an excuse to avoid the pointless exercise. He then asked Ghevont, but the scholar just laughed as though it were the funniest joke he had ever heard. As I expected, Cat seemed receptive to having Marcela around, if only to give her brother another target for his incessant mouth.

Once everyone became acquainted, I booked passage to Dranall. The soonest available ship was large, cheap, and crowded, but it at least looked sturdy enough to survive a storm, though I couldn't say I was an expert at evaluating boat durability. No tears left Marcela as the sails unfurled and the ship began to be steered by wind and rudder, but I had a feeling she was simply waiting for us to be out of sight.

Chapter Six

Odet

A fluttering pair of little legs roused me, as they often did throughout the night, but what forced me to stay awake was the harsh beam of sunlight inflaming my eyes. I pulled the blanket over my face. Elisa groaned beside me. I hauled her side of the silky covers to my own. She groaned more. I spun around so that the covers enveloped only me. My sister tried clawing back her share of blanket, but did not have the strength to drag it away from me. Her kicking legs then rolled me to the edge of the bed until I fell off it. I landed on the wooden floor with a stifled thud.

Elisa immediately regretted what she did and, looking over the brink, said, "Odet! Why didn't you stop me? Are you dead?"

I squirmed in fake pain. "No, but five ribs are broken. Oh no! I can't feel my legs!"

"You're a bad actress."

I shot a hand upward, curling my fingers for dramatic effect. "There goes my dreams of being on stage."

After unraveling myself, I did everything required to make me presentable to the outside world. I tolerated most of the hour long routine I had to endure to accomplish this mission. It wasn't so much the acts of bathing, dressing, combing, and teeth scrubbing that irked me, it was the obligation itself. Unless illness had me clinging to life's ever crumbling cliff, my parents become rather dismayed every time I neglected to keep up my appearance in public. My younger self experienced quite a few laughs when I exited my room wearing only my nightgown.

My more ostentatious mother never understood these sentiments of mine. In fact, the queen once told me that of every aristocrat she ever met, which included my sisters and some men, that I could most easily revert to living among the foulmouthed commoners. I think she was trying to scold me, but I took it as a compliment. I also don't know why she equated being foulmouthed to being a commoner. Nearly every filthy word I could recite came from overhearing it from my father. Honestly, she verbally slugged it out with the best of them when she howled at the king.

My itinerary for the day did not include going out of the castle, so I wore a simple green dress and kept my hair loose. The last donned item was an inch long crystal secured to a necklace. The normally transparent crystal was a rare mineral called vlimphite, though most people just called them prana crystals. Certain caves speckled throughout Orda held most of the world's vlimphite reserve deep within their bowels, a few holding several hundred pounds of the stuff.

The mineral was remarkably efficient at holding prana, getting several prominent scholars to declare the material as a new living organism. Their research even suggests it "grows" under the right conditions. But whatever its precise standing in nature, its importance to the magically inclined made sure a noble house always sprang up with the discovery of another crystal cave, sometimes after a battle or two.

Until the crystal caught an influx of someone's spirit energy, it stayed a translucent color, but as my particular gemstone possessed the pure prana of my deceased grandmother, it gave off a bluish hue. Like the current queen, my grandmother wouldn't have been regarded as a great caster. All the same, as a valkrean, every Astor woman had to learn to channel holy prana, the prana given to us by way of our family eidolon. Without mastering this power it would be impossible to summon the eidolon in times of great need. To help me in that endeavor, the crystal was handed down to me instead of Beatrice.

My mother noticed early on that my skills as a warrior-caster were far ahead of most children in my station and said the crystal would be better left with someone who could make use of its sacred potential. If a time ever came when my prana reserve dropped to dire straits, then I could use the prana stored in the crystal for an emergency spell or two. I first refused the offered crystal. Something in me said it was wrong for me to keep such a treasured memento, but Leandra's adamant bearing would not yield.

Her manner confused me. I plainly saw in her unsteady eyes that she did not like the reality that one of her daughters wanted to train in the art of blades and casting, but her open support contrasted that inner feeling. I concluded that my father convinced her it was best I learn to fight if I so desired it. Still, while the king enjoyed our sparring sessions—something I'm certain he feared he would miss out on with no sons—he carried a pang of reluctance as well. It seemed as though the gods themselves had persuaded them to train me, whether they enjoyed the idea or not.

Bell, who had been up for two hours before me so she could eat, put on her leather armor, and guard my door, handed me my letters for the morning as I sat down to eat. My family had already awoken an hour before me, so it was just us younger sisters at the table. Most of the two dozen letters came from friends, but one had the shield and crossed-blades insignia of the Warriors Guild. I pulled the string to allow the paper to unfurl.

The title of the letter was "A Business Proposal." The rest of it never stated his name, but reading through its contents soon had me realizing Mercer was taking advantage of my offer to help him. He explained that an old cult called the Advent were responsible for the valkrean attacks and that an important item of theirs was the original work of *Summertide*. This work was key to disclosing a possible stronghold of theirs. Anyone with this rare edition could very well be in league with the cult and should be treated with suspicion.

He entreated me to use my "very, very vast resources and feminine wiles" to "very, very quietly" seek out any existing copy of the poem in any collection within my grasp. If I found it, I was then to keep a close "eye, nose, tongue, and ear" on it until he retrieved it himself someday, as he knew someone with the ability to solve the mystery it held. As per his request, I threw the letter in a fireplace after I finished eating.

I next made my way up to the throne hall. This open-aired room had forty foot high marble pillars of glorious white supporting the squat domed roof. Enclosing the elongated space from three sides was a flight of steps one had to climb for ten feet to reach. My mother loved this high, airy room. It would have been her favorite if she didn't have to meet with a tireless flow of dignitaries every morning. Before I reached her at the other end, Elisa and I curtsied to the nobles waiting to be met with the queen, slowing my progress.

Standing alongside her, wearing an increasingly common expression of seriousness, was my eldest sister. I did not blame Beatrice for the change in her conduct the last couple of years. I would be much the same if I was next in line to become a ruler of a kingdom. Everyone expected her to continue the peaceful legacy our family have worked tirelessly to maintain. Everything would be scrutinized, from her choice of dress to the men she could make king someday. I knew of a close friendship that had recently become strained due to her turning down his requests for a more intimate relationship. She was already comparing young men to the standards of an old king.

I saw the weight bearing down on her every day, but she had all the support in the world, so I did not so much worry about her mental state as much as pity it. I strove to give Beatrice a flash of levity by telling Elisa to run as fast as possible to our eldest sister and hug her. With all her gusto in tow, Elisa did as I bid, almost making a giggling Beatrice tumble over when she embraced her legs. My older sibling, however, presented a playful scowl to me, knowing I had been the one to let the girl off her leash.

I waited a moment for Leandra to finish speaking with a man I recognized to be a financial advisor. When he left, I asked, "Can we still afford this place?"

"As long as I refrain from anymore major renovations for another decade or so. What is it you need?"

"There's a change of plans in my day. I've been given a top secret project that might require research outside the castle."

She frowned. "Are you sure this isn't merely an excuse to meet with Gerard? And what about the training session with your father? He so enjoys those, and he leaves for Brey Stor tomorrow."

"Gerard and I already have non-secret plans to meet later, and Dad leaves in two days."

"What? Gods, what day is it? Is it not Lindus? I swore your father told me he was leaving on... Oh! That wicked man! Never mind. Very well, go play whatever game you have planned."

"I swear it's not a game, Mother. I'm not even taking Elisa with me. Her orders are to keep Beatrice's spirits up for me."

"My spirits are fine," said Beatrice, picking up her smallest sister from the floor she had been sitting on.

My mother shooed me away when she noticed an impatient noblewoman creeping closer to us.

As we walked back downstairs, Bell asked, "So what game are we playing this time?"

"Ugh, you too? I'm being serious. Remember Mercer? He needs our help."

The first collection of books that came to mind was, of course, the two palace libraries. One collection mostly consisted of more modern works, but I still rummaged through it just in case. As expected, the well-ordered room allowed me to quickly determine that my goal did not lie there.

The second library contained a somewhat smaller horde of rarer scrolls and bindings. The head librarian, the middle-aged son of the former literature coordinator, was permanently ensconced within this circular chamber. Beatrice and I used to believe Hubert's antipathy to the outside world came from his secret vampire nature, so we often involved him in our scarier games without his knowledge. There was no reason not to trust him with my undertaking, but I played it safe and lied anyway.

On asking if he could help look for what I needed, I told him a friend of mine was seeking some rare works to add to their collection and so I wondered what writings we had extra copies of. He brought me the thick registry tome and we looked through its texts. While pretending to look through unrelated works, I scoured for the mention of *Summertide*, which I found under its proper category.

According to the archive, we had two of the three editions of the poem, neither of which was the original. The dead end meant I had to move on to other collections in Ecrin. Before I left home on horseback, I made sure to find a scroll written in Old Voreen so I at least recognized what the language looked like. To keep up appearances, I also marked down a pair of works I knew my "friend" not to have and said I would return later if a transaction would occur.

A similar pattern held in the next three libraries I visited with Bell, each located in the manors of friends near the castle. When noon arrived, which I concluded more by my gurgling stomach than the fiery clock in the sky, I decided we deserved a break. Owen's home wasn't far away, and since I figured I should check his family's collection anyway, I directed my steed to his sea-hugging house to fill my need there.

Western Ecrin didn't actually have many good beaches, but the Vealora family's Ruby Manor was positioned near a nice little strip of white sand. Even under the best conditions the Lucent Sea was always a bit rough on this side of Alslana, but a few of the more skilled servants could cast a calming spell over the shore if they had to. Giving it its name, the Ruby Manor was constructed from a combination of red brick and mahogany, and kept to Alslana's typical open-air style on the bottom floor.

The gatekeepers readily recognized me and had the entry opened before my horse broke out of his trot. As I handed the reins to a servant, he informed me that the older masters of the home were away, but the young lord was eating his meal on the balcony with a few of his friends.

Going up to the large, curved balcony revealed that his company included the Vernon siblings, two brothers who I didn't care for, and his cousin Sabrina. She had a crush on Owen that went back a few years. As an only child prone to bouts of illness, Owen picked up his friends from anywhere and the Vernon brothers had taken advantage of that. They never did anything overtly malicious, if perhaps act too much like uncouth tavern patrons at times, but the fact they sometimes neglected his easily granted friendship did not sit well with me.

Using my years of ingrained experience, I politely conversed with everyone and delicately ate my steamed fish until I excused Bell and myself. Owen's library was hardly large enough to fit six shelves of books and scrolls, something viewed as mildly embarrassing for such a prestigious family. At least it meant my investigation would be quick here.

Near the end of my search, Owen came in and said, "The brothers left. Sabrina was wondering if either of you would like to join us in a game of charades or cards."

"Sorry, maybe later. We're a little busy right now."

"Doing what?"

"Looking for a book."

"Which one?"

"Don't worry about it. It doesn't appear you have it anyway. I suppose I'd be a little worried if you did."

"You're not making sense."

"Good, then I'm being successful in my mysteriousness. We'll have to go once I'm done."

"Well, you're no fun today." He walked out of sight before I heard his steps come back in. "Oh, if you're *that* interested, my dad has a big shelf full of books in his study."

"He's not big on epic poems, is he?"

"No, but my mother is. She actually keeps her favorite in there."

Bell gave me a sidelong glance before asking him, "Do you know which that is?"

"Her favorite? That would be *Summertide*, though it's a weird version."

"Weird how?"

"As in I can't understand it. It's in another language, I guess."

"Can we get in your father's study?" I asked.

"Uh, sure. I'll get someone to unlock it."

I hadn't taken the search for *Summertide* seriously in this house. It was only as we walked to his father's study did it dawn on me that I could be inside a traitor's home. The real surprise came when Owen said it was his mother reading the poem when Lord Vealora worried me more, given his trade in military intelligence. Indeed, he was one of the head investigators my family trusted to uncover the truth about the attack in Qutrios. Of course, it could be that his mother innocently enjoyed the epic while his father used it for work, or perhaps they were each a part of it. I shook my head to remove these premature thoughts.

Seeing as it had no windows, the office door swung open into a dark room. The butler created the necessary light by using a fire spell to ignite a few candles and left us to our exploration.

"Do you see the copy your mother reads?"

"What's going on, Odet?"

"Nothing. Well, let's just say a friend of mine would give much to see an original *Summertide* work."

"Original? Oh, so the language is Old Voreen?"

"Yes, and I need to confirm it."

"You can read Old Voreen?"

"No, but I can recognize its alphabet."

"Oh, okay. Give me a moment." He examined the large shelf until his eyes reached the bottom corner. "Here it is."

He pulled out a fragile looking scroll and handed it to me in a way that made me cringe. With no identifying marks, I had to unroll a page to confirm what I didn't want to feel. I must have been standing there agape longer than I thought, because Bell had to say "Your Highness?" to snap me back to the normal flow of time. I had given myself away by this point.

"What's wrong, Odet?" asked a baffled Owen. "You're not acting like yourself."

I put the scroll back where he found it. "Listen, Owen, I need you to trust me. Can you do that?"

"Of course, just tell me what's gotten you so frazzled."

"I don't think I can explain everything to you right now. I'm not even a hundred percent certain this isn't a mere coincidence. Can you promise me you'll do as I say?"

"Sure, I promise."

"That scroll could be very important to a group of people, people who might hurt you if they discover you have it. At the same time, we can't get rid of it, so I need you to keep a close eye on it. This is where the trust part comes in, you can't mention any of this to your parents, do you understand?"

"My parents? Why not?"

"Because they might accidentally attract unwanted attention if they knew they had something this valuable. I'll also need your butler take an oath before I leave."

"What oath?"

57

"He knows we were in here. That could be enough to alert your parents that something is wrong. I need him to swear by my family's name that he won't say anything to them."

"Gods, Odet. This is as serious as I've ever seen you. Why can't you tell me exactly what's going on? Where'd you learn about this?"

"I can't confirm anything until I get more information myself. Will you do all this for me?"

"I already promised, didn't I?"

"Thank you, and I promise to tell you everything, no matter how it turns out."

Chapter Seven
Mercer

Dranall was about an eight hundred mile voyage to the north. A book I borrowed from the guild informed me of the city's disputable ownership over the last thousand years. More recently, Etoc forcibly claimed the port city over a century ago at a time when the dying Alslana Empire was otherwise freely releasing territories from their hold. The port had actually been the capital of Etoc before it was seized by Alslana, compelling the leadership to make the less developed town of Bukuna its new capital. Despite occasional efforts by Etoc forces to remove nearby Alslana forts, Dranall currently laid right at the edge of the Alslana border.

This latest voyage was no less turbulent on Ghevont's latest meals, but I felt more at ease than before. Clarissa's biggest problem remained finding blood to refill her vials. There were plenty of rats to be found, but the cramped quarters made it harder for her to hunt them down without being noticed. She was even caught draining a mouse's blood halfway into the crossing, but she used the excuse that she was collecting animal blood for the scholar's tests on experimental remedies.

Since the best way for Ghevont to thwart the expulsion of his food was to keep his mind occupied, he had sought the company of our fellow passengers. They acted as an attentive audience to his random soliloquies, which included his countless theories and all the ancient tales he knew by heart. This had made him well-known enough for the vampire's false explanation to ring true. It rang so loudly for two young brothers that the pair began to help Clarissa catch several more rats before their mother discovered the vile endeavor and spanked them in front of the whole ship. I laughed so damn hard when Clarissa told me that. I didn't know why I found children getting punished hilarious, but I did.

Early fall winds were filling our sails by the time we saw Dranall's six towers. I enjoyed the brisker breezes. They helped remove the perpetual stickiness I carried ever since summer began. As the ship started to dock in the packed harbor, I employed the morning light to see a city marked by two cultures. Following the northern style, the town's center was clustered with buildings of hardy stone, with the majority encircled by a thick rock wall forty feet high. Outside this imposing wall of gray were buildings following Alslana's wooden, open style. Many of these were encircled by a shorter wall of tanned brick.

"So you're not going to contact Malcolm?" Clarissa asked me.

Helping her step off the plank that linked ship and pier, I replied, "Not unless we have to, but I'll consider it if we can't find Magnus on our own."

We began the search for Tolosa's shipyard offices after regaining our bearings with a light breakfast at a tavern. Dranall had the resources and space to construct a steady supply of ships, so several companies operated in the wide harbor. Since I didn't want to alert any Tolosa collaborator of prowlers, I kept our questioning limited to lower management types, telling them I was a courier looking to drop off a letter.

The third company we visited bore a succulent piece of fruit. A busy dock worker pointed us to a man supervising the loading of a large ship. The stuffy man, who had never lifted a crate in his life, said he had dealt with Tolosa in the past and knew his usual workplace to be in the smaller of two administrative buildings located just inside the inner wall of the city. With a puffed chest he added that his son worked in the larger building.

We followed his directions to find a three-story wooden structure overlooking the Parsillion Ocean and erected next to a large warehouse. A wide road and pygmy wall separated it from the sea. I sat on the wall and watched the building through the busy street.

"Uh, are we just going to watch it until he comes out?" asked Clarissa, clearly bothered by the fact we couldn't at least find a spot away from the unobstructed sunlight.

"There's a higher chance he'll recognize me if I get too close."

"But not mine. Can't I at least go check if there's a Magnus Nissen working there?"

"Even if you confirm it, then what? Whoever you talk to will probably let him know that someone was looking for him. What if that's enough to scare him off?"

She frowned, but the downturned lips didn't stay dejected for long. "Oh! Ghevont and I will go together! Ghevont will say he's Vey's brother and that he has to speak with him in private at his house or something. Then you follow us."

I ruminated a moment. "Not bad, but if this private place just happens to be the office, then how will I get in? He'll become suspicious if you say you have to get somebody else. I also need to make sure we won't be disturbed. A public office is not the place to interrogate an enemy. I'm sorry, Clarissa, but I'm prepared to wait all of this day and the next to see if he comes out. If he doesn't, we'll take riskier measures."

She groaned. "I realize this is a delicate situation, but we've been waiting for a while already."

"Then a day or two more won't kill you."

"It might, Mercer, it might." She took out a blood vial and lapped up every drop.

Ghevont spent his time reading the time away while a hooded Clarissa stretched her legs with short walks, never going too far away in case I needed her. My expectation to see Magnus grew during the lunch hour, but he either had food already with him or it was the first sign he wasn't there at all.

The sun used its magic to cast longer and longer shadows, and the grand orb itself started disappearing behind the city skyline. It was in this dark orange tint that my unblinking eyes caught the hint of the familiar leaving the building—a red cloak. The figure was unhooded, allowing me to note the man's messy brown hair, small nose, and thin lips. It was him, my dusty ghost rushing back into my body confirmed that.

Still, he looked much older than I thought he would. My memory of Magnus was that of an unseasoned, nervy youth with little in the way of self-assurance. Now I was staring at a confident young adult walking with fortitude. How different would I look to him? It had been three years since we last saw each other, and even these past few months had me grow the couple of inches needed to wield my lengthy longsword with greater grace. I suppose how we looked to one another wouldn't matter once I placed Aranath against his throat.

I tapped Clarissa's shoulder. "The red cloak, that's him."

Magnus mingled with the crowd heading for the outer ring of the city. Staying well behind his range of suspicion, we started trailing him. My former handler occasionally stopped to look about himself, but his increased maturity did not translate to an improved talent for enemy recognition. To make sure the clumsy scholar did not attract my target's attention by tripping or knocking into someone, I made him stay a few yards behind Clarissa and I.

Not long after stopping by an open market to buy a pouch of walnuts and a small pumpkin, Magnus crossed into quieter, muddier streets, though they were populated enough to continue supporting our anonymity. He halted in front of a shabby little cottage of cold blue stone. We went around the corner of a nearby household once he disappeared inside. I called up Ghevont to us and directed the scholar next to the Magnus house. I next pointed Clarissa behind the house. From these positions we watched the place for over half an hour before coming back together.

"See anything?" I asked them.

"There's a little window on my side," said Ghevont. "He passed by it a few times. I think he's alone."

"Clarissa?"

"There's a backdoor leading to the alleyway. I got pretty close, but I didn't hear anything inside. I say he's alone, too."

"Then we'll start on your plan. You and Ghevont get him to let you in. Ghevont, once you find an opening, you paralyze him." Looking at Clarissa, I said, "Use your water spell to make certain he can't scream. Once he's secure, you let me in from the back, got it?"

"Uh, what do you mean 'use my water spell'? Like, choke him with it?"

"Yes. Cover his head in water until he breathes some of it, then come and get me."

"Oh, okay."

"I don't know what he's capable of, so do everything as fast as you can."

As Ghevont and Clarissa slowly strolled toward the front door, talking about what they were going to say, I sprinted to my station at the back. The mumbling murmur of the city was all around me, but it wasn't loud enough to prevent me from picking up the knock and most of the words that followed the opening of the creaking door.

"Can I help you?" asked the tenant.

"You may," said Ghevont. "My name is Ghevont Rathmore. I believe you work for my sister, Vey Rathmore?"

With a quieter tone, Magnus replied, "Yes, I do. Where is she? Did she send you here?"

63

"That's what we need to talk about," said a grave Clarissa. "Do you mind if we talk inside?"

"Of course, come in."

The door closed, muffling their voices. I don't know if it was actual time or my perception of it, but I waited a long while before I heard a loud thud, a short yelp, and Aranath being pulled out of my scabbard. The scrambling of feet reached my door. It opened to show Clarissa, the yellow light of Ghevont's paralysis spell, and a coughing Magnus on his knees. I entered a house with only two rooms—a bedroom to my left and the main living space, which had a small fireplace and two kettles hanging over it.

Pressing the edge of my longsword against his neck, I forced Magnus' drenched head upward and asked, "Do you recognize me, Magnus?" He was still ejecting some of the foreign water in his lungs, but he heard me and was skimming my face for the answer.

Giving him a bit more time to delve into his memory, I told Clarissa to shut the shutters and for Ghevont to ease his restrictive spell somewhat. When they were done and no answer came, I said, "It's okay if you don't recognize me. It's difficult to recognize a person when they were nothing more than a bag of bones in a dark pit."

With widening eyes and hoarse words, Magnus said, "You were at the Onyx base. You're the one with a fiend's tail around your arm." He looked at Ghevont. "Are you really Vey's brother?"

"That I am."

"Where is she?"

"She's dead," I answered.

Magnus' eyes glazed over with an anxious sheen, eradicating the thin layer of confidence he had been emanating up until that point. He reverted to the impressionable youth I had known in my earliest memories. "You killed her?"

64

"Yes, along with Corbin."

He hung his head with almost enough force to rip it off his shoulders. No spell could make him as static as he then became.

"I see, you cared for her."

"*Cared*?!" He snapped with enough savagery to force Ghevont to reinforce his spell. "I *loved* her. I loved everything about her—her determination, her smell, her hair, her ferocity. What other woman comes close?" His head drooped again.

"Strange," said Ghevont. "I was with Vey in her last moments and she never mentioned a great love. Were your feelings one-sided?"

"No… maybe. Well, they may not have been as strong, but she had her mind on other things, other goals. When those were done she would have seen what more we could be, but now… I don't understand, if you're her brother, then why are you helping her killer?"

"That answer might take longer than Mercer is comfortable with, but you can be assured that I do feel some animosity for the circumstances in which she died."

"You've never mentioned that before," I told him.

"Oh, it's nothing that interferes with my objectives or your own, so I never felt the need to bring it up."

Putting aside the fact that Ghevont was less of an open book than I first thought, I refocused on these objectives of mine. "Tell us everything you know about the Advent and my family."

"You'll get the same answers if you kill me, because I ain't telling you shit."

"Good, let's do this the more entertaining way." Turning to Clarissa, I said, "Drown him for a while."

She was halfway to gathering a ball of water when Ghevont said, "Wait a moment. Magnus, if you cared so much for Vey, then it's in your best

65

interest to aid my companion here. Yes it was his blade that killed her, but it was also her whip that saved him. Tell me, do you know where she went?"

"She said she had to get home."

"But not exactly where?"

"N-no."

"My sister trusted no one with her secrets, but she spilled all she could to Mercer and made him swear he would carry out her chief goal in life. That goal was to kill every last Advent cultist. The Advent killed our parents, you see, and this ferocious determination you so admired largely originated from wanting them avenged. Without her help, Corbin would have killed me and Mercer, taken Vey's home under his control, and probably have you killed, since it sounds as though your devotion went to my sister and not the Advent. Do you understand? Not helping us is the same as not helping Vey. So then, what do you know?"

Magnus digested this information slower than Ghevont's expectation, but there was eventually a reaction. He looked back at me and said, "This is bullshit. You kill her and you promise to kill her enemies?"

"I'm certain 'bullshit' was in her mind as well," I said. "Look at it this way, do you think we would know as much as we do if she didn't tell us everything willingly? I'll be honest, Magnus, the world is better off that a woman who helped take everything away from me is dead, but she saved my life from Corbin's final blow, so I owe her some measure of debt."

"And what will become of me?"

"You deserve your head to be rolling at my feet, but if I'm satisfied that you've given us everything, then I'll drop you off with the guild. They'll kill you if they discover your work in corruption, so all I'll mention is Corbin and the valkrean attacks. I'll even say you were too dumb to be nothing more than his assistant."

66

"The Advent will have me killed once they find out I've been captured."

"I'll tell them to keep your imprisonment quiet. In any event, you can either take your chances in a cell or find out now if your neck can resist steel. So last chance, what do you know about my family and the Advent?"

With callousness in his throat, he said, "Your family? That's right, Corbin went after them."

"Do you know what happened to them? Who went after them?"

"No. Other Advent took over the corruption project shortly after we sold you. Vey and I came here to work for Corbin more directly."

"Doing what?"

"Only Vey knows, *knew* the details. I got the impression he was smuggling something by sea."

"You must know some of Corbin's contacts, someone he would have trusted to carry out his dirty work. I imagine you still see a few every now and then."

"They mostly stopped coming over to the office when he left with Vey, but they do still leave messages."

"At his office?"

"Yes, but I gather them and take them to his mistress' house for safe keeping."

"Not his own?"

"He rented places sometimes, but he mostly used *The Blackfly* as his home."

"A ship?"

"Yeah."

"Where is it now?"

"You don't know? He and Vey used it when they left."

"Shit. Fine, so who's this mistress? Where does she live?"

"Bethany Lynd. She's some rich noblewoman who normally lives with her husband, but the house I go to is the one she uses for her erotic escapades with Corbin or any other man that says 'hello' to her. It's the tall brick house on Granberry Hill."

"Is she involved with the Advent?"

"No idea. I don't think she is, but who the fuck knows with those people?"

"How were you recruited?"

The corner of his mouth cracked a smile. "I was at the temple in Qutrios, praying for my shitty life to mean something. She answered my prayers before I rose from my knees. I didn't care who or what she worked for, I just wanted to be with her. I've never met another person as alive and real as she was."

"We need every document and letter available in Bethany's house and Corbin's office. I know you can get into the office at any time, but how easy is it getting into the lover's house?"

"I don't have a key, but the servants have been instructed to allow me in entry in the early afternoons. Any other time and Bethany might be there with somebody."

"Then we go to the office first."

"Ever heard of *Summertide*?"

"The poem?"

"Yes. Do you know if Corbin had a copy or ever mentioned it?"

"Why would he care about a poem? No, I never heard anything about it."

"I'm going to tell Ghevont to remove the paralysis spell. It should go without saying that any attempt at escape will be met with violence. I have connections with the guild, so there will be no consequences if I kill you in the middle of a crowd, understand?"

68

"Yes," he said gruffly.

I nodded at Ghevont. He looked confused at first, but then remembered what he was supposed to do. The scholar lowered his arms and the yellow circle of light under Magnus dissolved away. Our captive stood up like a slow raising marionette and smoothed out his cloak.

I sheathed the longsword and pulled out a dagger, keeping it hidden under my cloak's sleeve. "Lead the way, Magnus. We'll be on your ass the entire time."

The streets were still full of people heading for market stalls, shops, and taverns. It would have been easy for someone with any swiftness to make a break for it and hope to elude their captors. Yet Magnus seemed to take my threat seriously. He knew better than most what the corruption inside me could do.

Chapter Eight

There was no resistance getting into Corbin's spacious office. Once there, my eyes never left Magnus as he, Clarissa, and Ghevont rummaged through the desk, two cabinets, and a small chest. They collected every letter and loose document they could find, placing most of them in Ghevont's bag before leaving for Magnus' cottage. Then, as we waited for tomorrow afternoon to arrive, everyone sorted and read through the papers.

Much of it was months old business reports with jargon that would require an accountant to make sense of. A few personal letters told of an ex-wife and daughter that our captive said lived somewhere in Voreen. Magnus was uncertain how much they would know of the Advent, but as he rarely heard them mentioned, he assumed they weren't privy to any real information.

"Did the Advent learn anything new about corruption?" I asked our captive, who sat alone in a corner.

"I am also interested in that answer," said Ghevont.

"I'm not familiar with what was old about corruption," replied Magnus. "I just know you were by far our best subject, perhaps even better than Vey realized. In fact, I'd expect you'd be the one to uncover something new about corruption. You should barely be lucid by now."

"I only learned that the power of corruption can be held back by even greater power."

"Sounds like a precarious position to be in."

"Some men can handle a shitty situation."

"And some women," added Clarissa. She slumped in her chair. "I'm sorry, Mercer, there's nothing in my pile."

"Get some rest, then."

"Me? You haven't slept on land yet."

"I'm fine. I could go another day without sleep, easy. Trust me, if our friend here runs, I want nobody's blade but mine to catch up with him."

The next morning filtered through the cracks in the shutters. Clarissa heated cups of runny soup for our breakfast before we left for "Bethany's shack of extramarital affection," as the vampire put it.

Granberry Hill was not so much a hill as much as a big lump of pretty dirt within the inner city wall. The sea's rhythmic undulations could be heard a hundred yards away. Many of the buildings here were much taller than they were wide, with the rooftop terraces implying their builders had been drilled by their supervisors to get the loftiest possible view for their egocentric patrons. We passed a hired caster using a water spell to clean the paved streets of horse crap, giving the orange stones a bright sheen.

Magnus led us to a short walkway hedged in by tidy bushes, which were sprinkled with little pink flowers that Ghevont plucked for future examination. The path itself directed us up to the four-story brick home we sought.

I paused my walk when Magnus stopped in his tracks. "What is it?"

"Look, those two appear to be guardsmen." He was right. A man and woman standing at the front of the door were donning Dranall's distinct dark gray armor and green mantles. "Guardsmen usually patrol this district from the perimeter. Something is wrong."

"Lucky us. Ghevont, Clarissa, stay here a moment. We'll check what's going on."

The guardsmen quickly noticed us walking up to them. The woman was sent by the other to intercept us.

"Can I help you, gentlemen?"

"I'm an associate of Lady Lynd," said Magnus. "Can you tell me what's happened?"

"Robbery."

71

"Robbery? When? What was stolen?"

"The most valuable items appear to be silverware."

"And the 'less' valuable? I was keeping some of my boss' papers in there. Were any documents taken?"

"A few desks and drawers were broken into, but the servants couldn't say what they contained."

"Shit. May I go check if my papers are still there? The servants can vouch for my identity."

"Very well."

"Did anyone see the thief?" I asked.

"She was caught escaping through the second-story window by one of the servants. All he could say for certain was that she was a she. He also said her hair was long and either black or dark brown, but it was still too early in the morning for him to notice anything more."

Magnus thanked her and went up to get someone to confirm his identity. After a servant boy recognized him, we sprinted up to the second floor and entered a small study. Magnus did not need his key to unlock the already open drawer. He groaned when he saw its empty contents.

"This is not my fault," he said.

"Only your own crappy decisions have allowed your life to be determined by someone else's papers, so it kind of is."

"But why now?"

"Isn't it obvious? You must have been watched before we got here, meaning someone saw us going into your home and office."

"The Advent?"

"Doubt it. They would want you and any information destroyed, yet this thief merely stole them once she figured out you'd been compromised. I'm sure she cared nothing for you. Corbin must be her target."

"Wait! We can find her, or at least some letters."

"How?"

"Vey placed runes on some fake forms. I just have to recreate it and cast a spell to set them off."

"What happens when you set them off?"

"Depends on what spell I use, but I'll just have a pulse of prana burst out. I'll feel it if I'm close enough."

"How close?"

"I'm not sure, but I'm certain I'll be able to feel something if she's still in the city."

"Won't the thief sense this pulse?"

"Probably, but maybe that'll just convince her to leave the letters alone."

"Or convince her to destroy them." I sighed. "We have little other choice. Make some runes and let's get out of here."

I explained to Clarissa and Ghevont the situation when we went outside a few minutes later. Magnus then placed one of his paper runes on the ground and splayed his hand on it, focusing his prana into it. The triangular rune next lit up and the heat of the spell singed the parchment. Magnus stayed motionless a moment before turning to us.

"I got it. It's straight north of us. Can't be beyond the inner wall."

"Let's move!"

I forced Magnus up and pushed him ahead of me until we were at running speed. Our sprinting took us to the street hugging the coastline. It felt good sharply breathing in the fresh, salty air, but I was too busy to notice the invigorating sensation at the time.

Two hundred yards down the coast and I had Magnus try his spell again. The spark of prana told him we were on the right track. All my concentration went into my eyes, trying to get any glimpse at someone with long, dark hair, which accounted for half the women among the masses.

After the third spell attempt, Magnus said, "We're closer, but she's on the move. She's more to the west this time, deeper into the city."

"How far?"

"Like I said, closer. It's hard to give an exact distance. I only remember one more rune in the batch, so we have to make it count. Should have made more."

"You should have done a lot of things differently." Out of the corner of my eye, I noted that Clarissa labored under the clear noon sky. Whether she could keep the pace was irrelevant. There was simply no way to accommodate her. "Let's keep going."

It turned out we were forced to run slower in the congested, intersecting streets. I assumed the thief kept moving away from us, so I waited a good while before giving permission for Magnus to use the final rune.

Removing his hand from the paper, Magnus pointed southwest and said, "She's very close. Can't be more than a hundred yards off."

I scoured for a scalable structure. On spotting one, I used my most serious tone to say, "You two don't let Magnus out of your sight. Ghevont, if he tries anything, I'll allow you to do whatever you want to his corpse."

"Ah, excellent. Perhaps you would like to assist me, Clarissa?"

I heard the vampire exclaim an enthusiastic "Sure thing!" before I stopped listening.

The streets had fewer people here, but a handful of onlookers still wordlessly wondered why someone was climbing a small house. The thatch roof pressed up against a taller building I jumped on to. Keeping my profile low by crouching, I began to judge which building looked suitable for a wanted burglar. What ended up attracting my eyes was not a lifeless building, but a living creature.

It swiftly crept on a roof fifty yards away, so all I picked up was the rough shape of a cat-like animal with reedy legs, short black fur, and an

74

elongated body. It must have been three feet tall at the shoulders, and its large golden eyes had no trouble perceiving me. With supple fleetness the animal vanished behind a line of chimney stacks.

"Did you see that?" I asked Aranath.

"Briefly. Probably a zymoni. Sneaky little things."

"It's a summoned creature?" I asked, beginning a rooftop run.

"Yes. They're dangerous in packs, but as roofs make poor camouflage, it appears this one is alone."

A few hikes and drops soon put me in the same place the zymoni had been prowling. The creature remained undetectable, but there was an edifice that siphoned all of my scrutiny. Surrounded by a waterless moat was a temple of day and night. The reason I didn't spot it from a mile away was due to its lack of towers. Instead, six stony stumps stood in their place, with three on either side of the domed structure. It was apparent that the temple had been deserted for years. Black burn marks from an old fire peppered the white walls, and missing pieces of the dome allowed the weather to assault its insides. If this wasn't the perfect venue for an urban thief to set a trap for their pursuer, I didn't know what was.

A few buildings hugged the ditch, letting me get close to the temple's left flank. One building in particular rose ten feet above the temple's narrow balcony, which protracted just below the dome's curve. Along with eight glassless windows, a doorless entrance could be reached from the balcony. Thinking that starting my search from above would be better than walking in from below, I decided to take the leap. With a running start and prana-enforced legs, I hurdled over the forty foot drop and landed securely on the other side.

Anticipating that I had entered a cornered thief's territory, I took every step seriously and unsheathed my longsword. I judiciously looked through the little windows lining the wall, observing a typical temple layout that consisted of worn stone pews, crumbling pillars, and unlit metal braziers. On reaching the entry, I outstretched my left arm and cast my illusion spell, sending the visual copy of myself running inside. Nothing reacted to it.

For the next phase of preparation, I summoned a mix of explosive stones and fire stones. I then chucked them randomly into the religious construction. They rattled without interference, even their own echoes didn't blend into one another. There was nothing left to do after that but for my real self to go in.

Though no longer active, crossing the threshold made it the first time I stepped inside a holy place. I had gotten glimpses of it from the outside before, but my curiosity never reached a point where I listened to a sermon or experienced a priest's unearned hospitality. The pecking impression that my impure spirit had no business occupying the hallowed space was quickly replaced by not giving a shit. Blood was likely to be spilled, and I needed to make sure it wasn't mine.

The inner balcony continued to my left and wrapped around to the other side, expanding enough to fit more pews at its center. My right side held the stairs. Stepping toward the edge, I focused on the nearest stones and triggered them. The flash from the exploding rocks didn't die down before I saw the zymoni dash out from behind a balcony pew. It became a blur of shadowy speed as it charged my way, emitting a noise that sounded as though a saber-tooth cat was trying to bark like a dog. From this distance I saw that the beast had two trim tails and a wolfish snout. Before it crossed the range of my blade, it used its strange, gecko-like paws to cling to the wall behind me. The beast then leapt down and headed for the stairs.

"It's a distraction, boy!" said Aranath.

I was in the middle of coming up with that very same conclusion. I whirled back around just in time to avoid a thrown knife. At least, I avoided most of it. If I hadn't, it would have impaled my thigh rather than only grazing it. The thrower of the weapon stood behind a pew, a short scimitar in hand. She was a tall, lean woman in her early thirties. Her long black hair was tied into a ponytail and a light caramel color dyed her skin. The only defensive pieces of clothing were her steel gauntlets. Otherwise, she wore thigh-high leather boots, a dark blue corselet, and a short skirt. Even drenched in shadows it was plain to see that her composed face was the type men wanted to wake up to in the morning.

Knowing it wasn't a good idea to have the zymoni out of my sight, I started retreating to the stairs. As I did so, the woman strolled out from behind the pew with casual grace. Halfway down the stairway, I caught the zymoni staring up at me from the middle of the temple floor. I almost took a rough dive when my foot slipped on a step. I initially thought I suffered from a lapse of concentration, but the sudden wooziness overcoming my senses forced me to consider another possibility.

My wobbling knees struggled to keep me standing by the time I reached the flat floor. My forehead dripped thick beads of sweat and my eyesight only distinguished the thief as a descending blotch. As for my ears, they heard a slurring drunk when the woman said, "Don't worry, little man, my toxin won't kill you. *I* will if your friends show up and are dumb enough to attack me. Now, who are you?"

"Aranath!"

The dragon loosened its grip on my corruption. I still felt as though opening my mouth would allow my brain to fall out, but I could move, and that's all I cared about. I tossed an explosive stone at the beast and triggered both it and every other stone left in the area. The blasts and flickering fire propelled the frightened creature up a pillar. I caught her by surprise, but the thief was skilled enough to deflect an upward swing of my sword. She then pulled out a long, skinny dagger for her other hand to use.

As expected from a rogue, she used her limberness and agility for quick attacks and evasion. Even without the toxin in my bloodstream, I

77

doubted my ability to match her fleetness. Lucky for me, her lack of defensive strategy made my weapon more dangerous to her than hers were to me, forcing her to choose her movements wisely.

We were in a dead heat for a minute, steel sparking as they clashed in a flurry of tight slashes and narrowly missed strikes. The fight began to feel more like a high stakes sparring session than a life and death struggle. It would have been different if we were alone and pressured to come up with a plan to overwhelm the other, but both of us were waiting for reinforcements to break the tie.

"Kara! What's wrong, girl?! Get our ass over here and help me!"

The zymoni growled anxiously, her muzzle taking sniffs of the dissipating smell of dragon fire. She started descending the pillar, but her triangular ears picked up the incoming footsteps of my allies. A whip of water twisted out of Clarissa's hand and went after the zymoni. The creature growled and ascended higher. Ghevont kept Magnus in front of him, but he gained an angle to fire a bolt of lightning at my foe.

I knew that she knew it was over, but she still went through the trouble of evading the electric discharge, leaving her open for a sweep of my leg to send her on her back. Since she knew what was coming, she was able to maneuver her body to press her longer weapon under my ball sack at the same time I put my blade's tip to her throat.

"Let go of your weapons," I said.

"Will you kill me afterwards?"

"Depends. Are you Advent?"

"Advent? Never heard of 'em."

"Um, you okay there?" Clarissa asked me, keeping her other eye on the growling beast.

"Fine. All of you stay where you are." Back to the stranger, I said, "I don't think we're enemies. You've been watching Magnus, but I'm guessing you really want Corbin Tolosa, right?"

She licked her teeth. "Possibly. Why does that matter to you?"

"He helped fuck over my life, so I killed him, but there's still information I need. Why do you want his letters?"

"Corbin has fucked up quite a few lives, it seems. Strictly speaking, *I* don't care about Corbin, but one of my friends does. I was helping him out with his problem."

"Do you have any problems sharing?"

"Yes, but not about this."

I removed Aranath from her neck and stepped back. "Where'd you put the letters?"

She stood up and nodded toward the left line of pews. "Under the third one. Let's see if one of your fire rocks didn't end up scorching my satchel."

I sheathed my sword and she did the same. Clarissa let her whip of water drop and the zymoni's growl became a dull rumble.

"Come to mommy, Kara! You big pussy." The summoned animal scrambled down the pillar and whined at her master. Petting her, the thief told me, "You made her nervous. Haven't seen her like that since she was small enough to carry. Guess seeing you recover from my toxin so quickly freaked her out. How'd you do that, anyway?"

"I haven't recovered from it, it just doesn't affect me as much as it would normal people."

Stooping down to pick up her satchel, she said, "A little man who thinks he's special, huh? What's your name?"

"Mercer."

"Just 'Mercer'? No last name?"

"I would need a family for that."

"Orphan?"

"For all I know. What do we call you?"

"Lucetta Ambrose."

"Hi, Lucetta. I'm Clarissa Lorraine and the red head is Ghevont Rath-, um, yeah, Ghevont Rath. Sorry about Mercer, but he literally meets everyone by putting a blade to their throat. It's how I met him."

"Me too," said Ghevont.

Lucetta chuckled. "Sounds like a friend of mine."

"Have you looked at any of the letters yet?" I asked Lucetta.

"Just a few, but nothing interesting yet. Do you want to read them now?"

"I first want to leave Magnus with the guild."

"Wouldn't it be easier to kill him?"

"Yes, but he's merely an easily influenced fool, and I gave my word that I wouldn't kill him once he did all he could for me."

She shrugged. "Suit yourself, little man."

Ghevont cleared his throat and said, "Excuse me, Lady Ambrose, but Mercer is at least an inch taller than you, yet you keep referring to him as 'little man.' Is your sight well?"

She laughed. "'Lady'? That's a first. Aye, he's a tad taller than me, but I compare him to far larger men I know."

"I see. An appreciated insight."

I started to make my way toward the entrance, prompting everyone to follow me.

Before she strode outside, Lucetta kissed the zymoni's head and said, "I'll get a nice big fish for you next time you're summoned." In a puff of air, the zymoni's link to our realm was broken, sending it back to its proper home.

Chapter Nine

Braden was right about Malcolm, he was a dick. The curmudgeon was upset that I wanted to use precious guild resources to indefinitely incarcerate a man he had no information on. He openly stated that he didn't like the look of me and didn't trust my word that Magnus was indirectly involved with the valkrean issue, saying he would release him in six months if his own investigation on Corbin turned up nothing. He also said Braden now owed him a big favor. I was irritated that I would have to check on Magnus in six months, but I otherwise kept my mouth shut and handed the proverbial leash to the guild.

Once that chore was finished, the rest of us agreed to rent a room. By Lucetta's insistence, we found a nice chamber overlooking the sea. She paid for it herself with what I imagined were filched coins. The third-story space held two large beds I couldn't lay on without falling asleep, so I sat in a hard chair. I wouldn't have minded catching a few winks before plunging through the papers, but my corruption continued fighting off the toxin's effects. A good rest didn't seem possible for another hour.

Lucetta didn't concern herself with the threat of sleep and jumped into the bed nearest the door. She sprawled her lithe body onto the sheets and ruffled them under her. Clarissa, glad to have an adult woman to emulate for once, did much the same on the other bed.

After we each grabbed our share of papers, Lucetta asked, "What exactly are you guys looking for?"

"Corbin worked for a group called the Advent," I explained. "They're a cult responsible for the valkrean attacks and have funded experiments in dark magic. As I understand it, Corbin was responsible for seizing assets, living or otherwise. I'm sure no letter will explicitly state his or the sender's involvement, but anything that sounds vaguely cryptic should be put aside for a closer look. Names that come up often should also be noted." Lucetta had started reading her pile in the middle of my expounding, but it was easy to see she was the type who could take in information from different sides at once. "What are you seeking?"

"Same thing—weird stuff."

Getting more comfortable, she pulled her boots off her toned legs and tossed them aside. She then let her hair loose and laid on her side, her ass pointing straight at Ghevont, who sat by the window. Clarissa giggled when she noticed the scholar's unblinking eyes scrutinizing the shapely figure. Ghevont shook his head and focused on the task at hand when he learned what he could by simple staring. I was more subtle in the glances I garnered.

There was a good bundle to sift through, but between the four of us, it didn't appear so daunting. As before, most of it concerned legitimate business transactions, at least as far as I understood the convoluted verbiage of commerce. I set aside a few papers that seemed worth a second glance, but that meager stack didn't inspire confidence that there would be a trail to follow. That didn't matter. All I needed was a single letter. Half an hour after we started reading, I got it.

Ghevont gradually rose from the chair. He then just stood there, blocking part of the daylight. The meticulous man read it a second or third time before saying, "This is something." He walked over and handed me a short letter. It was dated a month ago and said:

To C. T.,

It took some time, but my informer found the family from Remron. They've settled in Bukuna. Don't know if you still want to add to your collection, but the job will cost extra if you do. They're within the walls and they've hired extra bodyguards. Things are only getting busier on my end, so respond quickly if you want this done. You can find them at a house they call

82

Equine Manor if you want your own men to handle this. Remember, the next drink is on you.

K.M.

"Can I see?" asked Lucetta.

"Is it something?" Ghevont asked as I stood to hand the letter over to the petitioner.

"It's the best we have so far."

"Wait," said Lucetta after reading the message, stopping me in my tracks. "Why do you care about this family?"

"I don't actually know if I should."

"What does that mean?"

"It means I have no memory of my time before the Advent experimented on me, but I know they got me from somewhere. Right now I'm looking to see whether Corbin went after a family I don't remember."

Lucetta sat up and swung her legs so they dangled off the side of the bed. She cocked her head and stared at me like a probing Marcela would. "This friend I'm helping, he's searching for his children, two brothers who lived in Remron with their aunt. One of them would surely be around your age, the first taken. The younger brother was kidnapped three years later. You don't look much like him, but he did say his kids took more after their mother. Hmm, if you're really his son, I guess that makes me your step-mother."

"So you're married to this friend of yours?" asked Clarissa. "To Mercer's maybe-father?"

"We never went in front of a priest or anything, but we basically are, as in I'll kill him if I catch him with another woman. At least not without inviting me."

"What's his name? What are the names of the brothers?"

"Lorcan Eberwolf is my man's name. Alexandros is the younger brother and 'Cyrus' might be your friend's real name."

83

Everyone turned to look at me, waiting to see what I thought of this possibility. The names did nothing to spur any memory or emotion, so I coolly asked, "Do you know if others were taken from Remron?"

"A few other kids, both in the first and second forays."

"Then I can be any one of them as well. Where's your friend now?"

"He's investigating a lead further south. He should be coming up to meet me in a week or two, but if you're thinking he'll be able to identify you as his son, I wouldn't count on it."

"Why not?"

"He told me the last time he saw his children was when the oldest was four years old."

"Then why does he care about his sons now?"

She shot up to her feet, looking serious for what could have been the first time in her life. "He might have not been there for his sons, but that sure as fuck doesn't mean he didn't care!" She realized her agitated state and relaxed her voice and shoulders. After a shallow breath, she said, "Lorcan wanted to raise his children, but their mother's stuck-up family wouldn't hear of a pirate getting involved with their blood, so they chased him off. I don't know if you're his son or not, but Lorcan is a man to be respected when you meet him."

"I'm sure he is," said Clarissa. "Mercer is sorry for the ignorant remark, right Mercer?"

"Sure," I said. "I apologize, Lucetta."

She sat back down in a huff. "No, don't be sorry. I'd normally slap a girl if she talked the way I just did about their man. It's vomit inducing, really."

"So Lorcan is a pirate?" Clarissa tried clarifying.

"That's the closest depiction most would brand his deeds, but he's no heartless brigand terrorizing every ship he sees. He's simply a man who has the spirit and capacity to live as freely as possible, and no one can tell one how to live in the open sea. If he has to support that life by stealing a few things from other thieves or defenseless ships of trade, then so be it."

"I believe you're gushing again," Ghevont pointed out.

"You'll be gushing blood if you mention that again."

Refocusing her, I said, "Lucetta, I've yet to hear about the mother of these brothers."

"Aye," she said dolefully, already answering my internal question. "Lydia Duncan. She died of illness soon after her second boy was born. It was a little later when Lorcan visited his children, but they were watched closely by their stuffy aunt, so he had no opportunity to take them for himself."

"I see." I sat down and pondered a moment. "Where's Remron, anyway?"

"It's a three or four day ride up the Dunmire from Bukuna."

Not liking my long silence, Clarissa asked, "Well, what are you going to do?"

"Assuming we find nothing else, I'll head to Bukuna tomorrow and find out what I can from Equine Manor. Lucetta, what's the aunt's name?"

"Rosemary. She's married, but I don't know her man's last name."

"You're not going to wait for Lorcan?" Clarissa asked me.

"Bukuna is about a three day trip by ship, so I should be back within a couple of weeks to see him. I'll know by then if I'm meeting my father or not. For now, let's just finish off these letters."

Nothing else in our piles pointed in another direction, though Clarissa found another mention of the "K.M." initials. They were referenced in casual passing from somebody who also only used their initials to identify themselves in their note, using the letters "F.L." The message itself appeared to continue an unassuming conversation between friends, but I was aware it could have been a cipher playing a deception. Any letters that looked suspicious in that regard I gave to Ghevont for further study.

Lucetta completed her stack earlier than everyone else, so she was free to do as she pleased, which included staring at Clarissa after coming back up from the inn's kitchen with a turkey leg.

"Hey, you're a vampire, aren't you?"

"Yes."

"Neat. My grandmother tried extending her life by becoming one, but it turned out she was too old to survive the transformation. Anyway, the vampire she found to infect her was a gentlemanly sort of fellow, and he knew so many jokes! Here's one—why is a man's pee yellow and his seed white? So-"

"So he can tell whether he's coming or going," I finished.

"Well look at that," said a surprised Lucetta, with Clarissa laughing in the background. "So you do have some humor in you."

"Spending a couple of years with criminals has one hearing every joke at least twice."

"So why don't you say any of them?" asked a still chuckling vampire.

"I'll have to get drunk first."

"Let's do that!"

"I think it's time I get some sleep."

"Oh!" said Ghevont. "I get it."

"Get what?" Clarissa asked.

"The joke."

While Lucetta and Clarissa snorted out hysterical laughter, I plopped into bed and said, "Congratulations."

I awoke several hours later in a dark room next to a sleeping Clarissa. Ghevont was snoring on the other bed and Lucetta was nowhere to be found. The pirate's wife returned at dawn, informing us that she found a ship leaving for Bukuna at noon. The vampire thanked her.

"Don't mention it. I just don't like sitting on my lovely ass for too long."

The three of us went downstairs to get ourselves some breakfast.

In the middle of eating my scrambled eggs and overcooked sausage, I caught Lucetta unabatingly staring at me.

"What is it now?"

"I think you really are Lorcan's son. Clarissa has kindly articulated some of your exploits while you were sleeping, and you seem to carry yourself very much like him. You also have his nose. It's a cute nose."

"I'll be sure to thank him for that."

"How did you meet Lorcan?" asked Clarissa.

"I worked for another pirate crew about nine years back. My former captain and Lorcan did not get along, so when she gained an opportunity to take his ship, she took it. Needless to say, we lost. After making the excuse that I was new to the pirate game and had no loyalty to the dead captain, Lorcan gave me a chance to join up with his men. I soon proved myself both at sea and in bed, becoming his right hand after a couple of years."

"And when did you realize you loved him?" inquired Clarissa, whose doe-eyed expression made it seem as though she was listening to the most romantic tale ever told.

Shrugging, Lucetta said, "There was no single moment, but I suppose it first entered my head five years ago. Our crew was leaving a brothel for the night, and since I was too drunk to walk, Lorcan was carrying me in his arms. As I watched his big, dumb face smiling down at me, I realized that I had been on his lap the entire night. We had always been openly promiscuous, but he had never moved to buy a night with somebody else. Neither had I, for that matter."

"And that's when you knew?"

"Well, first I waited awhile to make sure he wasn't just being lazy, but he simply stopped fucking other women, err, by himself, at least. I actually don't remember the first time I told him those three words. I was probably drunk. I do remember the first time he told me. We were on the prow of the ship as the sun was setting behind the open sea."

"Aww. He sounds romantic, doesn't he, Mercer?"

"I'd rather hear Ghevont talk about the digestive system again."

Ignoring my desire for their conversation to end, Clarissa asked Lucetta, "How does it feel like? To be in love, I mean. I thought I was in love once, but that didn't end so great."

"Mine might not end so great either. Look, all I know is that I love Lorcan, that's all. I don't know if it's real or if it'll last beyond today, so I sure as shit can't tell you what it'll take for other people to find it. I do know being a vampire won't make a man forget you have a good pussy, so your options are as high as any other girl. Better even. I'm sure Mercer here would love to go a few rounds."

"Oh, I've already offered."

"And he refused?" To me, she said, "Are your standards so damn high or do you only like other men?"

"Neither. As her question implies, she's still looking for love, I'm not. I'm choosing to refuse her now so I don't have to be crueler later."

"That sounds like too much thinking to me."

"Tell me, how many broken hearts have you left in your wake?"

Lucetta leaned back in her chair and looked up at the ceiling, looking as though she was actually counting those ragged organs. "Okay, okay, I *may* see a tiny bit of your side, but it still looks like she needs a good fuck."

"Who doesn't? Besides, no one's stopping her from doing anyone else."

"That's true. Hey, Clarissa, do you want to have a few nights with Lorcan and me? We can certainly show you a few things."

If a vampire had the ability to blush, Clarissa would be, but she just grinned awkwardly and said, "Uhh, no thanks. I mean, maybe later?"

"Well, think about it. I heard vampires have good stamina and can get rougher than most."

Shortly after Ghevont ate a light breakfast, we went over to find the ship scheduled to take us to Bukuna. I told Lucetta to check back at the inn for our return every day at noon. If she had to split for whatever reason, then I asked her to leave us a message with the front counter. Meanwhile, I also insisted she try and learn anything she could on *The Blackfly*. Once those basic instructions were arranged, we boarded our modest vessel.

Chapter Ten

It was on the second afternoon at sea when I let an excited Ghevont into my cabin.

"I think I have something," he said in a whisper, though Clarissa in the next cabin would have been the only one to overhear him if he spoke in a regular tone.

"Have what?" I yawned out.

"A possible answer to the vague letters. They're worthless."

"I hope that alone doesn't excite you."

"Hmm? No, no, of course not. They're worthless, but it's the business ones that might contain useful information. All those numbers would make a wonderful book cipher. And what book would the Advent use?"

I smirked. "*Summertide*."

"Precisely. I know it does us no good now, but this would mean the Advent are not destroying but keeping their copies. There might be a higher chance we'll find one after all."

"But if Corbin is receiving and sending coded letters, then it means he has a copy hidden somewhere."

"*The Blackfly*."

"Probably, but without knowing where it's docked, it'll be a bitch to find. We can only hope its crew will return to Dranall at some point. Nice job, by the way."

"I thought so."

The constant northern winds stalled us a few times, but the trip was completed as the third sun began its descent. Bukuna, though a capital city, was barely half as large as Dranall and its speed of life seemed cut in half as well. Merely moving through the dull streets made one drowsy. Querying a few dozy citizens soon had us walking up to the metal fence of Equine Manor. Standing on either side of the gated entrance were two life-sized horse statues made of copper, now green after decades of exposure. Erected thirty yards beyond the gates was the house itself—a large two-story home of gray brick.

Next to the animal replicas were a pair of armored bodyguards, both of whom marched up to us with stern auras. Fearing these obvious professionals could spot a vampire, I told Clarissa and Ghevont to stay where they were as I went up to meet them.

The bigger man, who only looked so due to his bulkier iron armor, asked, "Can I help you, sir?"

"Is Rosemary home?"

"Who wants to know?"

"I'm hoping she might tell me."

With a raised eyebrow, he said, "Don't play coy here, son."

"Yes, I understand. Look, I know about the tragedy she suffered in Remron. I've been looking for her nephews and I may know where one of them is. I don't even need to speak with her, just somebody who knows her and the family."

"And what's your name?"

"Mercer."

"Wait here, Mercer." Turning to the man in shining steel armor, he said, "Ask Cole if anyone will see a visitor regarding the Remron kidnappings."

The man clad in steel went back toward the gate, where he spoke with another guard within them.

Cole returned several minutes later with his answer, which was to allow me in. I wasn't permitted to go in with weapons, so I gave all the weaponries I carried to Clarissa. I next told my companions to wait at the end of the path for me. The iron man then patted me down, quickly noticing the padding around my left arm.

"What's under that?"

"An old injury."

"Prove it."

I unwrapped the cloth around my forearm, showing them the dark red chain-teeth rooted into my skin.

"The fuck is that?"

"As I said, an old injury. As much as I would like to, I can't remove it."

I was warily led into a cozy sitting room by Cole, where a small fire kept the space comfortably warm. Not ten seconds after taking a seat in a plush chair, a plump, old maid carrying a silver tray of tea cups entered through the double doors.

"Would you like s-" She was interrupted by her own scream and dropped tray.

An alarmed Cole unsheathed his short sword and shouted, "Madam Pharos! What's wrong?"

She ignored him and said, "C-Cyrus? Is that you? Or has madness finally overtaken me?"

Conscious of a confused Cole, I gingerly stood up. "I at least hope you're not mad, Madam Pharos."

She shook as she stepped up to me, her crinkly hand coming out to caress my face. "Gods, it is you," she said more to herself than anybody else. The short, corpulent woman embraced me. I hugged back, but out of pure courtesy than to a memory I did not share. Pulling away and wiping a tear, she said, "Cole, make sure Lady Winfield is on her way. Tell her it's Cyrus!" Once he was gone, she asked me, "What happened? Do you know where Alex is?"

"I'm sorry, I don't. I'll explain more when Rosemary gets here."

"Yes, of course."

I was helping the maid pick up her fallen cups and saucers when a thin woman in her early to mid-fifties entered. She had on a ruffling blue dress and her fading brown hair was braided tightly behind her. If she had been carrying a tray, she would have dropped it as well. She wanted to say something, but she instead choked up and burst into tears. I went to where she stood and brought her into my arms. She drenched my shoulder with enough salt water to make us smell like the sea.

The quivering emotion flowing out from her seeped into my skin, and for the first time in my remembered life, I shed a tear of my own. Not because I felt so much, but because I was feeling nothing at all. This was a woman who had raised me, yet her flower-scented perfume, firmly devoted touch, and the sound of her sniffling did not unearth that lost part of me, a part I now knew was truly gone.

When I sensed she had gained some composure over herself, I directed her to a small couch and we sat down.

Rosemary cleared her throat and said, "Look how much you've grown up! Leave us be, Sir Wesley. Phillis, inform the others that Cyrus has returned!"

"Hold on," I said. "Rosemary, there's something I need to tell you first. I wish I didn't have to, but I must. I don't, I mean, this might be difficult to hear."

Rubbing my hand, she said, "Gods, what is it, dear? Please tell me what's wrong. I will do everything to make things right again. The things you must have seen and heard. I don't want to imagine it."

"Have you wondered why you were expecting a man named 'Mercer' and instead got me?"

"I-I suppose that is strange."

93

"It's the name I gave the guards because it's the name I chose after I escaped my captors. I chose it because I didn't remember what my real name was. It wasn't until Phillis recognized me did I know I was home."

The housekeeper absorbed the information better than her mistress. She gasped and said, "A-are you saying you don't remember us? Your past?"

"I'm afraid I don't."

"Impossible! Then how did you find us?"

"By following a hard trail."

Rosemary's eyes were blank for a moment before she twitched them back onto mine. "Nothing? You remember nothing?"

"I'm sorry."

She embraced me again, tighter than the last. "What did those, those bastards do to you?"

"Don't distress yourself by contemplating such things."

"You're right. You're home, that's all that matters now."

"For a couple of nights."

"What?"

"I fear I have to apologize to you again, but I can't stay long."

"What?! Why not?"

"There's someone in Dranall I'm scheduled to meet, someone who might have more information about my kidnappers. Now that I know my brother is out there, I can't leave him to a worse fate than mine."

"Nonsense! You're not much more than a child and you want to fight?"

"I've been fighting for as long as I can remember."

"No, Cyrus, you can't."

"I know this is difficult to hear, but I've made too much headway to quit now. Besides, I sort of promised a dying woman I'd see this through."

"A dying woman? You surely aren't speaking like your old self." She ran her fingers through my hair. "And you're not bathing as often as you should. Gods! What you must have been through and I've yet to offer you water or fresh clothes!"

"Do you have enough for my two companions as well?"

"Companions?"

"Yes, they're waiting outside with my, uh, offensive items."

"I see. Of course they are welcome. Phillis, please instruct Sir Wesley to allow…" I told her the names when her expression implored me for the information. "For Lady Clarissa and Master Ghevont to be allowed inside."

Before she left, Phillis bowed and said, "It's wonderful to see you again, Master Cyrus."

"I must inform every one of the news," said my aunt. "Your uncle is in bed already, but he will gratefully be awakened for this, even if there is to be a sour note. Both of your cousins are also having dinner with some friends, and the Pendlecots also live with us. We wouldn't be able to afford this grand home otherwise. We pooled our resources together after the second raid and moved to a less exposed place. Perhaps once you are reacquainted with everyone you will see how foolish it would be to leave and have us all worry again about you. There's so much to catch up with. You yourself are an uncle now. Michael just turned two a month ago."

She never took a relaxing breath between any words, all in an effort to hold back more tears. Since none fell from her welled eyes, the strategy worked. I stayed listening until Clarissa and Ghevont entered the chamber. To prevent humans from noting her cold hands, the vampire wore her black gloves. This permitted her to shake hands with Rosemary, though my aunt still pointed out that a bit of makeup would do wonders for her pale skin. My aunt also appeared perturbed when Clarissa handed me back my blade and daggers, but said nothing.

It was decided that she would gather the family into the dining hall and explain my situation before I made myself known, saving me from the awkwardness of seeing their joy dwindle into muddled contentment.

A few minutes later and Phillis led Clarissa, Ghevont, and I to the dining hall, where Rosemary stood with my misplaced family. Next to my aunt was my uncle, Kario Winfield, a dignified man who looked a little less so in his oversized blue robe and nightgown. Their children, whom Rosemary considered my brother and sister, each looked older than I was, but not by much.

My two year old nephew was held by his father, Spencer, who appeared to be as stately as his father, if somewhat pudgy. His wife was standing in the background. Her face was the type that could easily get lost in a crowd, but even under all her clothes I could tell she had a toned body and an outdoorsy spirit. Our sister, Erica, had a foot over the edge of portliness herself, but I was sure Rosemary was doing her best to make sure her otherwise sweet looking daughter didn't cross over completely.

Erica made the first move. She rushed forward and used her youth to give me a hug stronger than anyone else's. The men were more subdued, including the toddler, but the older men also joined Erica in a fleeting embrace. The next few moments were similar to the meeting with Rosemary and Phillis, but once that passed, a smoother dialogue occurred. Our conversation was complemented with some plates of hearty steaks and tepid tomato soup.

"If you don't remember us," began Erica, "then how did you track us here?"

"I recently found the office of one of my captors. A letter of his mentioned this place. You see, it's actually my fault these people are interested in this family, why Alex was taken in the second raid. The spells they used on me made me a good fighter in their fighting pit and they believed someone else with my blood would also work well for them."

96

"So you know who abducted you and Alex?" asked Spencer. "Have you directed the authorities to them? Are they still at large?"

"The man responsible for sanctioning the kidnappings is dead. The caster who experimented on me is also dead. However, they were a small part of the operation."

"What do you mean 'operation'?" asked my uncle.

"I can't say much because I still don't know much, but what I do say can't leave this room, understand?" Everyone gave either a nodding or verbal signal that they did. "The Advent are not widely known, but they have a wide reach, though how they've obtained their influence remains a mystery."

"The Advent? Isn't that some mythical religion?"

"They are an old cult. They apparently wish to raise a dead being and are gathering power to do so. It's my belief they're responsible for the attacks on the valkrean. I've informed the Warriors Guild about them, but until more information is gathered, it's not safe to openly speak of them, especially for this family."

"Then you presume that Alex is being held by these Advent worshippers?"

I nodded.

"How horrible!" cried Erica.

"Indeed," said Rosemary. "I know you want to find Alex, dear, we all do, but you can't hope to battle an army of zealots on your own. Please, leave this to professional soldiers. Stay home with us. No more of this fighting talk."

"Are you joking, Mother?" rhetorically asked Spencer. "I wish I could join him."

"Spencer! Don't you start!"

"Don't worry, I'm no soldier, but it angers me that I can do nothing to help. Our family has suffered immensely and all we could do was run."

97

"Aye," assented his father. "My dear wife, I know you desire to keep on coddling the boy, but he has obviously matured into a man of conviction. I for one am proud Cyrus has risen above his severe trials."

"I'd rather keep him above the grave."

"That can come to us at any time. We kept to ourselves in Remron and were attacked twice for our trouble. Cyrus also has a right to seek reprisal for what has unjustly been done to him. He might be safe here, but it's a dangerous thing to allow a man's temper to fester."

This did not convince Rosemary to move on from her maternal opinion, but it quieted her down on that topic for the evening.

The rest of the conversation strayed away from my plight and to old family history, including learning that my uncle was a retired law interpreter. Spencer was following in his footsteps, but his real love was racing his horses. He was one of the reasons they bought the Equine Manor, which had been owned by a famous horse breeder several decades back. I got the sense Spencer and I had not been great friends when we were little, though I imagined we were both too much changed to evaluate the relationship fairly. Going by a handful of other comments from Kario, I concluded that I must have been a timid child. He appeared pleased that I grew out of what I'm certain he labeled as "feminine tendencies."

An hour after meeting my family, the Pendlecots entered the hall. They comprised of a quaint couple around the same age as my aunt and uncle, and a young woman. It was through them I learned that one of the children taken in that first raid was a playmate of mine, a boy named Nathaniel. They spoke as though we were best friends, and maybe we were, but it could have been revisionist history.

His sister was a beautiful black haired girl named Cecelia. According to my aunt, and supported by Lady Pendlecot, Cecelia and I had also been close friends. I had expressed this connection, as a young boy would, by

98

playing pranks on her, such as leaving frogs in her fruit basket and stealing her hats. It was embarrassingly obvious to the girl that my aunt hoped Cecelia's appealing presence would induce me to stay.

The talk became livelier as the night went on. It wasn't until the chiming of the grandfather clock informed us it was two in the morning did everyone elect to pause the reunion. We had been assigned rooms in the second-story and were told that a warm bath, clean clothes, and a robust breakfast would be waiting for us in the morning. My room had a glass door that opened to a small balcony and held the fluffiest and most comfortable bed I had ever touched, but I couldn't find sleep.

I responded to a light knock on my door by opening it. I let Clarissa in.

"You have a balcony?" she asked, walking toward it. She leaned on the railing to look out on the large garden below, where some animal topiaries traversed the landscape. The flickering torchlights in the corners of the yard made the topiaries dance eerily. When I leaned in with her, she asked, "You doing okay?"

"I'm fine. Just thinking."

"As always. What about this time?"

"My selfishness."

"Selfishness? When did that happen?"

"I basically came in and said, 'Hi family, I'm still alive, but I'm going to throw myself back into danger and have you worry about my death a second time.' I should've discovered whether they were my family or not another way, then it wouldn't matter if I did die."

"Right, because your death would otherwise mean nothing to everyone else."

"You know what I mean."

"I was only half joking. I don't think you did the wrong thing."

"Maybe not, but that's not the part keeping me up. It's wondering why I don't accept Rosemary's offer to stay."

"Don't you want to find your brother and friend?"

"There's no feeling for people I can't remember. And I probably should let the guild and military handle the Advent themselves, but when I think about living here, my blood cringes. At first I thought it was the pomposity of the people here, but it probably wouldn't have made a difference if they were farmers, artists, or kings. I would have rejected the notion of living a sedentary life. I think I'm too used to fighting at this point. Maybe I even enjoy it. You heard Kario. I was once a meek, unassertive kid. The Advent took that away, too."

Clarissa slung her arm around the back of my waist and placed her head on my shoulder. "I don't think the Advent changed you," she assessed after a pause.

"And what gives you that idea?"

"You're going to meet your father, aren't you? Isn't he someone who was told never to involve himself with his children? Yet he's in the middle of his own journey looking for you and your brother. I lived in an orphanage, and not every kid was in there due to dead parents. Some were very much alive. They simply didn't want any responsibility and dropped them off in the middle of a cold night. Your father is obviously not like that, so maybe you're just more like him than your uncle, or whatever the Advent wanted you to be. Can't that be right?"

I didn't think so, but I kissed her frosty forehead and said, "Of course."

She smiled and we spent a quiet few minutes letting the cool breeze ruffle our hair.

"Hey," she said, "What do I call you now? Mercer or Cyrus?"

"I like the idea of keeping a name I chose myself. Anyway, I don't want my real name to spread if I ever get this dragon knight thing down."

100

"Good. I like the idea of calling you by the name I met you as." She saw my mouth open for a big yawn. "Oh? I bore you, do I?"

"If helping to make a mind uncluttered is the same as boring it, then you're the most boring person I ever met."

Chapter Eleven

It was late the next morning when I became aware that I was eighteen years old. My nineteenth birthday landed on the twelfth day in the first month of the year, the Month of Ice. Other little facts made themselves known throughout the rest of the day—my favorite food apparently being smoked salmon, a steaming hot potato, and a cup of ice cold milk, for instance. This was confirmed later in the day when Rosemary ordered the cook to prepare it. It tasted pretty damn good.

As usual, Ghevont had no trouble running his mouth and finding somebody to listen to him. Clarissa stayed close to our red headed companion so she could guard against him spilling too much of our exploits. Thanks to my presence, no one paid too much attention to my companions' oddities or question their histories.

It was bizarre living with these people for a day while wearing elaborately expensive layers of clothing made from taffeta, velvet, and cotton. The only item I really liked, and ended up keeping, was a pair of black leather boots. They felt durable and fit much better than the tightening footwear I had worn for a year.

I think I was surreal to them as well. These were people whom a warrior melded into the background as a bodyguard or a soldier in a far-flung land, not a fellow family member. It didn't help that I wasn't being as forthcoming about my recent history as some wanted me to be. In any event, with everyone knowing I was only going to spend one more night in the manor, no member of the house acted aloof or drifted out of view.

Despite the formality of their words and garments, I began to sense a palpable connection sprout between the house and I. Perhaps they were the type of people that wouldn't have given me the time of day had I not been blood, but I, in turn, wouldn't have given two shits about them had they not turned out to be who they were. What forged the foundation of that link more than anything was the way poor Rosemary watched me with labored longing, hoping that the next idea her adopted son had would be to stay with her. I never before had someone behold me with such emotional intensity. It was a repressed passion that erupted in heavy tears when I met with her the next morning and told her I was glad to have a mother again.

The voyage back to Dranall gave me plenty of time to think about my expanding family. Not that I wanted the time to do so—I much preferred having battle strategy floating in my mind. Rosemary's maternal bond in particular made me wonder what my real mother was like, something I had now confirmed could be clarified by my father.

One lonely night, as I stared listlessly at the sea from the stern of the ship, Aranath asked me, "Do you wish for my view?"

"Sure, why not?"

"Dragon clans do not work like your own. Hatchlings leave the nest a year after they breathe the open air, and even with our long lives we will only sparingly see our kin, so I cannot say how a human should feel in a situation such as yours. However, I can say you now have more to fight for, which means you have more to lose as well. This circumstance has dictated the actions of many a warrior."

"I'm fully aware the Advent will use Rosemary and the others against me if they discover my connection to them. I'll guard for that possibility."

"You misunderstand, I am not concerned about your tactical mind. It is the emotional aspect that often leads to ruin. You may believe your lack of memory has detached you from your obligation to them, but I've witnessed the mere threat of endangered kin distract warriors long enough to get cut down. Do you believe yourself to be immune to such diversions? If you had to leave a battle to defend Rosemary, would you do it?"

"You can ask me the same of Clarissa."

The deepest part of his throat rumbled. "You are not as rationally developed as I assumed if you don't realize that the vampire would never forgive you if you left a vital fight for her sake. She is becoming a warrior in her own right, and a warrior would be insulted with the idea that one of their comrades sacrificed so much to save them. If you truly believe the vampire cannot fight for herself after this much time with you, then she has become a burden and is better left wandering Gremly. Conversely, your aunt has no capacity to defend herself beyond compensating others to do it."

"So what do you want me to do? How can I expect to know how I would react in your grave situation?"

"Your reaction should be restrained, but above all, it should not compel you to ignore your obligation as an aspiring Veknu Milaris."

"What do you mean?"

"Do you believe dragons and humans created pacts with each other just to have one abandon their duty in a time of crisis? You and I may be unique in the current world, and we've little other choice but to fight for what cause you alone choose, but that won't make it acceptable for me to someday see you act upon a reckless desire. Petty, humanistic reasons led to the War of Dragon Fire and to the separation of our races. If you wish for me to continue aiding you, then you need to accept that you can never leave a battle you have obligated yourself to. Few acts are as dishonorable to a dragon as that."

"Then I'll be sure to not obligate myself to any battles."

He grunted. "We'll see how that goes."

We arrived in Dranall nine days after leaving it. It was two or three in the morning, so there was still half a day before I expected Lucetta at the inn. As it turned out, however, she had left a note telling us to go to the docks and look for her on a two-masted schooner named the *Little Lydia*.

After asking around, a dock worker pointed out a ninety foot long ship docked nearby. We walked up the pier to see two people sitting at its end. One was a tall, lanky, clean-shaven man playing a game of cards with a stout, burly woman. A small candle between them lit their game. The woman noticed us first and stood up.

When the lanky fellow followed his companion's lead, he said, in a misleadingly cordial tone, "Whoa there, friends. May I ask who approaches?"

"Tell Lucetta that Mercer is here, and if your captain is with her, tell him Cyrus Eberwolf is here as well."

The two sailors glanced at each other with raised brows. The woman then said, "Lucetta told us to expect you. Come aboard."

As we followed her shorter steps, the loftier man used his gangly legs to race onto the ship. On boarding the quiet vessel, the woman told us to wait a moment as she tried finding her cohorts.

She didn't return, but the other soon came out from beneath the top deck. He was tailed by Lucetta and a mountain of a man. Not only was this man almost as tall as the long-limbed fellow, but was considerably more robust. Disheveled black hair and a short black beard outlined his broad face. His gristly skin was a dark bronze from his decades at sea. Considering he only wore a pair of black breeches and a puffy white shirt that exposed most of his hairy chest, I guessed he had been awakened from whatever dream his adventurous mind invented.

They stopped a few feet in front of us, and before a complete word could exit from Lucetta's open mouth, her man said, "There's no need, Lucetta. I can recognize my own son. I'm sure that's what you confirmed in Bukuna."

"Yes."

Neither of us knew what to do or say next, so a silence was birthed from the uncertainty until my father took the initiative a long moment later.

"You still don't have your memories?"

"No."

"I suppose I wouldn't be in there even if you did. Trust me when I say I wanted nothing more than to be there for you and your brother, no matter what you heard from your aunt."

"I heard nothing from her about you. We didn't even have enough time to talk about Lydia."

"Good. I'll be the one to tell you everything about your mother. There's much to catch up on."

"Including what you found on your end."

"Aye, we found something, at least we believe we did." He chuckled. "How strange it is! You were as big as my boot the last time I saw you, and now you're a fine young warrior. Lucetta tells me you fought her to a standstill even after she poisoned you. You also have your own crew following you to the ends of Orda, as I have mine. Lilly should be preparing our meals now. Come! We shall talk around a table."

All of us went below deck and entered what was probably the biggest room in the ship, which still wasn't all that big. Lilly, the stout woman from earlier, placed down plates of roasted duck and cups of red wine as we took our seats.

After my crew formally introduced themselves, Lorcan said, "Tell me, Lady Clarissa, what do you think of my boy? Does he treat his friends well?"

"Very much so. There's no one else I trust more."

"Quite a statement. Lucetta mentioned something about him saving your life, yes?"

"Yes. I was once foolishly part of a vampire clan. Your son could have killed me easily enough, but he kept his word to a despised creature such as myself and then tolerated my presence long enough for us to become friends."

"Good, good. And what of you, scholar? Did my son save your life as well?"

"Um, how do I put this? He has graciously tolerated my presence ever since I aided him in the killing of my sister."

"Now that sounds like a tale."

"One that helps explain how I ended up here," I said. "His sister was a false member of the Advent. It was she who told us where to find her assistant."

"You must tell me everything you do remember, Cyrus. What did these Advent do to you?"

In what was essentially a long sigh of words, I told a brief account of my history, including my corruption and the enchanted sword I used to keep it in check. For the purpose of brevity, I left out specifics like Aranath, Ghevont's family name, and not naming the noble I met in Qutrios during the valkrean attack. Notwithstanding the vicious way I attained my skills, my father sounded proud that I was a competent warrior, saying he couldn't wait to brag to his crew about me.

"If your brother is half as strong as you," he continued, "then I'd say we stand a good chance of finding him alive."

"I've perhaps been luckier than strong, but I suspect he would have a better chance if he were half as strong as you."

"Ah, mark it down, Lucetta. The first compliment from son to father!"

"I'll also have to request that you don't go explaining my corruption to the rest of your crew. I know you trust them, but-"

"Say no more, Cyrus my boy. I know it can't be comfortable living with that kind of power. I won't make it more so."

"Thank you. Well, Lorcan my father, how did your own search for me and Alex start?"

He gulped the rest of his wine down, shaking his head when he finished. "I have few regrets in life. My biggest is not ignoring your mother and taking her with me when I had the chance. We would all be at sea now,

107

living together and without the worry of this damned kidnapping business. My second biggest regret is not making my visits to Remron more frequent. If I had at least been there during one of the raids… Well, what's done is done. Alex had already been missing for five months by the time I checked in with one of your aunt's servants. I began my search right then and there…"

Lorcan went on to explain the rest of his hunt. One of the first things he did was sell his old ship, the original *Lydia*, and use the coin to buy his faster and more maneuverable vessel. He also cut his crew by half. The ones remaining were his most trusted friends, men and women who knew each other front and back, drank and fought together, and who would die for one another. With this lighter, swifter crew and ship, and using every connection to the underworld he had, Lorcan inquired in and around Remron about the raids.

He quickly realized that two raids separated by three years and which resulted in the abduction of two brothers couldn't have been a coincidence. So going on that assumption, he sought for anyone who had been in the area during each of those times. It took months of matching up stories, rumors, faces, and "politely" asking a few reprobates about the incident to pick up their most promising lead.

It then came down to tracking this elusive man, who turned out to be another of Corbin's lackeys staying in Dranall. The pirates, however, didn't learn about Corbin until after weeks of spying and stealing his correspondences. They moved in on this lackey and pulled out some information from him. They discovered that he was a member of the Blue Swords and was used by Corbin to send secret reports to a temple in Qutrios.

"A temple?" I asked him.

"Aye. That's where we were. We scouted the place for a while and stole the latest cache of secret reports he sent, but all we could get were some business reports. We figure they're encoded, but none of us have been able to crack it."

"Do you still have them?"

"Yes, but before we stole them, we watched them, hoping someone would come and pick them up. No one ever came."

He kept talking, but a couple of ideas meshing in my head stopped the words from making sense. After taking a glance at Ghevont and Clarissa, who each appeared to be sharing in my thoughts, I said, "The Advent must be using the temples of day and night."

"What was that?" asked Lorcan. His befuddled tone implied he wasn't accustomed to being interrupted.

"Vey's assistant told us he was recruited inside the temple in Qutrios. I think somebody didn't pick up the secret messages because someone saw you watching them, just like someone saw that Magnus was ripe for recruitment."

"Oh," said Lucetta. "You're talking about the priests, aren't you?"

"At least one of them in Qutrios has to be a cultist."

"It's ingenious," said Ghevont. "One can send messages all across Orda using the innocuous temples of day and night, and any ally of theirs like the Blue Swords can secretly share messages. Yes, that must be it."

"Gods, you're right," said Lorcan. "All we did was ask a quick few questions to them, but that must have been enough to tip off this infiltrator of theirs."

"If you were there for that long-" I began to say.

"Yes, we might have been watched ourselves, maybe even followed here. I expected our enemy to be nothing more than ordinary slavers or rogue casters, but they seem to be a little bit of everything. It's a good thing we found each other, or we'd both be in over our heads."

"We still might be."

"So what do we do about the Blue Swords?" asked Clarissa. "They seem to be working closely with the Advent. Do we tell the guild about the connection?"

109

"That would be of little use," I answered. "Their attack on Qutrios has already made them a target in this continent. Besides, their leadership is in Voreen. The guild there won't have the manpower to take down the leaders of a large mercenary group, not unless it receives aid from Voreen's military, but we already know Voreen won't do anything that helps Alslana."

"Ugh, that stinks."

"Anyway, the Blue Swords are still only pawns in this. All the effort it would take to get rid of them will accomplish little, and that's the kind of reaction the Advent want. They get to lay low while everyone else blames the Blue Swords or Sisterhood or anyone else they want, so as long as it causes more chaos and confusion. What we need to focus on is cracking their codes so we can find their base." I looked at my father to say something, but I hesitated when I noted his wry smile. "What is it?"

"A warrior with a cool head is more fearsome than one with a hot sword. Forgive me, were you going to say something?"

"Uh, yes. Ever heard of *Summertide*?"

"That long ass poem?"

"Ghevont thinks he can translate their ciphers and find their precious grave if he has the original copy. You don't have one handy, do you?"

"I'm afraid not."

"We need to find it."

"Hey," said Lucetta. "Should we check if this temple has an Advent person?"

"They wouldn't have needed your go-between if the Advent already had someone stationed here," I pointed out. "You can check, but don't scare everybody."

"Most people don't realize I'm scary until it's way too late."

"Then we go back to Qutrios," my father concluded. "If a priest there has been collecting coded messages, then it stands to reason that he can decode them, or knows someone who can."

"If you didn't already spook them."

I tried sounding more glum than critical, but Lorcan still said, "Aye, you have a point. I was careless overlooking the priesthood. The rest of my men are scheduled to return from their respite at noon. We can set sail right after."

Chapter Twelve

Lorcan woke me so that I could help with getting the ship aweigh. When I told him I knew nothing of sailing, my pirate father took it personally. He must have thought me a fast learner rather than the methodical one I really was, for he started stating the nautical terms for knots, directions, and commands in rapid succession. All this while also introducing me to his jaunty crew in the same lungful. The names were said as fast as his lessons, so I needed another round to get the names down and yet another later on to match them with the faces.

Including my father and Lucetta, there were a dozen crew members on board. The two I already met were Lilly Sundus and Athan Chamberlain. Lilly, I was told, rarely set foot beyond a pier. While not the oldest woman in the *Little Lydia*, she was viewed most like its mother figure. She conducted much of the cooking and scrubbing, and though seen as the weakest fighter in the group, could still hold her own in a brawl. Athan, on the other hand, was among the better warriors. His daunting height alone deterred most from taking on whatever group he joined up with. If violence did become necessary, then the ambidextrous pirate could counter any style with knife, spell, or bow.

The person Lorcan took the longest to introduce was Thoris Anworth. If I had to guess by appearances alone which man on the ship sired me, I would have chosen Thoris. His build resembled my own and his main weapon also happened to be a longsword, though he likewise carried a small axe for simpler enemies and jobs. In addition, he was clean-shaven and his brown eyes had a self-possession I would recognize in a mirror. My father placed an arm around his shoulders and declared him his most loyal friend, having known each other long before Lorcan became captain of the original *Lydia*.

The remaining crew was introduced with greater haste. Leo Brimsey, a balding black man of short stature, was their best all-around caster and the best candidate to give Ghevont a run for his coin when it came to babbling his mouth off. Menalcus Sheridan tried to stop himself from knocking things over with his bulbous girth or massive claymore, but he often failed. Making Clarissa drool all over herself was Aristos Kartini. His deep, sultry voice and chiseled looks allowed him to talk his way out of any situation and into bed with any woman.

The other married couple on board was Remwold and Athilda Osam. As the oldest and most well-versed seafaring members, Lorcan went to them whenever he encountered anything unknown in his varied travels. The ripe couple was a handful of years away from being unable to physically stand up to a competent opponent, but their casting abilities currently counteracted their slowing bodies. A gimpy foot and a bad knee on the same leg further slowed Remwold, but his proud walk never displayed these discomforts.

On the other end of the age spectrum stood the short-haired blonde Sophia McBoid. She was only four years my senior, but already had the reputation of being quite the nasty markswoman and an exceptional young caster. She specialized in trickier spells like water-breathing—which was really holding ones breath for much longer than normal—and detecting the prana of others from a distance. It was later obvious she saw Lucetta as a role model, though the older woman cared nothing for that kind of attention. I believed she would have gotten along with Marcela quite well.

The final crewmate was Yang Hur. All my father said about the soft spoken man was that one of his favorite pastimes included being alone with his thoughts. I immediately made him my best friend, even if he would never know it.

As expected from a pirate crew, they had been plucked from different lands and grew up with a different cultural landscape behind them. The only common thread they all shared was their love of the sea and the sense of freedom it gave, which my father expressed with every other sentence or deed.

As both my father's son and a fellow warrior, they all accepted me into the fold kindly enough. When it became obvious that I did not absorb my father's lessons as quickly as he supposed I would, they lent their expertise at a slower pace.

It was late afternoon when I next spoke with a secluded Lorcan. We sat in his cramped captain's cabin as he drank a bottle of rum behind a little desk. I took a presented cup. I ended up only sipping from it after taking my first gulp of the dark drink.

"Getting to know everyone?" he asked.

"I think getting their names down accomplishes enough for one day."

He laughed. "Don't think I'm trying to be pushy. Even if your vampire friend didn't tell me, I could see you're the loner type. I'd allow you to settle in at your own pace, but as your mother and I were never among the aloof, I know there's a part of you that can charm people with a simple smile. You'll need it to come out more if you want to lead men someday."

"I'll let you do the leading."

"I won't be around forever."

"We just met and you're already talking about your death?"

"More like my retirement. The more I think about it, the more I enjoy the idea of settling down on a little island with Lucetta and starting another family. Perhaps as soon as we find your brother."

"I hope to see that someday, but do you expect me to lead your crew or something? Because I don't imagine myself becoming a pirate."

"No, no, nothing like that. I only expect that you won't retire with me. Young warriors like yourself do not simply stay put, and you're certainly no follower. That only leaves leading men into battle, does it not?"

"I haven't thought about what I'd do if I live to see the Advent destroyed. To be honest, my planning has only gone as far as wondering what I'd do if the ship hits something and starts sinking."

"Ah, don't concern yourself with that. I'll swim right for you."

After forcing myself to take a bigger swig of rum, I said, "You mentioned how Mother wasn't the loner type. What was she like?"

The right half of his face grinned. "She was either the sweetest damn thing I ever met or the spiciest. How she ended up in that snooty family, I'll never know. Lydia was the one to drag her sister into the tavern I first met her in. She wanted adventure, she craved it. If her damn health were better, she would have made for a fearsome... well, anything she damn wanted to be."

"Lucetta doesn't seem jealous when you talk about her."

"If she was alive, then she would have plenty of reason to be jealous. As it is, she understands my first love simply left its mark on me, just as her own left his."

"Her first love?"

"Aye. A man not too different from Aristos. Made her think she was his everything only to take everything she had. Still, if that didn't happen, she wouldn't have become a pirate. Makes me think the gods do have a hand in how things turn out. Ah, that's another thing about acting a little more personable. A strapping young lad like yourself will only have to throw a compliment or two and-" He struck the table with his fist. "Bam! She's all yours. Or do you wish to someday let the woman of your dreams slip through your fingers because you didn't want to talk a little?"

"Again, never really thought about it, but I'll keep that in mind."

"Good, good. I don't like the idea that I've missed out on all my chances to impart my fatherly wisdom."

"I'd like to see how much wisdom you have with a sword."

"Ah, I would as well. Come! We have an old stash of training poles we can use."

We each drank the rest of our rum and stepped out. With mid-length sword replicas in hand, we made our way to the top deck. It was strange knowing I was outmatched before the sparring began. I deduced that I hadn't been the best swordsmen in all of my fights, but I had never before allowed that reasoning to negatively affect my outlook. Not until now. Did Lorcan being my father cause this sentiment? Or did he somehow emanate this to everyone he fought? The answer didn't ultimately matter.

For a man his bulk, he moved his feet as though he weighed a hundred pounds lighter. I still moved better than him, but the power he put into his swings went far above what I could produce. Besides the physical superiority, he had instincts honed by countless battles. Even my released corruption wouldn't have closed the gap by much. He simply reached a level I would need a decade of combat experience to equal. Of course, if the sparring session allowed for spells I might have been able to get in a few good strikes, but without my distractions available, all I could do was deflect and dodge his swings and kicks.

I perhaps wasn't giving myself enough credit, since half a dozen people who had gathered around us seemed entertained by our display, but that didn't ease the reality that every strategy I used was easily parried. It was as if he knew what I was going to do before I did it. In a way, I was glad to experience firsthand proof that I had the potential to become a much faster warrior. I had started learning to manipulate dragon fire ever since leaving Gremly, but that endeavor had me neglecting other aspects of my training. With a true sparring partner to go up against, I decided it might be time to go back to the fundamentals. My father and I thus spent the next few days at sea sparring between my nautical lessons and rest periods.

My mother's smaller namesake moored itself at the docks of a small city four days later. Qutrios still rested on the other side of the continent, but the landmass' width at this latitude spanned only about two hundred miles across. The reduced distance made it a significantly shorter journey than it would have been if we started from Dranall. Lorcan, Lucetta, and my trio was

116

joined by Athan, Sophia, and Aristos. The others were charged with guarding the ship. In the interest of speed, we bought a small herd of horses to take us to our destination. Lorcan seemed perturbed that I was not a master rider, but he expressed his amazement when I told him I walked most of the way to nearly every endpoint I chose.

Our troop of riders trotted for a full day, stopping only for brief periods of respite.

Not long after a stop for some breakfast on the forest floor, Aranath's voice grabbed my attention. "We're being followed."

I slowed my brown horse down so that I could speak without my father overhearing. "How do you know?"

"Do you see the small flock of sparrows flying overhead? I'm certain they've been frequenting our sky the past few hours. There is a way to reveal whether the birds are being possessed. Toss an explosive stone in their direction and ignite it. If the explosion does not startle them right away, then their senses are muddled by a possession spell. If I were a human, I would then move to an open space and wait for my enemy to come to me."

I made my horse stop in its tracks, letting the others in the convoy pass me. Clarissa stopped with me.

"Something wrong?"

Pulling out the explosive item, I replied, "Let's find out. Keep an eye on the birds above for me."

I hurled the rock fifty feet in the air and triggered its little blast. I heard other birds in the area react with squawks and flapping wings, but those in the targeted flock had an odd delay before they separated, almost casually so.

"Were you expecting that?"

Lucetta brought her steed closer to us. "What was that about?"

"We're being watched," I answered. "Tell Lorcan we have to get off the road. I'm heading for a hill we passed a hundred yards back."

117

The hill I spoke of was scarcely a rocky mound of grass and small trees, but it offered cherished high ground. The lack of mature trees also provided a clearer view around us.

When Lorcan joined me on the hill, he asked, "You're certain eyes are upon us?"

"I've survived this long trusting the voice in my head. There's no point heading for Qutrios now, but I have my own lead in Ecrin we can check with. For now, I'd like to see if our enemy is willing to show itself or retreat. Is that all right with you?"

"I'll give us until noon. We'll head back if nothing happens."

Everyone hitched their horses at the center of the hill and took a lookout point. I kept an eye on the shadiest part of the woods, setting up dragon stones nearby so I could light up the area at a moment's notice.

I stood at attention for over an hour before I heard Sophia call out a sighting from her position overlooking the road. Telling Clarissa and Ghevont to continue watching our backs, I sprinted over to see what was going on.

The short-haired blonde had her bow drawn at a solitary figure walking up to us with an outstretched hand holding up an active ward spell, which spread from head to knee. His ambling walk struck me as odd. He dragged his feet and swayed like a drunkard. Just as Sophia asked whether she should let her arrows fly, the cloaked stranger fell on his knees and put his free hand on the ground. Four pulses of air burst around him as he summoned his allies. What three of these allies ended up being shocked us.

They were humans, something that shouldn't have been possible if freewill had anything to say in the matter. A caster only carried the ability to summon creatures either too dumb to resist or who agreed to be bound, and few humans would allow the whim of another to determine their fates. Not to mention the long-term risks of being kept in an alien realm. The fourth being was an eight foot tall stone sprite, a faceless humanoid entity made from hundreds of peach colored rocks. They all mutely attacked in a single wave.

My father barked some orders to his men, which prompted an eruption of elements from both sides. Surges of fire met jets of water, colliding to become a gust of mist. Lightning blasted away hurled spikes of stone, and wind whirled around enough dust to create a miniature dust storm. I left the experience of the pirate gang to their own maneuvers. My focus stayed on the summoner, who hung about at the back of the pack. His magical shield remained up as he turned to stare at me with dead, hollow eyes. The veins in his face swelled with a dark purplish hue that reminded me of the corrupted I killed a lifetime ago. Yet he didn't appear insane like they did.

Just as I was about to impact his ward with my blade, the ward became enveloped in crackling lightning. I couldn't avoid it. The sword struck. While Aranath's power deadened the shock before it reached me, it was still powerful enough to force me to clench my teeth and twist my muscles for a painful moment. I barely recovered in time to roll out of the way of the lunging electric shield. His back was now exposed to an arrow from Sophia, who had been ordered to support me.

Although the projectile hit its mark, the enemy took no notice of the wound by his upper spine. He instead generated a spear of lightning with his free hand and swung for me. He did not have good control over his weapon. The electricity wildly frayed the clothing up his arm, blistering his skin on contact. Again, he took no notice.

"He's a puppet," said Aranath. "Just as the other humans are. Use only long range attacks or they will sacrifice themselves to injure you."

"Sophia! They're all being controlled! Tell everyone to keep back!"

She yelled my advice to everyone who could hear her high-pitched voice, advice that was easier said than done. My thrall swung away with mad abandon, dashing ever closer with every backward step I took. I would have

119

been hard pressed to come up with an unpainful strategy if I were alone, but since I wasn't, I maneuvered the tactless slave until I had him where I wanted.

"Sophia! Leg!"

The instant our enemy lunged, the back of his knee was impaled by her arrow. Whether it pained him or not didn't matter, the interrupted momentum tripped him up. Halfway to the ground, my sword swung upward and caught him by the neck. Aranath nearly lopped off his head, but a remaining strand of skin prevented a true beheading. The blood that had been boiling inside him came out in one big squirt.

I was disappointed, but not surprised to see that killing the summoner didn't release the others. The almost headless man may have called upon them, but he had merely been a mediator for the true-

"Get back!" exclaimed Aranath.

The dead body became sheathed in fizzing sparks before a shockwave of lightning exploded outward. I shouldn't have had time to dodge the thunderous outburst, but I found myself only feeling a mild tingle of electricity going up my body as I laid on the ground. I looked up to see a ward enveloped by water between me and the corpse. Looking behind me showed a relieved Clarissa and a surprisingly stoic Ghevont approaching me with spell-enwrapped arms. I gave my thanks with a nod and we moved to support the others.

With everyone switching to long range tactics, the worst injury anyone received from the human puppets was a gash suffered by Athan's thigh, which came from a shattering spear of ice. The stone sprite dished out a little more punishment. Offsetting its lumbering body somewhat, it could fling the rocks that made up its body with great force. A flung stone rammed into Aristos' gut, but the tougher than he looked pirate still contributed to the sprite's downfall. He and Clarissa joined their abilities and cast their water spells around one of the sprite's legs. The water then froze into a dense coating of ice, holding the brute down for the needed moment.

With the pinned sprite smashing pieces of the ice off its leg, Lorcan and Athan combined their spells, my father helping to fuel his subordinate's flame with a sharp outpouring of air. They gave it a second to further concentrate its vivacious heat before firing it at the creature's weakest point—a narrow waist where legs met torso. For good measure, Sophia shot an arrow she had wreathed in flame. The well-aimed flames burst forth at the target, the impact splitting it in half. The sprite's body broke apart into regular looking rocks.

As Athan's wound was being treated, Ghevont took the time to study the best enemy corpse available, which happened to be the one I first attacked. The electric surge had charred it badly, but it stayed in better shape than the others, all three having been burnt to near ash by a torrent of flame. I explained to the scholar what I saw when the puppet was still alive and then gave him a few moments to inspect the grisly, horrid smelling body.

When the red light of whatever spell he cast faded from his hands, I asked, "What do you think?"

"I would have once thought that too broad a question to answer, but now I really hear what you mean. I suspect a powerful mind rune was manipulating these people, but even that shouldn't have been enough to force the utter lack of consciousness these subjects displayed, not unless their will was destabilized beforehand."

"So you think they were corrupted."

"Not so simple as that." Ghevont pulled out a small knife and began to cut at the surface of the man's blackened chest. "Raw corruption spreads uncontrollably throughout the body, but I'm picking up a single concentrated point... Ah! Here we go."

121

He mined his knife in the bloody little hole and used it to dig out a half inch long object from the crater of seared flesh. He wiped off the blood with his cloak and laid it on his palm. The crystalized item emanated a red-violet color. I could feel as my own hungry corruption reached out, frantically attempting to add to its own influence. I clenched my hands to keep from snatching it.

"A corrupted prana crystal," I inferred.

"It seems the Advent's experiments on corruption are producing fruitful results. With a blend of mind runes and corrupted crystals to wipe away someone's resistance, a capable caster can link his prana with multiple subjects and accomplish much without ever having to endanger himself. All the same, I imagine the caster can't be too far away. I'm assuming I don't have time to do a complete dissection, do I?"

"No. Destroy the crystal, or at least bury it if you can't."

"Why can't I keep it?"

"Do you want to suffer your father's fate?"

"Excellent point."

Soon after Athan was helped back onto his horse, we began a hurried journey back to the ship. All of us knew it. If we had been attacked, then it was probable that the *Little Lydia* had also been made a target.

It was well past midnight when we reached the docks. The cloudy sky prevented a clean view of the ship until we came quite close. Even for my inexperienced appraisal of ships, I could tell that something was wrong with her. The shade of the upper masts had been made the same as the dusky sky and the sails were nowhere to be found. Almost all of the crew could be seen above deck. Thoris walked up to meet us on the pier.

"What happened?" Lorcan asked. "Were you attacked?"

"Yes. Menalcus and Leo were on watch, but some bastard with a halberd still set both sails aflame. He then almost cut Menalcus down, but the rest of us came up to chase him off. Both masts will have to be replaced. What about you? I assume you were attacked as well if you're back this early."

"Aye. There's no doubt we've caught the attention of these fuckers, so it's dangerous to split up. Cyrus says he knows of another lead in Ecrin. Take who you want and check the docks for anyone leaving for the capital today or tomorrow."

Chapter Thirteen

Thoris found a small cargo ship leaving for Ecrin at noon. I wasn't thrilled by its size. If the Advent had a ship nearby, it would be a simple matter of using their suicidal slaves to ram us and sink the ship. I was on watch as often as possible for this reason. Concern over Advent meddling also stopped me from sending a letter to the guild to let them know we were coming. Except for Lorcan's men taking over the sailing themselves, the trip ended up being uneventful, with even the weather staying abnormally calm during the shift of seasons.

While Lorcan and Lucetta went with my group to the guild house, the others stayed in Eastern Ecrin at a tavern called the Fat Witch. It was late in the evening, so I wasn't surprised to learn from the guild clerk that Braden was at home. I thus asked for Cat or her brother. Both ended up being present. They each came down wearing leather armor plated with thin sheets of steel on the inflexible sections. It was unadorned, standard fare, but Ethan walked in it as though he were royalty.

Cat hugged Clarissa and asked, "What brings you back so soon?"

"This is Mercer we're talking about," said Ethan with stern calculation. "He's here on serious business."

I shook his offered hand. "Only a true friend would have figured that out." I knew everyone but him picked up on the sarcasm. "Does Braden have any letters for me?"

"Uh, I'm not-"

"Yes," inputted his sister. "You can follow us to his office."

"Hey, why didn't you update me before?"

"I did, but I guess you didn't hear me when you were flirting with the stable girl."

"Err, well... So, Mercer, who are your new friends?"

124

Filling in for me, Lorcan pulled in Lucetta by her waist and said, "This is Lucetta Ambrose, my savagely endearing wife. I am Lorcan Eberwolf, infamous seafarer and father to your friend here."

Ethan stopped in the middle of the stairs we were climbing. "You're his parents?"

"*He* is," I clarified. "There's no blood relation to the woman."

"But I thought... So you-"

"Later, please."

We entered Braden's office, and using a key she had with her, Cat unlocked a drawer and grabbed some letters. She rifled through them until she reached the desired one. She handed me a rolled up paper kept curled up by a string. After reading the amazing penmanship, I regretted leaving Ecrin so soon. The letter was dated only a few days after I left, meaning Odet was forced to wait all this time knowing a traitor was possibly in her midst.

"Well?" asked Lucetta.

"It seems we might have what we came for."

"Really?" said Lorcan. "So where is it?"

"In a noble's home, but we can't get it just yet."

"Why not?" asked the piratess. "I can steal from anywhere."

"Stealing won't answer exactly who's using it. Besides, I doubt even you've stolen anything from a valkrean's home. No, first I have to get in contact with someone. Cat, can you use the guild's seal to send something to Odet tonight?"

"Probably. I'll even go drop it off myself."

"Good. Get me an inkwell and some paper."

"That's funny," said Lorcan. "I could have sworn you said 'Odet' just now."

"He did," said Clarissa.

"So your noble friend has the same name as the princess, then?"

125

"The same name, face, status, whatever you got."

I had begun writing my letter, so I only heard my father begin his bellowing laugh. "Why didn't you say so before?! My son knows royalty!"

"That's not the sort of thing I like shouted out in public, *Dad*."

"Yes, of course… They say the Astor women are quite the beauties. Hope you gave them a good impression of the Eberwolf family! Hey, do you think I could get all my crimes pardoned?"

"Mine too!" added his wife.

"Everybody's crimes!"

"I believe you're closer to being turned in by your son," correctly evaluated Ghevont.

I wrote what I needed to say—and what I didn't need to, such as Clarissa's regards—and gave it to Cat. She was off with it so splendidly quickly that she couldn't have departed the building any faster if she jumped out the window.

"Um, where's Marcela?" asked Ghevont.

"She's in a little place my sister and I rent not far from here. Do you want to see her?"

Ghevont looked for my approval, which I gave when I said, "We're done here until we get a reply. You and Clarissa can go, I'll be resting here." To my father, I asked, "What will you do?"

"I suppose I'll go update my men."

"If you can help it, I'd prefer you don't spread word about my connection."

He smiled. "If I can help it. I'll return at dawn."

Before leaving with Ghevont and Clarissa, Ethan showed me to a room being used by other guildsmen as sleeping quarters. Surrounded by stone walls and warriors allowed my mind to drift off faster than normal.

126

It was still dark when Ethan shook me awake from my unusually deep slumber. "Bell is here," he whispered.

I followed him into Braden's office, where the former guild master was waiting in his noncombatant dress. Waiting in her combat attire was Odet's royal protector.

"Hello again, Mercer," greeted the bodyguard with a small bow.

"Sorry for making your princess wait so long for a reply. Is *Summertide* still with Owen's family?"

"As of yesterday morning."

"I hope Ghevont is truly the best person to translate and decode this work," said Braden. "If the princess didn't instruct me to give you more time to reach us, I would've seized it myself and handed it over to our best men."

"I assure you, Ghevont is the best man for the job. Not only does he know better than anyone else what his father's line of thinking was, he can work with it far quieter than the guild can. Anyway, taking the scroll would force you to charge both Owen's mother and father, but they'll each have plausible deniability. I've come up with a way we can obtain the item and know whether one or both parents is the conspirator."

"How?"

"It was in his letter," explained Bell. "You didn't read it?"

"Catherine only woke me once the letter was delivered." Back to me, he asked, "What plan did you give the princess?"

"She'll tell Owen to make an exact handwritten copy of the poem when he gets the chance. This he will give to Odet and she will give it to us. After Ghevont translates the work, he'll be able to create an encoded message that we'll deliver to each of his parents."

"A snare, then. I suppose you do trust in this Ghevont fellow, but do you really wish to use Owen in this? I haven't seen much of the boy, but few sons would willingly help turn in their parents, especially if he knows something himself."

"Odet's letter specifically mentioned that he was the one to lead her to the scroll. So even if he is involved, then he's a very stupid fellow we can manipulate easily enough. As for his motivation, I'm certain Bell's mistress will see to that."

"And Princess Astor is fine with this?" Braden asked Bell.

"She is, but she sent me here with the express purpose of gaining your approval, guild master. She realizes that if your experience objects to the idea, then she will have to rethink Mercer's strategy."

A pleased expression flashed across his face before reverting to its former gravity. "Well, I don't see the harm in going about it the subtle way. We can always just barge in if something goes wrong."

"My thoughts exactly," I said.

"Who exactly is Ghevont?" Ethan asked me.

"Currently more useful than you unless you go find everyone and bring them up to speed. Bell, tell Odet that Owen has two nights to copy everything down."

"Why the time limit?"

"Mostly because I feel like it, but also because the faster we get this done, the better."

"I'll merely inform the princess of your preference."

Shrugging, I said, "I'm going back to sleep."

I spent the next two days sharpening my skills against my father. We sparred with real steel in an isolated slice of Eastern Ecrin's shoreline. The beach became too rocky here for regular beach going activities, so people were specks in the horizon. It was obvious that our first sparring session had him going easy on me. I was on my ass more often than he broke a sweat. His footwork was faster and his strength more ruthless. It wasn't until I shifted every drop of my focus into Lorcan's movements—and get punished more for it—did I learn how he did this.

As I laid on my back, attempting to regather the air Lorcan had kicked out of me, I said, "You're… using… wind spells to…"

"To quicken my steps, yes," he finished, grabbing my arm and pulling me back up to my feet. "I also use it to reinforce my slashes. Pretty nifty, eh?"

"I have further to go than I thought."

"Ah, don't be discouraged. My old man kicked my ass until I was thirty! He's senile now, but he's a tough son of a bitch, I'll tell you what. Anyway, you're farther along than I was at your age. Do you want me to show you how to cast some wind spells?" He opened his palm to allow a whirling ball of hissing air to form above it. "You'll be able to bust through boulders with this!"

"Thanks, but I have enough on my plate right now."

"Your illusion and fire spells are nice, but I feel you could use extra power in your attacks. You can't always rely on your corruption to bail you out."

"You're right, but once I master my fire spell, I'll soon succeed in summoning all the power I need."

"What does that mean?"

I mulled it over a moment, only to conclude that there was no reason to think it over. "My sword's name is Aranath."

"Really? I've never named mine. Maybe I should, except I replace or lose it every other year. Where did you get the name from?"

"Aranath told me himself. It's his power that removed the mind rune and keeps my corruption in check. This power belongs to a dragon." I showed him the hilt. "Here, take it and hear him for yourself."

He took the offered blade and listened to the dragon's words. I don't know what Aranath told him, but as I expected, Lorcan laughed. "Well, well! I

129

give you my thanks, dragon blade, for keeping my son sane and alive through all the shit he's been through." Giving me back the sword, he also said, "You keep surprising me, boy. I've seen a pissed off kraken sink a two hundred footer, but seeing a dragon will top that!" He raised his heavy cutlass and entered his stance. "Let's get to it, then!"

Chapter Fourteen

The afternoon after Owen's arbitrary two nights ended, Ethan came up to tell me that Bell *and* Odet were in Braden's office. He didn't even wait to see if I would follow him before he dashed back out the room.

Opening the office door revealed Bell standing next to a figure clasped in a dirty green cloak. Also in the room was Braden and Ethan. The door shutting caused the figure to turn around and confirm Ethan's vision.

"Do you have the copy?" I asked her.

"Hello to you, too," she replied. Her hand escaped her cloak to hand me a scroll.

"Thank you, and I am sorry I didn't wait a few days for your reply. I didn't think you'd find an original so quickly."

"You had places to be, I'm sure. So who is this translating friend of yours?"

"Riskel Rathmore's son."

Her head moved back. She then used the momentum to look at Braden, who simpered and said, "I've sent Catherine to retrieve the scholar if you want to meet him. Fidgety fellow."

Back to me, the princess said, "You make odd friends, Mercer."

"And your bodyguard friend looks competent enough to deliver scrolls, so why are you wasting your time here?"

"The benefit of being *second* in line to a throne is having more freedom to waste my time where I wish."

"Oh, so your parents know you're at the Warriors Guild helping to smoke out a traitor?"

"Well, I didn't say I *truthfully* wasted my time where I wanted. I'm 'officially' with Owen now. If they come looking for me there, then Owen will say I went riding with Bell."

"Why the lying at all?"

"Because I want to see this through myself. Or did you expect I'd stand idly by after you ask me to instruct my friend to help hand over his family?"

"I'm assuming you didn't actually tell Owen that much. What did you tell him?"

"He knows something is going on, obviously, but I haven't told him I suspect his parents of any wrongdoing. As far as he knows, *Summertide* is wanted by very aggressive art dealers."

"How long until Ghevont creates the false messages?" asked Braden.

"He's already studied some coded messages we took from Dranall, so it shouldn't take him more than a few hours to falsify similar letters. We'll send one overnight so it can arrive in the morning."

"What will these messages say?" asked Bell.

"Something simple, yet mildly menacing. Something like 'We have to talk about your husband and son,' along with a meeting place and time."

"And the meeting place?"

"The Advent seem to enjoy using temples, so we'll set the first meeting at noon for whatever temple the Vealora family uses. Noon is when we'll also send the second letter. This second one will be addressed to Owen's father and will call for him to come to the temple in the evening. Whoever answers the missive will be our traitor. Does that sound okay with you, guild master?"

"Aye, so far so good. I imagine the Vealora family uses the more intimate Western Ecrin temple, right?"

"Yes," answered Odet.

"Then I'll take a couple of guildsmen there before the noon meeting. I sincerely hope we don't have to apprehend anyone of that high a station, but it would confirm the Advent as major players in the attacks. We'll then be able to make this line of investigation more official. Mercer, do you mind if Ghevont does his work in my office?"

"I can't think of a better place."

"I can think of way more places," said Ethan, simply trying to add something to the conversation.

The room became too crowded when Catherine brought over Ghevont and Clarissa a few minutes later, so Braden decided that Ghevont and Catherine would stay with him. Everyone else would wait for a result in the sibling's home nearby. I didn't want to wait in a cramped room with Ethan and Marcela, so I slinked away by saying I needed to inform my father of our current status.

It was a slow walk to the large, cheap inn the pirates occupied half a mile from the guild house. Lorcan wanted to basically bring his entire crew to the temple, but I insisted that no battle was imminent and that he and Lucetta would be more than enough.

I didn't go back to the guild house until after I ate supper with the buccaneers. When I checked back with Ghevont, he said to carry a couple more hours of patience. I tried spending these hours on a nap, but I had trouble getting my eyes to stay closed. I gave up after an hour and instead went to wait in the office. Ghevont had asked for Braden and Catherine to leave as he worked, but he said nothing against my presence.

It was soothing watching and hearing him scribble away, enough so that I was almost slumping with sleep in my chair. His "I did it!" exclamation rid me of my snooze craving.

"Did what?"

"I decoded one of Corbin's shorter messages. Someone evidently denied a financial request from him. Some Old Voreen words are unknown to me, but I've proven I can at least translate eighty-five percent of the language. I've also learned that the differences between the original and newer editions are substantial. I can see why the changes were made. The original is quite dull compared to the newer versions."

"Feel good enough to start working on those fake messages?"

"I'll have them done in an hour, and then I'll start translating Corbin's messages and then see what *Summertide* is hiding."

Braden and Ethan came in to check on Ghevont when he was halfway done making his first encoded letter. When he finished it ten minutes later, he handed it to Braden so he could start the delivery process. Twenty minutes after that and the scholar turned code breaker finished with his second letter. This second snare we left in the drawer for future sending. Without missing a beat, Ghevont went on to studying the poem's deeper secrets. I agreed to Ethan's request to join him in updating the girls back at his place.

The room he rented was located above a little woodwork shop a strange old couple owned. I knew they were strange due to the fact the still awake woman was told us to keep our "erotic endeavors" quiet with the girls upstairs. She sounded serious, but a nearly toothless little grin crept up on her face as we climbed her stairs.

On opening the door to his room, Ethan proclaimed, "Don't worry, ladies, the men are here!"

"Hit him for me," Cat entreated me.

My harder than necessary punch landed behind his upper arm. He wanted to curse from the pain, but seeing Odet on the floor braiding Marcela's hair stopped him.

"Guys, we're supposed to act like civilized people."

"Then you should rent a more civilized place," I replied.

The room was too small and packed to do anything but stand. There was a single bed by the tiny window Bell and Clarissa sat on. Cat sat in the only chair in the room, which was next to a small-ass table to my right. To my left, Odet and Marcela were on a squashed pile of straw covered by a bristly rug that must have acted as an extra bed.

Odet, without taking her attention away from the girl's hair, asked, "Did Marcela's friend succeed?"

"The proverbial wheels are in motion, Your Highness," I answered.

She sighed. "Then there's no going back."

"What you should do now is fetch Owen and take him back to your palace until this is done. He'll need your support if we discover what I expect to."

"I told you, I want to see this through myself. I have to be there to see who shows up. Besides, Owen is stronger than you think."

"I suspect he's only strong when you're around him."

She looked up at me with a face mildly scrunched by incertitude, not knowing how to respond to what was a compliment to her and an insult to her friend. Not having the conviction to look at me, she said, "I suspect you're wrong."

We would have continued our discussion if we had been alone, but current company stopped me from what I was going to say to actually asking, "Do you believe it's only his mother?"

She held her tongue a moment and paused in her braiding. At the same time she restarted weaving the hair, she said, "If this isn't all a coincidence, then yes, I suspect Lady Vealora more than her husband. Lord Vealora was a comrade of my father's when they fought in the special units together. His loyalty and skill earned him the role of royal spymaster, a role he's held since my father became king. Lady Vealora is more of an unknown to me, but I do know she's of valkrean blood, so I don't see why she would work for the Advent if she's what they're after."

"She wasn't there to help protect her son during the attack on Qutrios. You still don't believe that was a coincidence, do you?"

Odet's silence allowed Clarissa to ask, "I don't know about everyone else, but I think we can leave grim news for later. Mercer, I was just telling Odet a little about your father."

"He sounds like a charming man to meet," said Odet. "He is near, I understand."

I mentally chuckled at the image of a drunk pirate meeting a refined princess. "I fear the state he's in at this time of night is no state to meet a lady, much less royalty."

"Then he sounds as though he'll get along wonderfully with my father. Perhaps once Alslana is allowed to breathe a moment, we may all meet more officially."

"You get right on planning that."

The others began trickling in their input on different topics, which mostly came back to Odet explaining how palace life worked. I was certain the princess had heard every question imaginable regarding her aristocratic life, but she answered everything as though she had only recently become royalty and was describing her new experiences to close friends. I expended more brain power than I should have trying to figure her out, and I concluded that she must have truly appreciated not being first in line to the throne. As a result, she didn't mind trading the pressure of someday leading an influential kingdom for the little annoyances that came with intermingling with us lowly commoners.

The overfilled chamber was losing its air too quickly for my liking, urging me out of the room. I hoped to get some proper sleep in the guild house before we all made our way to our respective positions in the morning. After a few good yawns and stretches, I succeeded in entering a dream world where I struggled to swim in an endless field of fire.

Ghevont was still working when I made my way down to get some predawn breakfast. I ate with Braden in the corner of the mess hall before the others began showing themselves. As the siblings were not official guildsmen yet, Braden ordered them to stay at headquarters in case he had to send a message to his other comrades. For my part, I told Clarissa to move Ghevont in with Marcela and keep an eye on them. She didn't like the babysitting duty, but I assured her that if I were anticipating trouble, I would have undoubtedly brought her along. Including the two guildsmen Braden was going to take, the temple group stood at eight strong.

Thanks to Odet not wanting to make it known that she was at the guild, my father's introduction with the hooded princess was subdued and pleasantly short. The preparation we were in the middle of also cut off any casual conversation he wanted to get into. Nearly all the planning was done by me, Braden, and Lorcan, but the princess tried her all to add her input. To eliminate any doubt as to why she was there, I resolved to be the one to act as the letter sender and get Lady Vealora to spill her secret to me. When I extracted it, I was to signal Lorcan and Lucetta, who would be waiting in a nearby pew. Their getting up would prompt the out of sight guildsmen to come in for the arrest.

Odet wanted to be the first person to encounter Lady Vealora if she appeared, but not only did Braden point out that he would be beheaded by the king if he allowed his daughter to head into an unpredictable situation, he also rightly identified that her relationship with the noblewoman would fetter both mouths. She also couldn't argue with the fact that it was my plan and my digging that led us here in the first place. The princess gained a victory when she convinced me to allow her to stay close to the trap, since someone needed to let me know who the lady was.

The eight of us rode guild horses to the western temple two hours before noon. We arrived minutes after the morning sermon ended and with plenty of time before Lady Vealora made a life altering choice. Any non-highborn believers who wandered in during our operation were kindly told by one of the two priests on staff that the temple was closed for a couple of hours,

137

keeping away as many prying ears and eyes as possible. The priests themselves were told nothing other than this was guild business and to only allow nobles inside. Luckily, few nobles entered a temple when it wasn't obligatory.

The temple's size was much cozier than its grandiose sibling in Central Ecrin, but it was still spacious enough to have a quiet conversation and not have it resound across the echo friendly room. The pirates sat themselves at the front pew while the guildsman disappeared into a small hall. Odet and I sat on a pew close to the entrance, with Bell watching her highness from a nearby hallway of her own.

I grabbed a pair of holy books from a priestess, *The Tome of Duality*, and gave one to Odet so we could pretend to read. However, I did begin reading through a few passages for the first time in my life when Odet and I weren't talking. The first half of the book was dedicated to the three gods of day, who were led by their chief god, the god of sun fire, Tahlous. His underlings were the god of stone and the goddess of sky. Ylsuna, goddess of night and wife of Tahlous, held domain over goddess of the sea and god of luck. To further emphasize the duality of these gods, the first half was written in black ink on white pages while the second section had white words on pages of dark gray.

Sprinkled throughout both halves were references to the four gods of strife. War and lust were among the most commonly acted upon disharmonies, thus making them the most malevolent and prominent of the immoral deities. Not to be outdone, the goddess of curses and the god of madness focused on making their rarer evils more corrosive to the soul, making them as reviled as any other ills. Despite their bitter intents, the tome explained that even these evil spirits played an important part in keeping balance throughout the physical and spiritual planes. I believed the parts citing these depraved immortals to be the most eloquently written and interesting.

A few minutes into our vigil, Odet asked, "What will you say to her?"

138

"I plan on playing a blackmailer."

"Ah, I see, that is a good tactic."

"I'm aware."

She turned away from her book to look at me with the corner of her green eyes. "You really don't want me here, do you?"

"It seems you're mistaking my indifference for something else. Still, since Bell also knows Lady Vealora, I do feel you're somewhat redundant."

"Oh, right, you still think I should be with Owen."

"That would be the logical place to be, but it seems you're allowing yourself to be a bit selfish."

"Selfish?"

I rose my eyes from the holy pages. "Tell me, do you think Owen will wonder why you *had* to be here to see his family detained? I doubt it, he'll have more things on his mind by that point, but you know the answer to that. You don't *have* to be here, you *want* to be. Don't get me wrong, I'm not maligning you. If you your friend was more than just restless, then I'm sure that would outweigh everything else, but you can't convince me that this act right now isn't a little selfish."

"No, I suppose I can't convince you, especially if you might be a smidge correct, but I still say you are disregarding his own strength."

"How many people around his age would you say with certainty is stronger than him? Three people in this room are clearly so. Include Clarissa and the figure only grows from people you just met."

"I just happen to know a lot of strong people. Moreover, you're concluding all this from a single circumstance. I've known him far longer."

"Most meetings between warriors will be a single circumstance. Perhaps there is a level of strength I have not yet seen, and I am not saying he is weak in will, but even the way you defend him only tells me he needs it."

139

"Until he proves you wrong, it appears we will remain at an impasse on the matter."

"I can agree to that."

"Does this still count as a business conversation?"

"Yes."

"Do you only have business conversations with Clarissa?"

"I'd say forty-nine percent of them still are."

"Ah, so she is worthy enough to be considered your friend. That's good, she speaks highly of you. It'd be a shame if that wasn't reciprocated. It's also a shame Clarissa would be condemned by many, no matter how good-natured her persona is. Did you know early Alslana was once ruled by a vampire? He ruled it well for about five years until a knight discovered his feeding pit full of live prisoners. Anyway, it says much about your own character that you would befriend a vampire."

"Her state and my own aren't so different."

"Yes, she's told me a little of your current condition."

"Is there anything she hasn't told you?"

"There must be, for I can tell she wants to say so much more. She did say that as long as your sword is with you, then there's nothing to fear, right?" I nodded. "I know a few enchanters who would give anything to examine a sword that can suppress corruption."

"They'll then quickly learn why they can't mimic that power. I'm afraid my method for keeping sane cannot help others."

"I see. That is a shame." We were quiet for a few minutes before Odet said, "Your father keeps looking back at us."

"I know. I'm ignoring him."

She gave him a little wave. "Clarissa said he was a 'maritime adventurer.' Was that her way of saying 'pirate'?"

"Yes. Be warned, he'll try to get you to pardon known crimes against him."

"What are his known crimes?"

"Never asked."

"I've never seen someone smile so widely. I'll laugh hysterically if you do that right now."

"Don't hold your breath."

"Come on, just a teeny smile."

"Invite me to your room one night and you'll get your wish."

With a mock tone of girlish fretfulness, she said, "But then someone would surely see us and my beloved will strike you down! All your blood will ruin my floor."

"You believe him good enough to accomplish the task?"

"You'd give him a good fight, but yes, I believe so. He was trained by some of Alslana's best warriors and casters from an early age. He currently belongs to Alslana's High Guard as one of the youngest members to ever be accepted."

"Sounds like the type of person I'd prefer backing me up at the moment. Where is he now?"

"Unfortunately for you, he's with my father's escort while he visits with the southern nations."

"When does he return?"

"If the schedule is kept, within two weeks."

"Then it sounds like we have a fortnight of nights together."

"But my floor."

"It would be worth it."

The next five minutes or so were filled with only intermittent comments. The next real interaction came when she nudged me harder than she probably meant to and whispered, "That's her."

141

A woman with graying blonde hair had passed to my left. I allowed the ambling woman to take a few more steps down the center aisle before standing up and saying, "A pleasure to meet you, Lady Vealora."

She turned with a surprised spin. Most of her face was still smooth, but a few creases around her eyes and mouth could not be halted. "C-can I help you, young man?"

The twitchy manner of the thin, dignified woman told me how to proceed. I had to hit hard. Loosely resting a hand on my sword's pommel, I said, "You're a busy woman, so I'll get right to the point. I would like five hundred gold standards delivered to my ship by the end of the week. In exchange, I won't deliver the evidence I have of your involvement with the Advent."

Her mouth opened, but nothing came out. She turned a shaky head, but no one was coming to her aid.

"Do we have a deal or not?"

Finally, she stammered out, "W-what proof do you have?"

"Are you joking? Everything I have on the Advent leads back to your family. I know about the original *Summertide* edition you own and how to use it. I even know you keep the scroll in your husband's office. Enlighten me, how would a spymaster feel when he learns his own wife is a traitor? Or is he part of this conspiracy as well? Or maybe you don't care about what happens to him at all. Does the same go for your son? I know an Advent worshipper attempted to take him in the Qutrios attack you were mysteriously absent from. Was that to take the suspicion off you? Or were you serving him up as an offering?"

"Never!" she exclaimed louder than she desired. She cleared her throat and composed herself closer to the highborn she was. "You obviously have little idea what you're getting yourself into."

142

"Perhaps. I'll admit to being intrigued by this cult. I've seen them use corrupted puppets and even heard they were the ones to truly defeat Riskel Rathmore."

"Hmm, it's unusual for an outsider to learn so much of our work without either being turned or... disappearing. Who are you?"

"A simple sell sword who perhaps has gotten in over his head."

Her dauntless smile made a few more wrinkles appear. "We can always use capable young men in the fold. A new age is coming, you see."

"As long as this new age has coin, I'd rather have the coin."

"I've had a well full of coin my entire life and it has never quenched my soul. It will be the same for you."

"Are you trying to recruit me, Lady Vealora?"

"Even if I gave you every coin I have, you'll be caught in the change we will bring to Orda. Why not benefit from this change on a level far deeper than most mortals will experience? To inherit the power of an immortal?"

"And you were recruited this way? With the idea that awakening an old god will bring about your immortality?"

"Idea? I've seen that power for myself. I've seen *him* for myself. You will it as well if you prove yourself worthy."

"And what would be the first step toward that?"

"This is no place to talk about such things. You know where my home is, correct? Why not come over this evening? We'll talk. I'll even be able to gather fifty gold standards so you may waste it on drink and whores while you think things over, hmm?"

In theory, it sounded as though I could get her to spill more on the Advent if I continued the ruse, but in practice, I was pretty sure she would have me killed. The cue to get everyone to reveal themselves to a traitor was for me to say "It's over, Lady Vealora" loud enough for all in the temple to hear. A stamping of boots came first from the pirates and Bell. Then the guildsmen

143

made themselves known. The noblewoman was surrounded before she could comprehend what was happening.

Her eyes fell on Odet when she let her hood fall. "P-princess Odet," she gasped. "What is happening here?"

"I would like to know that as well, Lady Vealora. How could you betray Alslana? My family? Your son?"

"Betray!" She swiveled her head around again and sighed. The Advent in her reappeared. "You think so small, Your Highness. We are both small players, but you will soon see that my actions will save my family while no action you take can save your own."

"What do you mean? What did you do?"

She looked away from her. To the armored men, she said, "You are here to arrest me, are you not? Get to it, then."

"Wait a moment," the princess requested of Braden, who was about to give an order. "Are you saying the Advent will target my family?"

Her wrinkly grin grew again. "How many people do you truly trust in your father's escort? Perhaps word of some tragedy is on its way right now!"

I foresaw a cackling laugh about to spring from her, but I didn't let it get that far. I stepped up and planted a punch squarely on her stomach, sending the delicate woman wheezing to the floor. "Get her out of here as fast as you can," I told Braden. "We can't have word spreading about her arrest."

A thin rope was bound around the noblewoman's hands and a piece of cloth was used to gag her mouth. She was then led out the back where Braden and his subordinates would take her to a guild cell.

Glancing at Odet showed her to be in deep thought. "Are you all right, princess?"

"Yes, but I must go update my mother about everything we have so far. I will return in three hours. Let's go, Bell."

Chapter Fifteen

The group had decided beforehand that we would meet at the temple again in four hours for the next traitor-luring operation. The pirates and I wasted much of that time at a tavern discussing what had happened over a big stack of meat. Both my father and Lucetta laughed their asses off every time they described me hitting the old woman. I allowed myself to snicker once or twice with them.

We met up with Braden at the temple in the hour Odet said she would make her return, but we had to wait a half hour more before the royal actually arrived. When she did, Braden informed her that Lady Vealora was secured in a cell and that a binding spell would prevent her from summoning her eidolon or cast any spell of note. He also took great care to make sure few guildsmen saw her, hoping word of her arrest wouldn't spread to her husband and make our operation pointless.

Since spymasters weren't prone to declaring their location, the courier was forced to send the encoded letter to his house. Braden probably did have the pull to find out where Lord Vealora was, but as that in of itself might be seen as suspicious, we elected not take that route. We just hoped he didn't work too late.

It was the same setup as before, except the pirates and guildsmen were waiting halfway down the pews instead of nearer the podium as before. If a spymaster attacked me, it was in my best interest to get backup as quickly as possible. Once again, I was in a position most men would strangle a fluffy kitten to be in—sitting alone by an Astor woman.

"How did your mother take the news?" I asked her.

A little smile formed at the brink of her lips. "She acted as though she knew all along that Lady Vealora was not an honorable woman, but she was hiding her shock, I'm sure. I've informed her that the guild still needs time to determine the honesty of her husband, so she won't decree anything today."

"And she still doesn't realize you're helping?"

"I know she suspects, but without Dad around, she knows she can't stop me without getting *really* upset. I'm in Ecrin surrounded by our armies, so she won't go that far. She was more worried when I told her to send a letter to Father. I assured her it was only precautionary."

"Do you believe that?"

"Now I do. The more I think about it, the less it makes sense for the Advent to target him. It would take an army with a significant strategic advantage to overwhelm his escort. And even if the Advent hire every mercenary in the Blue Swords they won't have the manpower they need for such an attack."

"I don't think the noblewoman was talking about an army."

"I know, but I'm even less worried about a traitor within his escort. They're severely underestimating the king if their traitorous plan involves anything less than three elite warriors. If I believed there to be that many conspirators in Alslana, I'd be absconding with my family at this very moment. I'm more concerned about my mother. She's the one with valkrean blood and without a warrior's instincts. The queen would also be easier to get to if my father isn't around to help defend her. Of course, they both could be targets."

"You said the king will arrive within a fortnight, correct?"

"Yes."

"And our new prisoner sounded quite confident that arresting her would change nothing in the grand scheme of things."

"Yet I'm certain she fears the ultimate penalty her crimes will bring. She wants to be immortal, after all. Her poise must then come from believing the Advent's plan will soon avail her of her situation. Even if we were assured tomorrow that she couldn't provide us with any useful information, her status as both a noble and a valkrean will stay her execution for many weeks."

"So we can guess that if this plan exists, then it'll make itself known before your father returns."

"I'll see to it that my family is well defended by extra guardsmen until Dad can see to the defenses himself."

I blankly regarded my open book for a moment, mulling over our circumstances. Then I said, "Until Ghevont discovers what my next goal should be, you can consider my blade added to whatever protection you wish to give your family. I'll be a poor substitute for your paramour's sword, but it's all I can offer."

A sugary chuckle escaped her. "Thank you, but it's clear your sword is not all you've given in this quest of yours. For instance, I would like your prediction on Lord Vealora."

"My prediction? Okay, hold on… Well, the fact that Owen doesn't appear to be in league with the cult implies that at least one parent isn't a member. He would've been born into it if they both were. There is the possibility they didn't want their son involved in this mess, but the Qutrios attack implies otherwise. I expect he won't show."

"I'm leaning that way, too, though his career will be ruined once it's known a traitor lived within his own home. Owen will be devastated… and stop thinking what you're thinking. This situation would affect anyone. Well, everyone but a completely practical business man like yourself."

"And as I hope our professional partnership continues a little longer, I will go ahead and ignore my thoughts on Owen."

"Are you really still… Oh, your father is waving at us again." She once again acknowledged his wave with her own. "Is he always so jovial?"

"I hope not."

"You don't know?"

"Clarissa didn't tell you that I just met him?"

"Now that you mention it, she was quite ambiguous when she spoke of your relationship with him. Is that why you were in Dranall, to meet your father?"

"No and yes. I was looking for family, I just didn't know which ones were still out there. He was searching for my brother and I when we ran into each other on the same lead."

"Clarissa mentioned that you were still looking for somebody. So it's your brother?"

"Yes. It was my resistance to corruption that attracted the Advent to him. The others I found settled in Bukuna."

"You don't sound like a man who's found his family."

"I suppose Clarissa has been better than I thought at keeping my privacy intact."

"Really? I'll need to give her a stern talking to, then. But what does your privacy have to do with your family?"

"Because I would need to remember them to care as much as I should."

"Oh… Now I see what she meant…"

She was going to say something else, but then thought better of it. I inferred she had figured out why I didn't go on telling everyone I met about my memory loss. I appreciated her holding her tongue on the matter.

We spoke less as the spymaster's time neared, but he remained an absentee. There came a point when a few people began trickling into the temple for the evening sermon, and though we waited even as several more people came in, the lady's husband never showed himself. When other nobles Odet recognized came in, we thought it best to end the operation before someone spotted the princess and spoke to her in that flamboyant voice nobles used when trying to attract attention to themselves.

Even knowing the separation was coming did not lessen the disappointment I felt go up my serrated arm. Why the prickle came from there, I didn't know. I did know I would have to find an opportunity to be alone for a while so I could relieve the uncontrollable restlessness a girl like her fostered.

What happened to the Vealora family did not interest me all that much. As far as I was concerned, unless Lady Vealora spilled her guts literally or metaphorically, my business with them had ended. Braden explicated some of the psychological, physical, and magical means the guild could implement to extract what information they could from her, but the process would be a slow one, particularly when that person was of high status. It didn't help that her husband's last ditch effort to save his own career would be to defend his wife from these "fraudulent" accusations. Lord Vealora didn't show up, but he would still have to be treated with suspicion. Perhaps even his son to some extent, but Odet would be there for him.

Publically, the word "Advent" wasn't used to describe Lady Vealora's crimes, since few would even comprehend what that meant. And while the public would express some anger over the noble traitor, I doubted they'd be incensed enough to push for a quick execution, especially without tangible proof of her misconduct. Her own vague admission to being involved with the Advent simply opened the investigation.

All in all, this amounted to putting my full attention to Ghevont's progress. The original *Summertide* scroll in the Vealora manor was given to the scholar, which he valued greatly, knowing it was an item his parents had lost their lives over.

Two days after the Vealora operation, I entered the siblings' room, where Ghevont had made his new work space. He had etched a glowing rune in a wall to provide the light a few candles were too weak to give. Reminding me of the first time I saw them, Marcela was taking an afternoon nap on the bed as

149

Ghevont scribbled away on one of his papers, many of which did not fit on the tiny table and were thus piled around his feet.

I said his name. I lobbed him an apple when he looked up. His reflexes were better than yesterday, when it was his lap that caught it and not his hands.

"Oh, yes, thank you. Marcela gives me oranges, but I find they make my fingers too sticky for my work, though I suppose I enjoy their flavor better. I've noted most fruits-"

"How's your work going today?"

"Wonderful! Well, not if I include Corbin's letters. They are a dead end unless we can find dozens of more coded letters to complete the largely incomplete thoughts and responses. However, thanks to some books your guild associates have given me, I've translated almost every Old Voreen word with great accuracy. I am now consolidating all my time on a single *Summertide* theory. You see, I'm now quite positive that *Summertide* doesn't lead to a map, but is itself a map!"

"It mentions the grave?"

"No, but it points to it nonetheless. I've held this theory for some time, of course, as even the newer editions of the epic lend well to that idea. Jages Mar, who's really Jagstonius Marcunis in the original, visited many lands across Orda, and I've concluded that these locations, when aligned properly with one another, will pinpoint the exact location of the grave. What I have to figure out is learning which sites are relevant. Using them all leads to mixed results, so there's a specific pattern I need to find. We'll otherwise be forced to individually check over seventy different possibilities."

"I'm assuming you'll be able to narrow that down."

"Yes, yes, no worries. In two days I'll cut the possibilities by at least half. It'll get a little trickier after that, however. Since many of these ancient places have been lost through time, obtaining precise coordinates will require actually finding out where some lie. Being off by just a few miles in any one of these positions will deviate the final objective by hundreds more."

"How many of these lost places would we have to go to?"

"Eight as of now, but, again, getting more maps and the appropriate literature should make things clearer for us in the coming days."

"Fine work, scholar."

"I thought so."

The day after this update, Bell came to inform us that Odet had arranged for my group, which included all the pirates, to move into a large home in Western Ecrin. Going to it that evening revealed the three-story building to be a small mansion standing within half a mile of the Diamond Palace. The reason a home was even available at this prized a location was due to it only being midway through a renovation it needed after the half brick, half-timber structure suffered a fire. Still, enough of the rooms had been rebuilt to accommodate everyone, as long as some of us shared. It helped that everyone had different sleeping schedules.

I felt our relocation wasn't only a reward of comfort, but also a way for the princess to expediently gather more allies in case an attack occurred. Moreover, Bell came with news that Odet had invited everyone who knew me to a dinner with her family to take place in two evenings. To help the girls buy the best clothing they wished to wear, the bodyguard came with a pouch of coins. I had never heard such piercing screaming in my life. The offer to join Clarissa and the others in their hunt for already dead furs was tempting, but presuming I would get enough of everybody at the dinner, I resisted and settled for continuing my training.

I ended up regretting being a killjoy, since, as any good seer would have foretold, I never made it to that dinner.

Chapter Sixteen

The day before the fancy dinner, a vibrating house jostled me awake. I had a late training session the night before, but the pounding mirth coming from downstairs meant I wasn't going to experience a full morning's rest. Going down to the lowest floor had me smelling the various dishes some of the pirates had heated up in the kitchen.

Walking within sight of the dining hall had me spotting the little princess Elisa, the ever wary Bell, and my business partner sitting among my usual group. The princesses' refined garbs marked them as ladies of import, but their jubilant manner blended well with the rambunctious swashbucklers. Most of the current laughing and witticisms originated from the fearless Elisa trying to strictly instruct the uncouth pirates on table manners.

Lucetta was the first to spot me. Possibly afraid I was going to stand there the whole time, she pulled me into the merry fray. I was at first genuinely depressed that I wouldn't be able to add to what everyone else seemed so naturally good at—even Ghevont was unintentionally funny—but Clarissa helped force out some form of amusement from me.

"Tell one of your jokes, Mercer!"

The entire table suddenly became silent, the only sound being their necks pivoting so that their eyes fell on me. I marked this instance as the first state of embarrassment I had ever felt. I reminded myself that I had slain worse things than humiliation and said, "What does the sign of an out-of-business brothel say? Beat it, we're closed."

The bawling laughter tickled my eardrums. It arose from the fact that I told a joke at all rather than the stupid joke itself, but I felt encouraged enough to say a couple more, including one about sagging breasts being mistaken for nuts. Odet didn't seem to be all that perturbed about her younger sister hearing these inappropriate one-liners. Anyway, seeing Elisa's scrunched face made me think that most of the jokes had gone over her head, so there was little harm done to the pristine mind.

There came a point when the single collection began fragmenting into smaller ones and intermingled with the others. When Odet's cluster walked into mine, she and I broke into our own group.

"I thought you'd still be with Owen," I said.

"I was, but he requested some time alone. It's odd, with his father under suspicion, he's become the effective head of his family. It's an unexpected pressure."

"Have you told him your part in this?"

"That be a little overwhelming at this point."

"So he believes his mother could still be innocent in all this?"

"I didn't want him having too much false hope, so I told him I knew the evidence was damning. Of course, as any son would, he still hopes it was all one big misunderstanding."

"At this point, I wouldn't mind if this all turned into one big misunderstanding, too."

My unrealistic desire for such a notion held even less water when the air and ground rumbled around us twenty minutes later. Seconds after that and snarling animalistic screeches and booming roars came from every direction. Human screams and detonations of spells erupted in the near distance.

I told Ghevont to keep hidden with Marcela in the deepest part of the home. The older princess instructed her sister and Bell to stay with the scholar as well. Bell protested the idea of Odet leaving, but the royal wouldn't hear of it. She needed to get back to the palace.

Lorcan reassured the bodyguard, saying, "Your lady is now an honorary member of my crew! And we defend our own with our lives. She won't get a scratch with us around!"

Before we left, Bell had Odet put on her oversized leather cuirass over the princess' unarmored torso, since the only defensive items she wore were her tall leather boots and the leather gauntlets hiding under her jade sleeves. We then ran to the stables to get on our anxious horses.

Going under the clear blue skies also cleared up some questions as to who are enemies were. A large shadow swooped far above us, heading directly for the large crystal spire topping the highest palace tower. The blocker of sunlight was only a blurry silhouette that looked a bit like a thin spider with four furry wings, but this was enough for Aranath to identify it.

As the creature dove toward the palace walls, firing a greenish electric flare from its mouth, Aranath said, "That's a bazeeba. An eidolon."

After telling Odet this, she saddled her horse and said, "That's one of the eidolons involved in the valkrean abductions... Gods, is that what the Advent were doing all along? Gathering valkrean to use their eidolons in this attack?"

"But shouldn't that be impossible?" asked Clarissa. "Eidolons only follow a valkrean's orders."

"But we already know the Advent can control people using corruption," Athan pointed out. "We fought some."

Looking at me, Clarissa said, "So they experimented with corruption to control valkrean? But why? I thought they wanted to raise a dead god, not attack a nation."

Instead of answering the vampire, Odet snapped the reins of her horse and steered him in the direction of her home. The princess knew the answer, as did I. The Advent were indeed still interested in obtaining power, and Odet's family had a link to one of the most powerful known eidolons in any realm. The Advent were after her mother.

Our horses charged the streets, their riders pushing them to reach the palace gates as fast as their hooves could go. I saw several more winged eidolons nosediving over Western Ecrin, two of them joining the bazeeba in its attack of the palace grounds. They indiscriminately fired caustic spells on anything that moved. The oscillating impacts created shockwaves felt as far as Voreen. Human incantations from below tried bringing them down, but they were either too slow to hit the swift creatures or the hardy eidolons simply brushed off the attacks.

A ground-based eidolon was easy to spot a thousand feet behind us. It looked like a walking hill that stood twice as tall as the community of manors surrounding it. Four thick legs of stony skin supported a tortoise-like frame. Its small, spikey head didn't appear to offer much in the way of facial features, but as we moved farther away from it, it was too difficult to know if it had any face at all. Going by the outbursts of chaos that thumped the ground and quaked the sky, there must have been more summoned beasts wreaking havoc across the city, but they were not within sight.

When our stamping herd entered a hundred yard clearing of grass that separated the palace's outer wall from the nearest neighborhood, another stony eidolon crossed into view. It appeared to be heftier and taller than the last, and it used that bulk to push against the first barrier in its way. The eighty foot wall and the enchanted metal gates it encompassed held firm for now, but large cracks were already forming where the beast had slammed into it. Guardsmen shot arrows and spells from higher up, but its hard skin-shell shrugged them off like it would raindrops. The defenders also couldn't concentrate their fire as much as they wanted to due to the eidolons above, who would decimate a line of soldiers with a single attack if they didn't evade it or create a ward spell quickly enough.

Down below, some sixty soldiers who wished to attack the massive eidolon's stumpy feet had to contend with about four dozen hound-sized, lizard-like animals, though their glossy skin looked more like silvery fish scales. They darted with great speed and their bulging eyes would target a

155

soldier or horsemen before spraying a yellow goo at them. This sludge would either blind someone or stick their feet to the ground, making them easy targets for the lizard-fish to bite down on head or limb with their needle-like teeth.

Through the bedlam happening on all levels, what caught my attention the most was seeing who stood directly underneath the giant eidolon. I would have initially missed him were it not for the sharp streams of flame he blared out at any soldier who managed to get within his wide range. His fire-wreathed halberd was all I needed to see to confirm his identity, but his long white hair and nimble movements likewise reminded me of the Advent cultist from the Qutrios attack.

Three of the lizard-fish saw the newcomers and began to fire their sticky spit at us, but Odet cast her crystal shield over a wide area to prevent it from catching anyone. Proving his worth as a captain of men, sea or not, my father barked a few succinct orders that sent his crew flanking the princess' faster horse. The pirate crew next spread outward from the main assembly to make certain no foe reached the center squad, which consisted of Odet, Clarissa, Lorcan, Lucetta, and I. This strategy created a hole in the battleground for us.

Seeing our intrusion had the Advent fearlessly dash up to my group. A spinning line of his fire impacted Odet's shield. She resisted it for a moment, but the heat was far too powerful to withstand for long. Her crystalized ward shattered, startling her horse enough to make it rear up. She slipped off the animal and let it go its own way. Knowing I was no horsemen made me do the same. The next thing I saw was a wall of fire. Like a waterfall breaking on a boulder of glass, Odet's recast shield diverted the infernal blitz. The giant eidolon next made a noise that sounded much like a dying whale and crashed its enormity against the wall, sending debris and a handful of screaming soldiers tumbling to the ground.

When glare and bellowing subsided, I saw the Advent stop fifteen feet away from us and give the princess a little bow. "Your Highness, it will be an honor to be the one that kills you." He gave a glance to the three horsemen flanking him. "But it appears I am outnumbered once again! Why do you always surround yourself with such scary friends? I know! Does one of you want to join my side?" Then, looking at me, he asked with grave seriousness, "How about yourself? Your corruption will fit well with us."

Aranath growled. "How does he sense your corruption?"

I didn't get the chance to ask. Lorcan used a swing of his sword to propel a slash of air at the Advent, which he proceeded to seamlessly counter with a flame that burst forth from the pole end of his weapon. The explosion of dusty smoke hid him from everyone but the princess and I. He used the debilitating cloud to sprint, not to Odet, but straight at me. I expected to dodge blasts of fire, but he focused on pure speed. The halberd's tip clashed onto a defensive Aranath, and before I had a real chance to deflect his next swing, his weapon's staff swung and struck my ribs, sending me to the ground. I barely rolled out of the way from a downswing. His sheer speed and mastery over his weapon made him little more than a haze to me.

Not wanting to hit me with an errant spell or knife, Lorcan and Lucetta dismounted their horses and tried coming to my aid. Strangely, the Advent used a steady stream of combustion spells to keep them and everyone else back so that he could continue to focus his heatless strikes on me. At one point, when my father came close to adding his blade with my own, one of the fish-lizards mindlessly closed in on him. His wife's warning had him escape some incoming spit. Clarissa used a ball of water to trip up the beast enough to allow Lucetta's scimitar to pierce its flat head.

It was at this instant that the Advent struck the ground with his halberd, causing an opaque smoke to overwhelm us. I recognized the action from my first meeting and was prepared to counter it. I summoned a pile of explosive

157

stones and triggered them. The blast wave pushed away the smoke in time for me to see his smiling face rushing at me. I used my slashing sword to push away the halberd's spike, but the axe part gave me a nice gash in my lower ribs. However, the halberd was not his main weapon this time.

The Advent clutched a new weapon he had obtained from somewhere within his cloak—a glass-like dagger that carried a familiar dark purple hue. He lunged this knife at my open chest. I saw Odet's shield form in front of me, and while it slowed it some, it wasn't yet strong enough to stop the dagger from making a wound deep enough in my chest for it to stick to. The Advent leapt backward, looking quite satisfied with himself. He turned away from me and made his way to my father.

I was confused at his sudden disinterest from me, but as I went to pull away the crystalline dagger, a surge of acquainted pain clenched every muscle and nerve in my head. It was as though each of my teeth ruptured at the same time and now someone was pulling out my tongue with their bare hands. I think I screamed, but I didn't hear it. I may have shed blood from my eyes, but I didn't feel it. All I sensed was the dagger adding new corruption to my soul, using my blood as its link.

My sight blurred as another tortured convulsion constricted my stomach and forced me to expel vomit and humanity. The corruption's takeover was quick, for I already recognized a sick form of pleasure coming from the agony. I overheard Odet yell a muffled form of my name, the name I gave myself when I thought I had freed myself from my oppressors. If her voice was the last sensible sound I ever heard, then I suppose there were worse ways to go.

158

Chapter Seventeen

Odet

I hardly saw it through the smoldering dust, but something dark glimmered in the Advent's hand. Assuming it to mean nothing but misfortune, I cast my shield in front of Mercer. The Advent was too quick for me to completely fabricate the singular ward, but it slowed his thrust. The Advent, however, still had the strength to stick it in his right shoulder. I dispelled the ward and expected the relentless enemy keep up his assault, but he instead hurdled backward and turned his attention to Mercer's father.

As I tried gaining a new bearing on my surroundings, somebody howled in heartbreaking pain. I knew it had come from his direction, but I couldn't believe that spectral sound came from Mercer. When my eyes went to confirm what my ears heard, they saw Mercer's body twitching and his mouth expel a bloody mix of yellowish bile and half-digested food.

"Mercer! What's wrong?! Mercer!"

I started running up to him, but stopped when every hair on my body crawled in the opposite direction. A perceptible shift in the air's weight fell over me when it became thicker with a foulness I did not recognize. Mercer's jerking body then became entirely still, as though he had died standing at his feet. I couldn't help thinking this was indeed the case. A signal of life expressed itself when he took a deep inhale, but another sign that contradicted both sacred life and warm weather came out of him when a frosty mist left his lips.

As I cast my shield in front of me, I said, "Mercer?"

He responded like a rabid animal who had heard his prey whimper. The blood vessels around his eyes were pronounced and dark, and a tear of blood had slithered down his cheek. He transformed into a wild blur as he came at me with speed equal to that of the Advent. I had the time to make my shield as strong as my skill could make it, but his blade carved through it as easily as a fine drape. I was still far away enough to avoid its slash and the next, but each wild swing cut the distance more and more.

He was quick, but his senselessness made him somewhat predictable, giving me a small opening to unsheathe the long knife I had tucked within my boot's shaft. I used it to repel a swing, but my body's bones quivered violently from the impact. When I raised my knife for another deflection, the next swing knocked it out of my hand. The corrupted Mercer then slammed his body into mine, getting me flat on my back and pinning my legs under his own as he sat up.

Just before he slammed the point of his sword down, Mercer's torso and arms became wrapped in water. The envelopment of liquid tried to push him off of me, but I actually felt an outpouring of his dark prana resist Clarissa's spell. The spiteful prana iced some of the water and gave him the strength to continue bringing down his blade. The best I could do was cast my shield, but the sword's point pierced through the magical glass effortlessly. I shrank the ward to focus its power around the blade, but all I managed to do was redirect its path from my heart to my left shoulder. Bell's cuirass provided no resistance at all.

The steel's point punctured my left shoulder. Despite bracing for it, nothing prepared me for the bitter, raw pain that snapped one of my shoulder's tendons. I cried out, but an oddly pleasant burning sensation just below my neck dulled the blade's bite. It took a second to realize it was my grandmother's crystal. An even stranger sensation occurred from the sword skewering me. A scorching power far different from Mercer's corruption began intermingling with the crystal. These two influences prevailed over the impression of pain the physical frame of the sword still tried to bring. They churned and flowed in both me and Mercer. I shut my eyes tight.

160

When I opened them next, a sky of absolute darkness reigned unconditionally. Mercer was no longer above me and no battle was taking place. In fact, nothing was happening around me. The darkness simply continued for a long way. My natural reaction was to think myself blind, but when I turned my head far enough, a kind of horizon with a soft red glow eventually appeared. Despite it being too far away to provide any real illumination to my unnatural expanse, it still made me feel better.

My teeth unconsciously chattered when my brain realized I was someplace very cold. I expected to see my breath in the arctic temperature, but no fog formed. I noticed two other conditions as I tentatively sat up. First, I laid in half an inch of water, water that perhaps should have been frozen in the glacial air. Second, a pinching pain ran up and down my left side from the still open wound the crazed Mercer gave me. I couldn't tell whether I was bleeding or not.

Fear ran amok in me. Was I dead? Or was I on my way to being corrupted?

Startling me further was a deep, growling voice that asked, "Do you wish to save Mercer?"

I didn't know where to look. Each word, each letter seemed to come from a different direction. "Y-yes."

"Behind you, girl."

I looked to see an unconscious Mercer on his back, the real Mercer, except his body laid deeper in the water than mine had been. Only his face and chest remained clearly visible. The rest of his submerged body rippled with the water. I carefully walked up to him, hoping I too didn't sink in the deeper water. When I didn't plummet to his level, I kneeled beside him. He wasn't breathing.

"How?" I asked the invisible entity.

"The holy prana you carry."

161

I took hold of the crystal and snapped it off the necklace. It was glowing with a soft blue light. "I-I can't really control its power yet."

"I can aid you in that endeavor, but you must first release it."

"Who are you?"

"There's little time, girl. Release it and I can rein in his corruption enough to pull him out of this place. Place the crystal on his chest and begin channeling your prana into it. Do not react when the power is released, for I will manipulate it from there."

I laid the crystal down and placed my hands over it. It took a moment to calm my anxieties enough to connect to the holy power stored in the crystal, but once I did, I let every emotion in me fade. At that instant, the crystal blinded me with an outpouring of blue light. The voice growled to remind me to not lose my nerve. My eyes were shut, but a gasp of breath lifted my hands and rang my ears.

Chapter Eighteen
Mercer

A watery hand was enveloping my limp body before it tossed me aside. I rolled over several times on the verdant ground. When my head stopped literally spinning, I rose to my hands and knees, trying to figure out what in Orda just happened. Flickers of memories danced in no real order as I tried extracting the last one. Grabbing my attention was a familiar woman yelling for someone named Clarissa to stop what she was about to do. I looked to see a white-haired young woman holding a ball of water a few yards away from me.

Another young woman sluggishly sprinted up beside her. This second woman was bleeding from a wound on her upper shoulder. On the ground next to me was a longsword stained with blood at its point. The blonde woman— Odet! Her name just came to me—looked at me warily and asked, "Is that you, Mercer?"

Many names entered my head, but I liked the sound of "Mercer" so I nodded. I also liked the look of the sword and went to pick it up. A relieved Odet fell on her knees, breathing hard from some great exhaustion. Gods, everything fell into place when my fingers grazed the hilt. I remembered there was no memory to recall before the fiend's tail wrapped around my arm. I remembered the defiling pain from each inpouring of corruption, and I knew I would gladly take that pain for the rest of my life if it meant not seeing a terrified Odet as she resisted my attempts to kill her.

When I grasped my sword, Aranath said, "I still carry some of the girl's holy prana. Cut your hand against the edge of the steel and pour all the prana you can into the blade. Then, instead of focusing on the dragon stones, focus on summoning a dragon."

I ran the edge of the sword against my palm, the hot sensation of cutting myself a paradise compared to what I had experienced moments earlier. I then pressed this bloody hand into the ground and used the foreign power inside me to call upon an ally not witnessed in centuries. A great pulse of wind blew in front of me as something as large as a whale pushed away the air the freshly summoned dragon now occupied.

For the first time since knowing him, the great beast growled outside of my head, vibrating the ground and my blood. The smooth, lustrous scales running down the serpentine creature were of a dark blue hue, dark enough that the dragon might look black from afar. Making Aranath appear many times larger was when he stretched his forelimbs, which spread his vast, bat-like wings. Three sharp claws stuck out from the wings' central peak. The fleshy membranes looked large enough to lift a dragon thirty feet longer than his forty foot long frame, which didn't include a tail that doubled the greater part of his length. This tail lashed the air like a whip and ended in a bony point shaped like a spearhead.

On the other end was a fearsome head that hung from a uniformly long neck. Two curved horns of pearly white extended from behind the top of his swept-back skull. His eyes were of a burnt orange and had that black vertical slit slicing down their center. They looked as if they could see into souls as easily as I perceived flesh and flame. The tremendous roar he produced made me forget that he was my partner and quieted everyone else who heard it.

Keeping his voice within my head, he said, "Keep sending your prana into the sword if you wish to keep me here. This will not last long, but it should be enough to give you an opening."

With a few powerful flaps of his great wings, the dragon took to his proper domain. I wasn't the only one captivated by the awesome sight. Watching the nimble dragon treat the heavens like a dolphin whirling in water, I could see why he had been given the title "Sky Lord" in his younger days.

His first targets were the comparatively ungraceful eidolons in the sky, who responded to his appearance with alarmed screeches. The bazeeba fired a blast of its green discharge, but Aranath evaded it by rolling out of the way. To my surprise, the dragon didn't emit fire of his own. He instead slammed his body into the somewhat smaller beast. The dragon then used his teeth to bite down on one of the bazeeba's wings and used that as leverage to fling it against a palace tower. As it wailed out with high-pitched squeals, the eidolon tried regaining the sky with three good wings left.

With a dragon near the clouds, I refocused on the Advent, who was fighting evenly with Lorcan and Lucetta. Every step I took toward them had me better sensing just how much pure prana stirred inside me. I weighed nothing and the palpitating power made me feel as though I could thrust my feather-light sword through a slab of steel. More than that, I knew I had the capacity to kill the halberd-wielding cultist.

"Dad! Lucetta! Get back!"

The pirate captain uncrossed blades with the Advent. Following her husband's lead, Lucetta jumped back from the Advent and asked, "What the fuck is going on?! First you go insane and now you can summon a bloody dragon?"

"I'll explain later."

My father slapped me hard in the back and said, "Yes, explanations for later. For now, let's get a bit of revenge against this Advent fellow, eh?"

"No, you and Lucetta help Odet and the others."

"You sure?"

"For the next few minutes."

"All right, then. Let's go help our men, darling!"

As they turned their backs, the Advent fired an inferno he had been gathering at the head of his halberd. I felt it within my dominion. Raising my left arm, I evoked my meager training with dragon flame. However, with her

165

hallowed power enhancing mine, this paltry control over dragon fire resulted in total domination over regular flames, no matter how brutally hot one made them. Before the enemy blaze made the surrounding air a degree warmer, it died in an explosion of a million embers that landed on the ground as harmlessly as snowflakes.

The Advent didn't look worried about his flame dying in front of him. He actually took a moment to look up as Aranath glided over the stone eidolon and released a shower of dragon fire upon it. The pungent burning produced a mad groan from the lumbering body as it backed away from the wall with a few earthshaking steps. The eidolon then attempted to shake off the fire, but it found no relief.

Two other flying eidolons pursued Aranath. The first looked like a vulture with short yellow feathers, but it had four long legs curled beneath its belly. Except for the shaggy fur and the mammalian features outlining its form, I couldn't take more than a rough glance at the second eidolon before I noticed the Advent staring back at me. After a deep inhale, he charged.

He seemed to be half as slow as before, and that accounted for the fact that he abandoned his fire spells and sent all his spare prana into his body. Of course, I knew it was I who had sped up. I not only deflected his swings, but evaded them entirely. Small pieces of his halberd chipped away when we clashed weapons. To not have his speed and fire threaten me the way they once did and yet still not become overwhelmed was a testament to his high skill. Nevertheless, when I finally obtained a small measure of control over Odet's waning power, it was over.

I let his halberd glance off the fiend's tail before sending a burst of prana to my feet, instantly closing the distance between my sword's tip and the Advent's upper stomach. We were eye to eye as his back gained a new hole. He was strangely serene as he coughed up blood and lost the color in his cheeks and eyes. I pulled the sword out of him and let him fall to his knees.

166

"How many of you are there?" I asked him.

He looked up at me and cocked his head. "Strange question. I'm one of a kind."

"How many Advent are here?" I asked more firmly.

"My wound hurts. Are you going to end me, or shall I do it myself?"

It was obvious he was not afraid of death, something I admired. With time being precious in an ongoing battlefield, I decided to end it myself. As fast as I could swing it, the blade slashed his throat open. Not two seconds after his body crumpled to the ground, the remaining lizard-fish and, more importantly, the mansion-sized eidolon were unsummoned back to their realms. The ground soldiers gave a quick cheer.

Those with able bodies started moving toward the heavily dented metal gates to get some cover from the monstrous battle still happening above. They then surrounded Odet when she revealed herself to them. Exempting a couple of pirates getting viscous spit on them, my group came out intact.

After some difficulty, one of the twenty foot tall gates was pushed open. Meeting Odet on the other side was a small group of steel plated knights, one of whom kept a thick ward above them. In response to Odet's question, an older knight with a thin white beard told her, "The enemy has infiltrated the palace, Your Highness. I'm afraid the queen has met them in combat."

"What!? Then why are you not with her?!"

"Every man we can spare is trying to reach her, but a powerful barrier blocks us."

"Take me to her!"

I gave the situation in the sky another glance once we ran past the shorter but thicker inner wall guarding the true palace grounds. The glimpse I caught had me seeing the eidolons continue to be pestered by the dragon, enough so that they could no longer attack Odet's home without exposing

167

themselves to Aranath's attacks. I sensed the dragon continuing to siphon huge chunks of prana from me, helping to give his sky-rendering roars their strength.

The knights led us into the main edifice—a broad, tanned building with a curved wall making up its facade. Our full speed run did not allow me to catch much of what I otherwise expected to see in the grand halls, namely, too much grandness in what should have been modest things. After a few turns down passages and through lavish rooms full of either very hard or very cushy items, we entered a domed dance hall.

Soldiers and casters filled our half of the enormous ballroom. They all faced an almost wholly black barrier that divided the room in two parts like a smooth curtain. Knights and casters hurled spells and arrows at this magical wall, but for all their trouble, only small ripples appeared on its peculiar surface. Once the throng made way for the princess and her group, I came close enough to see through the vaguely translucent barrier.

At each end of the barrier stood an Advent. To my right was a blonde haired woman clad in the silver armor the royal knights wore, implying more treachery within Alslana. To my left stood another armor-wearing, blonde haired man who looked very much like the woman, each having small noses, slightly slanted blue eyes, and thin lips. The woman's hair was significantly shorter than the man's curly mane. If I had taken quicker glimpses, I would have mistaken each of them for the other gender. At their feet were seven dead soldiers, one of whom I recognized as Sir Stone. The possible sibling duo were the obvious casters of this singular barrier.

Behind these Advent was another figure cloaked in bright red. With her hood down, I saw that she was an older woman without a strand of hair to speak of. Oddly, I only assumed her to be old. I couldn't actually pick up all that many wrinkles and she might not have been that much older than my father. She was simply someone who commanded the respect a veteran of war and life demanded from those around her, all without her having to say anything of her past troubles. Both of her hands held lances made of lightning itself, which she was using to ceaselessly strike a half sphere of crystal.

Standing on one knee within this crystal ward was Odet's mother, Queen Leandra. Her quick, shallow breaths and clammy brow told of the heavy strain the other woman placed on her spirit. Her family shield flickered like a failing torch in a hurricane from the lightning it refracted and absorbed with diminishing effectiveness.

As I charged a swing, the head knight said, "Wait! Hitting the barrier with physical attacks will cause your body to become numb. Those who have dared strike it half a dozen times either pass out or seize up. It's like nothing I've ever seen before."

Taking his word for it, I joined the casters in their fight. I summoned as many dragon stones as possible, teleporting them alongside the barrier. Their initial flare-ups rattled the black ward, giving it a lighter shade I used to see through it better. I noticed both siblings were giving their attention to me. The brother turned his head back and moved his mouth. The barrier prevented me from hearing what he told the old woman, but she responded by giving her lances more vigor. Her next lurch with them tore some of Leandra's shield.

I felt the gifted power within me sharply dwindle away as I attempted to give the dragon flame more prana to fuel its burn. The other casters fused their spells with my own to further weaken the wobbling ward, but still it would not fall. As I tried giving the melting stones another surge of prana, my link with Aranath abruptly ended. I had lost both the prana and focus to keep him in my realm. My inexperience also had me lose most of the hold I had over the flames.

"Mother!"

Passed the dying dragon flames and the splatter of spells happening over me, I saw the queen's shield had been broken.

Down to her final option, the staggered queen put her hands to the ground. Everyone turned away from the brightest light anyone could ever experience, not unless the sun replaced the moon. The brilliant intensity steadily condensed to form a snowy outline of a feminine figure of pure crystalline glass. The hard light hid any notable features, but one could see her head rose nine feet above the ground. It was the Astor family's eidolon, a legendary being said to be a servant of Ylsuna, just as the dragon lord served Tahlous. She went by many names, but the one used by the royal family was Mytariss.

The old woman leapt back and cast a ward spell. It might as well have been a piece of parchment. Without seemingly taking a step to appear before her enemy, Mytariss had used a spear of glass to impale the woman's heart. As she turned her formidable attention to those at the barrier, she and her light vanished.

With a splintered scream I wish I never heard, Odet shouted, "Noooo! Mother!"

Piercing out through the queen's chest was the point of a blackish blade. Its cloaked wielder gradually became visible as his invisibility spell ended. Leandra's body and his brown hood prevented me from seeing most of his face, but the fairly robust figure told me this Advent was a man. The Advent's corrupted blade began turning white as it absorbed the queen's holy prana while she yet lived.

Sharing Odet's desperation, I plunged my sword into the barrier with everything I still carried within me. The steel cut through, but it became lodged between the Advent's side and my own. The numbing sensation the knight spoke of coursed up my arms. I didn't care. Neither did many shouting knights. Seeing my sword's relative success had others do the same. A handful were able match my accomplishment. Meanwhile, their comrades put all they had left in their spells. And while it quivered and the blondes became restless, the fucking barrier still wouldn't fall.

The now pure white sword slipped out of the motionless queen, letting her body slump callously to the ground. The light from his glowing blade illuminated a surprisingly youthful face under his hood. A fringe of sweaty black hair could be detected, and stubble lined his cheeks and chin. The hooded Advent then walked up to his dead comrade and placed a hand upon her. She was gone in a blink. He used the same teleportation spell on his living allies before he placed a hand etched with a bloody rune on himself and let air take his place. Only then did the barrier fade away.

Odet's sprinting steps and those of some knights were all that echoed in the quiet chamber. When they stopped, it was Odet's tears that rang loudly as they dripped onto her mother's body. I hated it when my father placed a consoling hand on my shoulder, for it made me feel even more like a helpless child.

Chapter Nineteen

Without the Advent supplying the corrupted valkrean with orders, all the eidolons were unsummoned. To keep the corrupted valkrean from attacking with their bare hands, all eight found inside Western Ecrin had to be killed. My group were given horses to get back to our borrowed house. With the dangers of the eidolons gone, Bell and Elisa returned to the palace. I told Bell what happened, but Elisa would be kept in the dark awhile longer.

I didn't chase updates over the following days, but I heard from Clarissa that the guild had found a vacant ship drifting near the eastern shore, a ship owned by Lady Vealora. This piece of news came shortly after she was found missing from her cell. There was a frantic search for the Advent. No known teleportation spell could take someone as far as a few hundred yards, but with an unknown enemy using unknown barriers, it didn't come as a surprise to me that not even a destination rune was found anywhere.

As for that barrier, Aranath stated that the power he sensed when I stabbed through it was not fed by corruption or by any kind of power he encountered before. "I am certain it's not a power a mere human could discover on their own," continued the dragon.

"So you believe another realm's power is involved."

"Most likely."

"Is my corruption purified now?"

"Neither the girl nor I had the skill for such a feat. I was able to seal it away, meaning my own power is free to aid your prana with less resistance. However, I can no longer release any corruption without breaking the seal. There's simply too much added corruption to suppress if it were to escape."

"So no more trump card, huh? You know, for as much as it hurt to use it, I actually liked knowing it was an option. By the way, are you fully grown? Not that I'm implying anything. I just heard some dragons can get pretty big."

"My growth has slowed the past two hundred years, so no, I do not expect to get much larger over my lifetime. Nonetheless, as I prefer keeping my status as a dexterous flier, I'm quite pleased my frame won't swell with more bulk. I wouldn't wish to be any smaller, either, as that would limit my power. You will come to see that my current size will bring you the best of both speed and strength."

"How close am I to summoning you without help?"

"You are nearer without the corruption hindering us, but seeing you practice with dragon fire will help me determine how far you are."

That's what I did over the next four days as Ecrin awaited Odet's father to return from his journey.

The day after the king arrived, Bell came to inform us that we were invited to the memorial service, which was to take place after the morning's funeral procession. Whether we came to the memorial service or not, we were entreated to show ourselves afterwards in the throne room by the king's request, who wouldn't be a king once his first daughter had her coronation.

We went to the service, of course, along with half of the city's nobles. It took place at the palace's central garden under a sky as cloudless as the days before. Many people spoke, which included the king and his two older children. Their stirring eulogies made me glad I did not know such a wonderful woman. Even my father shed a tear, though I believe that came from being reminded of the woman he lost years before.

It was after Odet stepped down from her verbal tribute that I saw her current paramour for the first time. He was in emerald armor engraved with a rearing stallion at its breastplate. I then expected to identify a face fashioned from the gods themselves, but he was closer to mortal than not. His boyish face was topped with tawny hair and his fair skin carried a tanned tone thanks to his recent trip to the south. He might have been an inch or two taller than me, but even in the armor he looked leaner than I. I think Clarissa told me at some point in the past that his name was Gerard.

The sun had begun to drop from its highest point by the time Lorcan, Lucetta, Clarissa, Ghevont, and I made our way up to the throne room. Lucetta wasn't specifically invited, but she came anyway. We were led there by Bell, who had previously told us to meet her by the copper garden door. We used this door to enter a small storage building that helped us bypass the crowds. The throne hall was located at the top of the same building I had witnessed the death of the queen.

We climbed a spiraling staircase to reach the sought after height. The great hall was exposed to the elements on three sides. Its single wall stood behind two hefty thrones that sprouted directly from the marble floor. Along with the two heavy wooden chairs placed alongside them, the seats were cushioned with thick fabrics.

Sitting on three of these thrones was a grave King Eudon, soon-to-be-queen Beatrice, and Princess Odet. Standing to the king's right was a heavily armored, heavily bearded, brown-skinned man with a weighty lance in hand. Our introductions had me learning that this knight was captain to Alslana's High Guard, Bernar Savoy. Gerard was to Odet's left.

"I wish our meeting were under better circumstances," said the king after introductions.

"I'm sorry for your loss," said Lorcan. "I too know the horrendous pain you all are going through."

Stroking his short gray beard, the king nodded. "Aye, and you also know our enemy better than most."

"And most of that comes from my son."

His grim gaze fell on me. "Yes, Odet says you've been tracking these so called 'Advent' for some time now. She also says you're responsible for the dragon in the sky that day."

174

"And she's the reason I was able to summon him at all."

"So it's true, then? A dragon knight is among us after all this time."

"I am no true Veknu Milaris yet, Your Highness. I could not summon him now if our lives depended on it."

"Nevertheless, I'm now in the position of either having to confirm or deny the existence of a dragon knight within my kingdom. How do you wish for me to handle this situation? Do you wish to declare fealty to Alslana?"

"I'd rather you not confirm that I exist at all. As far as I'm concerned, that was a wild dragon the Advent failed to control. Even if I wished to declare my existence at this moment, I would only swear fealty to individuals, not any nation. Your second daughter might be a princess of Alslana, but to me she is simply a friend whose support I will lend when I can." I wanted to make eye contact with Odet when I admitted we were more than business partners, but her father's severe scrutiny forced me to keep my focus on him the whole way.

"That's good enough for me," replied the king. "I've heard that you're close to discovering a map of sorts to the Advent's main purpose."

I slapped Ghevont's back to make sure he understood his cue.

Bowing awkwardly, the scholar said, "Oh, yes, your mighty majesty. All my research the last several days has led me to believe that *Summertide* is a map. Based on the related pattern of words and stanzas in the poem, I believe there are four sites in Orda that can be linked together on a global map to pinpoint a new location. Unfortunately, I've come close to doing all I can on paper. There are still two sites unknown to me that need to be found."

"Which locations are those?"

"The first is a place Mercer and I are hoping Your Highness will hire the guild to locate. Somewhere in the southern reaches of the Rezundari continent lies the lone battle site of the mythical Solstice War. This is where the Doomhammer was said to have been forever lost with its master. The battle is only mentioned in one other reputable account, but it too describes the battle taking place on a small crescent harbor. It wouldn't hurt to find the Doomhammer itself. When you hire the guild, be sure to stress that they need expert cartographers plotting the site. The more accurate their readings, the better. The fact the Advent found it must mean we can at least get quite close to discovering this real site to a possibly fictional battle."

"I'll be sure to stress all I can. And what of the second site you need found?"

"I will have to go personally, unless Your Majesty doesn't mind invading the Hadarii Desert, of course."

"The Hadarii? What do you wish to find in that barbarian infested place?"

"Ah, if Your Highness recalls his history lessons, then you will remember the capital of Old Voreen lies somewhere there. Kitiri'mor was abandoned to barbarians and sand soon after Old Voreen's collapse. The city has been lost to modern mapmakers ever since. Any maps that do have the lost capital are purely speculative and lazily place the city roughly at the center of Niatrios. No, someone must learn of its true location."

"I see, then it seems I've little choice but to allow you to search on your own."

"What?" said Odet. "There has to be a better option than to leave them to explore that desolate land on their own."

"It's not ideal, but sending the guild or our soldiers will only draw unwanted attention. Few barbarian tribes are friendly to outsiders, but they'll stand a better chance traveling in a smaller, more innocuous group... What? Did you say something, Beatrice?"

His daughter did indeed say something, but she had been too quiet to hear. Even when she spoke again she was barely discernible and her lips appeared to be going through the motions of talking.

Trying hard not to fumble with her fingers, Beatrice said, "There might be a better way. I remember an academic gentleman came over from Prusal last year requesting funds for an expedition into the Hadarii. I do not recall if he sought Kitiri'mor, but it must have surely been one of his goals. We did not end up granting the request, but I do remember him explaining to mother that he had gained support from a few tribal leaders. They were to help him traverse the wastes in greater safety. If we can search our records, I'm certain we can learn the gentleman's name and find out if it's not too late to fund his project."

The king had been nodding proudly as his princess pushed through her still enfeebled mind. "Yes, every few weeks we grant an audience to some scholar or adventurer seeking a hefty investment on our end. They always promise us a portion of the treasures they'll find in whatever ruin they'll surely discover. So even if Beatrice's academic is not available, I'm certain we can find someone else to fund. Would being part of an academic expedition be acceptable for the rest of you?"

"As long as it doesn't take too long to set up," I replied.

"We have a good standing with Prusal and they'll have no objections to sharing any information they have on their academic expeditions. A response from them will be swift."

"If you can, your grace, treat this matter as a mundane topic that holds little of your personal attention."

"Yes, young dragon knight, I am well aware how to go about this business quietly. I realize it will seem strange to outsiders that Alslana royalty has suddenly concerned themselves with a trite matter after an attack such as this. I will work through our respective universities and make it appear as though this was nothing more than a long scheduled application. Does that satisfy you?"

I bowed.

"Now, you may not declare your allegiance to Alslana, but I don't mind lending my support to you. The next time you move out, I would like you to take one of Alslana's finest young warriors." Gerard stepped up and bowed to my group. "Gerard Safrix is part of my personal escort and is determined as anyone to repay the Advent for what they've done. Will you accept my offer?"

I thought over a moment, looking over both him and Odet, then said, "As long as he agrees that the orders of my father and I are the same as those from a superior officer."

"Then it's agreed. Alslana would also like to give a future dragon knight more permanent lodging whenever you or your allies visit my kingdom, but for now, you may keep using your current accommodations as you see fit."

"Uh, thank you, Your Majesty, but if you insist on giving me permanent lodgings here, then I must insist on a quiet, modest place."

"You can speak to our architects later for the details. Meanwhile, as you follow your *Summertide* lead, I'll get my people to openly hunt the Advent. If we're lucky, then maybe we can find the cult's hideout without the need to go into barbaric wastelands. If there's nothing else, my family has much to do."

More bows were given at our leave.

The majority of my time over the following days was spent in training, either alone or with a sparring partner. I even amused Ethan's whims a few times. I expected for Odet to bring over Gerard soon after the throne meeting, but they didn't show that first week. She must have truly been troubled for her sisters' mental state to not feel as though she could leave their sides for a few hours. Her own mind must have not been too keen on leaving as well.

My own concern lied with Clarissa's reaction to what I had to tell her. I knew it wouldn't make that much of a difference, but I chose to give her the news when she was at her most tired. This meant speaking to her before she was to get her afternoon sleep. I entered her candle-lit bedroom to see she her gulping down a pre-sleep blood vial.

"We need to talk."

Her experience with me had her pick up the subtle difference between my regular serious tone and the one I used when an argument wasn't going to be possible. She took some seconds to swallow the remaining blood before sitting at the edge of her bed.

"I knew this was coming," she said unhappily.

"Then you should also know that I want for you go with us, but a desert is no place for a vampire. Something goes wrong and you'll be the first to suffer. I don't want to see that and you don't want to become a burden."

"No, I guess I don't." She stared at the window, not caring there was nothing to see beyond the heavy drape. She sighed and looked back at me. "You promise to come back?"

"It'd be a shame if a dragon knight died in the heat."

"I was thinking more about pointy things and hungry barbarians."

"I'm still more concerned about the heat, but yes, I promise to come back."

"Good. At least Gerard's skills should make up for my absence."

"No it won't."

Odet and Gerard did finally show themselves eleven days after the meeting. Gerard was predictably pleasant when he was introduced to everyone. Along with the knight, Odet brought over news that contact had been made with Beatrice's academic over at Prusal. He was a scholar for the Behar-Dural's College of the Arcane named Fardin Bhoju. According to the response, Fardin would be ecstatic to revive his dead venture, a revival that would "only" take as long as getting into contact with everyone previously involved.

As the pirates gave the new guy a bit of grief to get to know him better, I asked Odet, "How are your sisters?"

She sat down on the chair beside mine and answered, "Elisa is a little better, but Beatrice only started crying a couple of nights ago."

"I'm guessing her coronation won't be for a while."

"No date is set yet, and with everyone trusting Dad to keep the ship going, I doubt a date will be set anytime soon."

"Between Owen and your sisters, I can't imagine you're getting much time to be with your own thoughts."

"Trying to help others helps me, so I'm doing exactly what I need to do."

"No, what you really need to do is join me in my Advent hunt."

"Right, I'm sure you'd love the added pressure of keeping a princess safe."

"Forgetting what I would like or what's practical, I'm only saying you're the type who works best being out in the world, whether that be as a traveling minstrel or leading an army. Your abilities are wasted stuck in Ecrin. Frankly, without Clarissa joining me in Niatrios, I wouldn't mind if you came along, princess or not."

"Well, you're right, I wouldn't mind using my training in a more proactive manner, and while I can't use it how I want, it's nice to hear it acknowledged. My father helps me train, but doesn't exactly encourage me to become a real soldier, and no one else dares imply that I be anything but a lady. I envy your freedom, though perhaps not in the way you've attained it."

"If you wish, as a thank you for saving me, I'll someday have Aranath come to your window and he'll fly you away to wherever you want."

In what was probably one of the few times since her mother's death, she chuckled. "That will be quite a sight, actually. Everyone will think a dragon is taking me to his lair until a hero comes to slay the great beast."

"Then I hope you believe Gerard is good enough to accomplish the feat."

180

"Hmm, I suppose I'll have to rethink who would win in a match between you and him if you can summon a dragon."

"I'm serious, you know, about repaying you for saving me. I haven't had a chance to properly thank you for that."

"No thanks is necessary. Anyway, it was Aranath who really saved you."

Sighing, I looked at my hands. I was thinking about telling her how I remembered slashing away at her, how I could see my corrupted self in her petrified eyes as I lowered my blade. I even remembered every muscle twitch my body took to pierce her flesh.

There was a good chance I would have told her my guilt if we had been alone, but as we weren't, I only hinted at it when I said, "I'm guessing you didn't tell your father about the wound I gave you."

"He has enough on his plate, besides, it isn't too bad. I honestly haven't been bothered by it too much after my healers tended to it."

"However you feel about it, I feel like I owe you one, so if there's anything I can do for you, just name it."

"I'll ke-" In one of the few times Clarissa drew anger from me, the vampire came over to join us. "Mercer tells me you won't be able to join him in the Hadarii."

"That's right," replied Clarissa. "Constant sunlight isn't exactly good for my kind. I'll be staying here and helping the guild siblings and Marcela however I can."

"I'll be sure to visit with Bell and Elisa whenever I'm able. If your discovery wouldn't cause a scandal, I'd bring you over to the palace as well."

"Thank you for the imaginary invitation, Your Highness. Mercer, have you decided when you'll leave yet?"

"I'll tell either Lucetta or Lorcan to find passage as soon as I get the chance."

"You want to leave for Behar-Dural already?" Odet asked.

"I realize the scholar's plans might fall through, but I need to get to Niatrios at some point anyway. Besides, going on a seventeen hundred mile journey should give Fardin enough time to give me a solid answer about the state of his expedition. If it looks like he won't be able to get everything done, we'll go at it alone. If he needs a little more time to bring the whole thing together, then I'll wait there."

"That makes sense," said the princess. She stared forlornly at Gerard, who was in the living room laughing at something Aristos said. "I really do wish I could go with you."

"Aye, same here."

Chapter Twenty

Since Behar-Dural wasn't a major trading partner of Alslana, it took two days to find a ship that would take us that far south. We then had to wait two days longer before the ship was ready to sail. A few hours before I boarded, I sent a letter to my rediscovered family, telling them I was still breathing but would be unavailable to send another message for a while.

When I first decided that Clarissa wouldn't be accompanying us, I had to get others to act as Ghevont's protector. The most natural pirate for the job was Leo. Battle-wise, his casting abilities complimented Ghevont's spells well, and while they were still far from being actual friends, Leo was the only crewmember who could handle both Ghevont's talkative and silent shifts in mood. For the benefit of us both, I pushed Ghevont and myself to train more with the others.

My favorite sparring partner turned out to be Thoris. His style fit mine the best and didn't carry my father's vexing habit of repeating his advice from earlier sessions, or that very same one. My least favorite sparring partner was Sophia. She treated everything too flippantly for my liking, not to mention that her hand-to-hand skills and non-bow weapon talents were below average. Nevertheless, I soon found her to be a better partner in another area.

We had finished our first sparring session on the top deck when she said, "Sorry your vampire girlfriend couldn't come with us."

"We're not actually together in that sense."

"What? Really? The way you two were always together, I just assumed... And Lucetta told me... Wait, so I could have tried, you know, messing around with you and she wouldn't have sucked me dry?"

"As far as I know."

She considered the situation a moment, then said, "You have to understand something, I'm not the kind of girl that just gets with whatever guy is around. You're not even my type. I prefer older, more experienced men."

"All right, so why the interest?"

"Uh, hello? You're a dragon knight. How many girls will get to say they've been with one?"

"Hopefully plenty."

"And they'll have me to thank for your experience. So you want to?"

I looked up and down at her lanky frame. She was too skinny for my ideal body type, and her face, while not unattractive, wasn't anything that would garner a second look from me if I passed her on the street. Of course, these minor quibbles weren't enough to get me to say no. In truth, even major quibbles wouldn't get me to say no at this point. People don't simply come out of near-fatal situations and not take advantage of the more pleasant things in life when opportunity allowed. It helped me understand why Francine relieved her carnal tensions on me after the vampire problem was resolved. I had always been a little confused about that until now. At any rate, being with Sophia helped time move along quicker.

Slowing time back to a normal pace was anytime I saw Gerard. The man himself was genial enough, but the effervescent feelings of jealousy and envy could not help but boil up into my brain every time I saw his placid face or heard his mellow voice. I mindlessly cracked my knuckles every time I thought about his hands or lips planting themselves somewhere on Odet's face or body. Lucky bastard. I only allowed these sentiments to expose themselves in the times we sparred one another.

As Odet had declared, Gerard was an elite swordsman. If I hadn't learned anything from my bouts with my father, he would have soundly beaten me every time we crossed blades. As it was, he was only better after extended sessions allowed him to read my tired movements. He was the type of fighter who would wait for his enemy to make a mistake, so he used his prana to extend his endurance further than most in our generation. When he saw the mistake, he used a flurry of quick strikes to end the contest. The times I beat him came out of a mix of luck and hitting him hard early.

It was after one of my wins that Gerard stood back up on his feet and said, "Good thing the first dragon knight in half a millennia is on our side." He adjusted his green gauntlets, which were green due to a thin layer of combat-glass magically infused over the steel. The rest of his outfit was currently an informal tunic and breeches, but he was never without those gauntlets.

"I'd rather say my enemies and your own are the same."

"And once those enemies are no more? What then?"

"Good question. I suspect I'll become a potato farmer up north. Where will you be in ten years?"

"All right, all right, your point is taken, but then I recommend you see Alslana's royal seer. He hasn't been at it long, but he's supposed to be good."

"So he saw the attack in Ecrin coming? He foresaw the Advent taking and corrupting valkrean?"

"Everyone expects seers to predict everything, a power reserved for the gods, but Odet tells me it's more about trying to reveal the reality in a sea of dreams. In fact, it wasn't so long ago that I was as skeptical as everyone else, but the king recently told me something that convinced me there's something to their gift."

"And what was that?"

"It was actually just before I joined up with you. He said the last royal seer heard a great roar when she looked at a newborn Odet's future, a roar he's now sure came from a dragon. He told me this because he also said that this dragon had been attacking Odet and everything around her. Sound familiar? Do you know what the queen did to help protect her daughter from this future danger? She gave her a holy crystal, a crystal Odet told me she used to make you sane again. Without the seer's warning, Leandra could have very well kept that crystal with her and, well, I don't like contemplating what would have happened to Odet. Do you?"

"Of course not… But if you're right, then you're saying the queen didn't have an item that could have helped save her own life."

"Maybe. Maybe the gods needed to trade one life for another, but if we have to make sacrifices to stop chaos from spreading, then we can't shirk away from that responsibility. You probably weren't planning on being a dragon knight, but you are now, so I would like to see someone with this power do all they can to make certain they're guided in the best way possible."

My throat grumbled out an imperceptible sigh. "You make some sense, knight, but perhaps I'll see a seer with a bit more experience than Alslana's."

"I'll leave that to you."

Between the bruising sparring sessions and the allaying lovemaking, I'd objectively say the eleven day voyage was productive.

With the early stages of sunlight behind us, Behar-Dural's tannish coastline revealed a sprawling city assembled largely of mudbricks, though a few of the more important looking structures had hardier materials either reinforcing them or adorning their exterior. Unlike what I expected to see deeper in the continent, there were clusters of tropical trees dotting the landscape.

While most of the city worshiped the six gods of balance, no towers of day and night could be seen. The holy places of Niatrios followed more modest techniques in their construction, as the religious leadership believed that the gods favored humbler temples compared to what Iazali usually erected. I figured they were either too cheap to build them or didn't have the resources to match Iazali's grander examples. Probably some of both.

We docked an hour after dawn, so we had plenty of time to search for the academic institution with the aid of light. I didn't think it necessary, but

186

after the assemblage chose an inn to stay in, Lorcan had Leo back up me and Ghevont in our walk to the college. The college was among the most respected institutions in Niatrios, so the residents of the tidy, if dusty, city had no trouble giving us directions.

Despite its cultural and educational significance to the nation, most of the college's buildings didn't stand out all that much from the others around it, except they were broader, taller, and had painted floral designs wrapped around their roofs. Only the center building carried the distinguishing features of a clock tower and a small dome at its top. This central building was the one we chose to inquire about Fardin.

The first floor was lit with plenty of sunlight by way of several long pane windows lining sections of the six-story high ceiling. Stairs in every corner led up to the upper floors, which only extended its walkway a few yards away from the walls. A plethora of books and scrolls filled the shelves lining the walls. In front of us was the largest grouping of gray haired people I had ever seen. Like much of the city's inhabitants and the population of Niatrios' eastern coastline, the robed elders were a mix of dark and light-skinned people. They were, however, dissimilar to the other half of the populace, in that I did not spot a single woman in the group. Many sat by lengthy tables and were either talking amongst themselves or reading to themselves.

On inquiring to a group of old men if they knew Fardin, the disgruntled response from one of them was, "Who wishes to know?"

"We have business from Ecrin to discuss," I answered.

"Ecrin, you say? Is this about his expedition into the Hadarii?"

"It may. Is he here?"

"So it's true?" asked another scholar. "Alslana has granted him funds? Impossible! How many of my requests have been rejected? And Enchanter Bhoju doesn't even deserve that title! His theories on-"

"As much as I enjoy hearing the grievances of others," I interrupted, "I would like an answer to his whereabouts."

The first old man said, "He should be in his office now. It's on the second floor. His door will be marked by a painting of the Hadarii hummingbird. It's not to be confused with the large-breasted hummingbird, which has a shorter beak and blue plumage."

Leo laughed. "Just how large-breasted is this bird?"

I pulled the pirate away before he caused the old men to indignantly mutter themselves to death.

Once we found the described door, I gave it a hearty knock.

"Come in!" said a good-humored voice. Opening the door showed an ivory colored, portly man sitting behind a desk. He didn't appear as old as the others. Indeed, he would look younger if he shaved off the remaining gray hairs clinging to the sides of his head. He would also look more proportioned if his head were bigger, as it was too small for even a thinner man's frame. The hefty gentleman blinked rapidly when he noted the unfamiliar faces staring back at him. He lost the jolliness in his tone when he asked, "C-can I help you, gentlemen?"

I stepped forward and handed him a little rolled up paper with the Ecrin Academy's thunderbolt seal. "I and fourteen others have been sent to check how your expedition plans are going."

He read the little document asserting my identity as a trusted sell sword and regained the color in his fat-filled cheeks. "Ah! Splendid! You've come earlier than expected, but I'm encouraged that Alslana shares my eagerness."

"How far along are your plans?"

"Far indeed. There's still some things to do, of course. For instance, I'm awaiting to hear from a few Hadarii guides who had previously agreed to aid me. Meanwhile, I've already purchased a good batch of sariff to see us through the first half of the journey."

"Sariff?" said Leo as he scratched what little hair he had left on his own head. "You bought that with your new funds?"

"Why yes. That's what the majority of the coin needs to go to in order for this expedition to survive."

"Why does the expedition need sariff?"

"As a trade commodity," replied Ghevont.

"Well done," said Fardin. "Someone has done their due diligence. Sariff is essentially the only legal good we have that just about every Hadarii tribe will accept. They may take other items like spices or wine, but they don't exactly value them as we do. Sariff, on the other hand, is now integrated into their society. I mean, it takes no great mind to imagine its value here. Wouldn't you want a plant that helps prevent pregnancies in a land where having too many mouths to feed will endanger the livelihood of the clan? In darker times, tribes often cut the testicular organs off an entire generation of boys to hinder them from breeding."

"So we're trading sariff for safe passage," I tried clarifying.

"Precisely. Most other kinds of caravans would simply be attacked, but most of the Hadarii people are sensible enough to allow the sariff trade to spread across the wastes."

"And the less sensible ones?" Leo asked.

"Well, that's why you and your men were hired, no? Speaking of which, I also need a little more time to find more mercenaries to help defend the convoy. I understand why Alslana forbade me from hiring the Blue Swords, but that has made finding another reputable source of men difficult. Still, you say there are fifteen of you in total? That's a good start."

"How confident are you that you can find Kitiri'mor?" I asked.

"Do you think I would waste time, resources, and possibly lives if I did not think the venture worth it?"

189

"I'm certain the leaders of a hundred expeditions before you thought much the same."

"First of all, most of those 'expeditions' were severely underfunded at best, misguided at worst. With Alslana providing the funds and my mind providing the guidance, we are well prepared to make history."

"So you already have a good idea as to where Kitiri'mor lies?" asked Ghevont.

"More accurately, I believe I know where a nearby settlement lies. If we find that, then the lost capital herself can't be very far."

"And how did you learn of this adjacent ruin?"

"By asking, of course! Most of the old men here don't dare step outside this town, but I have a more adventurous spirit! A spirit that has earned me some respect from some local tribesmen, and which has thus led me to learn a few of their dialects. You'll find that the majority of people here speak of the Hadarii as being filled with violent savages, and no doubt many are, but even a savage can be tamed when one shows attentiveness to their peculiar culture. You should see as young and old gather to see me write! It's as though I'm casting a mighty spell!"

"They are illiterate?"

"By and large. At any rate, once I established that I was merely a curious intellectual with no interest in their demise, I gained a few contacts who brought back word to me about various points of intrigue. After a decade's worth of substantiating these words with other contacts and trying to crosscheck their locations on maps, I've long concluded that it's time for my work be validated in reality."

"It seems like a lot of effort to find some artifacts," said Leo.

"Ha! You think all my sleepless nights and sweat have been in the hopes that I strike it rich by selling some old trinkets? A sell sword might think that way, but not a respected scholar. What I want is to confirm my theory, which will in turn have fledging academics learn of my work and thus develop historical thinking for generations to come! That is far more precious than any rusty relics that might be buried far too deeply to reach."

"What is this theory of yours, exactly?" asked Ghevont.

"Ahh, yes, you should know what you are truly defending. Through the use of language, I will prove that the people of Old Voreen came not from a first wave of Iazali settlers, as everyone assumes, but from Efios hundreds if not thousands of years earlier!"

"Efios?" said Leo. "You believe they had ships strong enough to make a journey of over five thousand miles at that time?"

"Obviously, I do. It's difficult to prove that aspect, however, so all I can focus on is the language the Efios people would have brought over with them. But do you understand what I imply with my theory? Everyone's perception is that Old Voreen was formed by the Iazali people trying to graciously bring civilization to this wild land, but I believe the barbarian hordes and Old Voreen are one and the same. I believe Old Voreen collapsed not from an onslaught of savages, but from civil war and a growing desert. This would make the Hadarii tribes of today descendants of that once proud nation."

"But did not the leadership of Old Voreen move eastward and begin today's Voreen?" stated Ghevont. "The Iazali people inhabiting the area would not have allowed themselves to be ruled by foreigners."

"I hypothesize that no leadership of Old Voreen survived the downfall, which just leaves some Iazali men lying about their origins. If I can find the oldest version of the Old Voreen language intact on murals or stone tablets, I can compare it to the old Efios languages and prove the connection. Currently, every enduring document we have on Old Voreen can be traced back to the early new Voreen, so they are considered by me to be little more than hearsay. Or perhaps they were repurposed as propaganda for the new government."

191

"Yes, yes, that makes sense. Saying you're the last of a royal bloodline has often proved advantageous in the attainment of power. There are several families still living that claim to be descended from the ancient Voreen kings, so showing their bloodlines to be nothing special will certainly anger a few powerful people."

Fardin raised his eyebrows, having clearly not thought the consequences of his theory through. "Well, I'm willing to put my life on the line in this expedition, so a few more perils won't hurt."

"You don't know how danger works, do you?" I said. "How public is your theory?"

"Not very, which I believed unfortunate, but I'm currently reevaluating that conclusion. My own colleagues think I am erroneous and so only scoff at my ideas if they speak of me at all. They are quite jealous of me now! How many of them have gotten support from the richest nation on this side of the world?! Ha!"

We left after telling him that I would continue to check up on him every morning. He in turn informed me that the wait to get everything in order would be no more than a fortnight.

I saw other individuals involved in the expedition meeting with Fardin over these next two weeks. Among them were three traders experienced in desert transactions and two female assistants of the enchanter. I was sure that each woman must have paid a "heavy" price to join the career-enhancing mission. The younger of them, Janna, was in her mid-twenties and had her sienna hair cut quite short. The other, Clio, was a dark-skinned woman in her late thirties. While the younger had the firmer body that youth provided, I thought Clio's soft face and fuller lips more pleasing to the eye. I felt sorry for both of them.

Fardin had hired thirteen other mercenaries by the end of the fortnight, several of whom seemed to be former barbarians. The sell swords rounded out the thirty-four person assembly. It felt a little dreamlike as everything came together one predawn morning. We all met at the outskirts of town, finally forming the caravan of camels, mule-drawn carts, academics, and warriors who had agreed to head into a scorching wilderness that held a greater promise of death than treasure.

Chapter Twenty-One

The goal of the excursion's first week was to gather a pair of tribal guides, both of whom were waiting at a village fifty miles from Behar-Dural. Their skin was of a dark brown and had tattoo markings imprinted over parts of their bodies. The younger man—whose name may have been Yallie'cor, but he corrected me and others too often for anyone to be certain—only had tattoos on his arms. Conversely, his older partner, Banering, had them on his arms, upper chest, and back. Whether to compensate or a personal preference, Yallie'cor had a red rune-like design painted over his chest, though Ghevont doubted it was an actual spell rune.

The general plan was to go in a northwesterly direction for about thirteen hundred miles, stopping by tribal villages and oases to trade the sariff we carried for safety and more food. There were twenty-two camels and mules in our convoy, and though the methodical speed of the expedition allowed me to walk under my own power, I spent more time than I thought I would riding these animals. I found them each to be less jumpy than horses and thus better suited to absorb my amateurish riding skills with greater civility.

As common sense expected us to do, we traveled as much as possible during the morning and evening hours to avoid the hottest part of the day. Giving us shade in the high afternoons were two canvas sheets we raised on tall wooden poles. Putting them side by side created enough of a shadow that most of the human explorers could fit under it. I felt hotter when I was with everyone else, so I often avoided the artificially made shade and tried to find a natural source to have for myself. That was becoming harder to find with every passing day.

The lack of privacy and the imperious heat prevented Sophia and I from finding any more physical relief. I think we were both glad to have an outward reason to break off our "relationship," a relationship we would have kept up simply for the sake of amatory benefits. We had gotten what we wanted from one another and were able to separate without having to delve on the parts of our personalities that were never going to be compatible for a long-term match. Still, it was frustrating to know that she was *right there* for the taking and I couldn't do anything about it.

Due to the equatorial scope we traversed, going deeper into the fall season did nothing to quell the Hadarii's midday fervor, but it did make the nights colder than it would have been earlier in the year. The acute temperature differences experienced within a single day bothered the others more than it did me. According to Aranath, this enhanced toleration to the environment meant my prana was linking better with dragon flame.

"A Veknu Milaris who masters dragon fire is never troubled by the light of Tahlous," continued the dragon. "And as you already experienced, even the dying embers of my flame can keep your blood warm during the harshest winters. Relish how your skin blisters under this sun, boy, for I suspect this will be the last year you experience such a thing."

Helping to keep everyone quenched were the casters who had the ability to pull a few cups of moisture hanging about in the twilight hours. Consequently, most of us were more concerned about our food supply than our drinking water. To save as much of our more endurable food as possible, the tribal guides often pointed out edible plants and little animal dens we took advantage of. This life of simplicity suited me and the pirates well enough, but the academics were little used to the punishing conditions. To their credit, they didn't gripe much. I was sure that would change the longer the Old Voreen ruins remained veiled.

There wasn't much sand at first, just dry dirt that gave way to cracked topsoil. It was three days into the second week of travel that we felt the chafing sand coming in the breeze. Then it seemingly just dropped out of the sky one morning, proclaiming the true beginning of the untamed Hadarii and its rugged people.

Our first encounter with a tribe large enough to give us trouble if they chose to came two days after traversing the sands. Our traders met their own just outside of a lush oasis as the sun dropped below the horizon.

After the transaction finished without incident, we began to head for a small knot of palm trees to set up camp. It was here when Fardin walked up beside Ghevont and said, "It's said all of Niatrios was once an oasis. Oases were also known to be more common as recently as a few hundred years ago. As a fellow scholar, I'd be interested to know your theory on the matter."

"I'm afraid I have too little information to form anything that would satisfy someone who's been living and studying this land all his life."

The pleased enchanter waved off the accolade. "Perhaps not, but different perspectives are always welcomed in our line of work, no?"

"Ideally. I for one have never bought into the notion that the gods are disciplining these savages. In fact, I've read that many deities in the Hadarii are not too dissimilar from the gods of day and night. It's only their worship of them that differs."

"Yes! Precisely! I believe them to be the very same myself, only with different names and different customs. In any case, even if the gods were fussy enough to care about the particulars of worship, I doubt they'd make it even harder for civilization to spread by creating a destitute land."

"Yet it's difficult to imagine a continent losing much of its biota in a relatively short span without some magical influence coming into play."

"Ah, one would think. I theorize that physical forces are stronger than many realize. Perhaps spells helped nudged the change, but what we see now is primarily a result of a great climate shift caused by natural forces. If I'm also correct about how early the first peoples arrived here, then we might also include agricultural negligence to the list of suspects. The only question now is

196

wondering whether if it will continue to shift or eventually rebound to a rainier environment. The answer will determine how much future trouble the barbarians will bring upon the coasts."

"Do your assistants agree with your climate shift theory?"

Fardin yowled with wheezing laughter. "Oh, Master Ghevont! They might be able to hold a decent intellectual conversation with the amateur scholar, but commenting on continent altering matters is quite beyond them."

Fardin's aides were not far behind us, and I was sure at least one of them had heard the enchanter's assertion. The pity had built up to the point where I later asked Aristos if he could humor them.

"My standards are usually aimed a bit higher," said the pirate.

"I'm not telling you to marry them, or even touch them. Just make them forget for a while that they're working for a fat ass in the middle of this damn desert."

"Why don't you?"

"Charm is no weapon of mine."

"No better time to practice."

"I have enough things to practice."

Overhearing us, a pipe smoking Thoris said, "You're going about this the wrong way, Cyrus. Aristos has no ability to minimize his philandering to mere humor. Set him upon those women and you'll only succeed in breaking their fragile hearts. They want to be treated seriously as academics, do they not? Get your scholar friend to speak to them as such."

"It might be too early in the expedition to take that extreme measure, but I suppose it's better than having him talk my ear off."

"In any event," began Aristos, "I'll keep an open mind and give them a few reasons to move on in this sandy world." The heartbreaker right then moved to speak to Clio.

Watching his comrade begin talking to the woman, Thoris said, "I should tell you, your father has noticed your preference to keeping to the periphery of the caravan."

"I prefer meeting opponents head on. I'm guessing Lorcan has asked you to keep an eye on me."

"Yes, so it's something to keep in mind if a battle were to occur, though I'm certain a father's worry would have asked me the favor no matter your preference."

"Thanks for the heads up."

"I don't know how eager you are to get in a fight, but I propose letting the mercenaries meet whatever enemy comes at us first. The rest of us will support them from a distance, of course, but your father would prefer not exposing us to any needless danger, particularly over a mere point on a map."

"I understand, but you should know that I've been pretty much conditioned to attack the first thing that moves. So how are you and the others handling a sea of sand?"

"It reminds me of a time when we were shipwrecked on a deserted island for a few weeks. Lost a good young woman there."

"Sorry."

"A risk we take in our line of life. Our crew has seen some good people's lives cut short, a few of which would have surely joined your father in the search for his sons."

"How did that go, exactly? Did anyone think twice about joining Lorcan?"

"I didn't. I'm not sure about anyone else, but I'm never surprised by Lorcan's ability to draw people to him. It's something he's always been able to do naturally. Honestly, I don't think he even realizes it. If he does, then he doesn't use it to his advantage much."

"Something I didn't inherit."

198

"Maybe not, but from what I've seen from the vampire and Ghevont, you can inspire your own form of loyalty well enough. Your status as a dragon knight alone will incite quite a reaction from people all over Orda. They'll see you as something as a champion of justice or some nonsense like that. There's much potential in being able to call upon support from across the world."

"They'll have to see a dragon first."

My talk with Thoris motivated me to spend some travel time talking with his comrades. I was intrigued by my father's capacity to get people to follow him, and it was an opportunity to learn more about the man himself. I already knew Sophia's situation wasn't so much about my father as it was about finding adventure. She was the type of girl who couldn't sit still when she didn't have to, which was why she left her well-to-do family when she turned sixteen. The others had gathered enough experience to be a little more thought-provoking.

The people that surprised me the most were Remwold and Athilda. They told me they had two children, a girl and a boy. Both youngsters lived on an island off the shore of Somesh, a country lining the northern coast of Kozuth.

When I asked why they left their children to help Lorcan, Athilda replied, "Well, if it weren't for your father, we wouldn't have met in the first place. I was planning on quitting the life, you see, but Lorcan had become a new captain and begged me to stay to assist in the transition. A year later and he recruited this cranky bastard fresh off the Somesh Navy."

"It was fuck at first sight!" said Remwold. "It was difficult to leave the little tykes behind, but we see this as our last opportunity to give your father a proper thanks. What better way to thank him for our family than to help save his own?"

"Granted, the thought process might have been different if we knew beforehand that we'd be fighting an enemy who could manipulate valkrean."

199

"Nevertheless, darling, we don't go back on our word. Well, sometimes we do, but not when it comes to Lorcan… Except the time with the dog, but that couldn't be helped."

With a raised eyebrow, I said, "A dog?"

Athilda shook her head. "Sorry, we don't speak of that unpleasant incident. Poor thing."

Surprising me less was learning that Aristos had two children of his own, each with a different woman and both born within weeks of one another. He had sired them when he was young himself, younger than I, in fact, making them almost as old as I was at this point in the calendar. The pirate spoke facetiously about them, treating them nothing more than mistakes he had learned from.

As for why he was aiding my father, he said, "I've found no man yet who has helped me win over so many girls as he has. It's somehow even better now that Lucetta is with him. I believe he enjoys living vicariously through me. Of course, they occasionally enjoy the girl themselves once I'm through. Have you ever been with more than one woman?"

"No."

"It's fun every now and then, but I actually don't fully enjoy being in a group. I prefer putting all of my attention on one woman and thus pleasing her with every fiber of my being. I suppose I'm sort of a romantic in that sense."

"So because he supports your womanizing you feel obligated to help him now?"

"You say that as though bedding a woman is a mere pastime! What greater goal is there in life but for a man to spread his love to all the tantalizing lovelies he can? The aspiration to impress a beauty has led to the birth of civilization itself! If a time spell allowed us to see the first kings and casters, I'm certain you'll see they were persuaded by a woman's splendor to conquer lands and fire alike."

"Then becoming a pirate doesn't seem to be the best way to meet as many women as possible."

"There are stints when seeing a new woman becomes as scarce as a blue rhino, but that is a temporary disadvantage to being a pirate. If I were a dull baker or an obedient soldier, for instance, what stories could I bring that would stir a woman's heart? In the pursuit of this, I long ago lied about my profession to ladies from all walks of life. When I said I was a pirate, every one of them reacted very well. That's when I decided to become a seafaring brigand and collect as many stories as I could. Even now, wandering a sandy wilderness under an unforgiving sun hoping to find my friend's child will garner much sympathy. I'm excited to try it out. It doesn't hurt that the profession itself is quite liberating from more mundane work."

"Or that you happen to be good at it."

"I'd master any vocation if it led to a single night with a beauty, preferably as tall as I am, but those are hard to find when one is over six feet."

A few minutes after speaking with Aristos, Lilly had noticed my sudden talkative spurt and asked what I was doing. She laughed when I told her Aristos' reason for helping my father.

"You really had to ask him why he was here? He's as shallow as he appears. Still, there's something sweet about him, isn't there?"

"That's not the word I'd use, but sure, why not?"

"So were you going to ask me about your father as well?"

"Sure, why not?"

"You know, I've never thought much about it. I kind of just fell in with his crew when he became captain. I respected him as soon as he got rid of the true reprobates on board. It showed me he wouldn't suffer any fools that might get us all killed. I may not be as physically or magically useful as the others, but I do my part to keep everyone full and comfortable."

"You don't strike me as someone who wanted to be a pirate."

"I still don't count myself as one. Never even stabbed anyone. I've knocked a few on their asses, but never with the intent to kill."

"But what made you join a pirate crew in the first place?"

"My brother. I idolized him when I was a wee lass and followed him wherever he went. We ended up working for the last captain. I soon started acting more like his mother than a sister. That attitude just kind of spread to everyone else."

"Where is he now? Is he…"

"Dead? No, he was one of the reprobates Lorcan dismissed. Best thing that ever happened to him. He was too old for anyone else to take him in, so he's back home. Last I heard, he found an old widow to leech off of. He'll be well off for the rest of his life once she croaks, well, if he doesn't end up gambling it all away. I'll hopefully be back with him before he does something as stupid as that."

"You mean after you help Lorcan?"

"Probably later than that. I say I still have a good five years left out in the open sea, whether that be with your father or whoever takes over afterward. That won't be you, will it? A dragon knight pirate sounds like the king of both the sea and air."

"The sea isn't my thing."

"Too bad. Hey, you're not planning on asking Yang anything about his past, are you?"

"Your tone implies that isn't a good idea."

"Oh, I wouldn't be afraid of him or anything, it's only that he doesn't open up to us about it, so I doubt you'll get much. And I'm certain his answer to why he's here would be something like-" She cleared her throat. With a mannish tone, she said, "Lorcan good man, so I help."

"I have no idea whether that's a good impression or not."

"I don't either. Another piece of advice, I wouldn't mention anything about children to Menalcus. He has a young daughter, but the mother won't let him see her. The big guy starts bawling the second he thinks about her. I would try to keep as much water as possible inside his body."

Lilly's advice compelled me to save the rest of my inquiries for a later date.

With energy being a precious resource out in the desert, my training eliminated sparring sessions and focused on manipulating dragon fire. I had progressed in my dragon flame enough to make it last twice as long as before and with a stronger burn. Smaller stones dissolved completely under these more intense conditions. Casting it on heavier stones gave the flame either a more vibrant light or a bigger ear-ringing blast.

When adding more heat to my day became intolerable, I went to practicing my illusion spell, which I had neglected for the past several weeks. It seemed my sealed corruption benefited this spell the best, since I found I could keep it together for up to half a minute and send it as far as twenty yards before it distorted out of existence. The tribal guides didn't like it when I cast the extra copy of me, going as far as breaking up my illusion with their bare hands.

Fardin found their reaction fascinating and asked them in their long-winded language why they were offended by the spell. The answer had something to do with believing the spell infused a bit of one's soul into the mirror-mirage, so it was something to be done sparingly. I didn't stop practicing it, but I respected their view enough to keep my mystic clone away from their sight.

While some days were harder than others, we by and large kept a steady pace as we zigzagged between known oases and tribal encampments. It was on the twenty-first day of the expedition that the first sign we had truly entered unmapped territory came within sight.

Below a fifty foot tall cliff grew an oasis that hugged the shade of the rock wall for five hundred yards. A few trickles of water leaked out from fissures on the wall and filled a pair of little narrow ponds. Neither the cliff nor the oasis appeared on any known map. Enforcing the idea that we had stumbled on another realm altogether was the absence of any human activity, meaning even the enterprising barbarians hadn't found this piece of tranquility yet.

Supporting Fardin's theory that this place had recently germinated was the fact that few plants were tall enough to give us shade. Our grateful animals ate and slurped up everything they could in the half day we rested there. Giving all the scholars further pause was when Yallie'cor spotted the partial skull of a cow a few hundred yards away from the oasis. This fascinated Ghevont enough to pick it up for a closer examination. I asked my scholar what his fascination with the skull was about.

"Well, have you seen any bovine around?"

"No, but don't the tribes breed them?"

"Not many, and they'd be much closer to the coasts where grasses would be more inclined to grow. Why would they bring a beast this far out into the Hadarii?"

"It can't be a stray?"

"It's possible, but what are the chances one walked this kind of distance without dying sooner or being caught by a hungry tribe? What's also interesting is that the skull shows obvious signs of abuse. It's only half of one, after all. Where's the rest of it? It isn't that old and brittle. It might have even been using the oasis to live. This would mean something killed it while it was living healthily enough. It's a strange set of circumstances—an undiscovered oasis and the half-skull of an animal that simply isn't seen this far inland…"

"You have a theory?"

"I have many, too many for your tastes. It would help if we find more bones like these, or none at all."

"My theory is that your theory won't be so pleasant if we find more battered skulls."

"And I can confirm such an outlook."

In anticipation of finding a ruin, the guides and scouting teams spread farther out from the main group. For a solid six days we found nothing but orangish sand dunes and skeletal shrubs. Then, shortly after an early morning sandstorm—the brunt of which was held back by air spells working together to create a clear bubble around the huddled group—a hazy silhouette of a tree line materialized. Sure enough, the large oasis turned out to be no mirage. It held a little spring at its center and the shade generously bestowed a comparatively cool place to sit.

The haven provided both a nice respite and a base to return to after an excursion, but that was tempered by the discovery of more animals bones scattered about the immediate region. The bony pieces of cows, goats, and ponies laid half-buried in the sand, indicating they were recent leavings. These lost beasts compounded another mystery. The last week was devoid of any humans other than ourselves. Fardin expected to see members of a tribe that had years before informed him of the ruins we sought, but the uninhabited oasis seemed to confirm that they no longer occupied the area.

I didn't believe the Advent would go out of their way to eliminate a tribe to keep Kitiri'mor secret. Such an act would simply invite other tribes into the territory. Ghevont shared my view.

As he examined a goat vertebra, the scholar expounded his view by saying, "They likely didn't eliminate any tribe, but I'm sure they have a hand in this. The dead beasts have all suffered violent deaths... Something is out here."

"So the Advent find Kitiri'mor and then leave either a spell or creature to deter anyone from getting too close."

"The likeliest scenario. Whether the Advent force them to or not, I speculate that the animals are brought here by tribesmen as a kind of offering."

"At least this means we're getting close to something important. Tell everyone to keep their guards up and that we need two more volunteers for the night watches."

Helping to keep an eye out for danger at night was Kara. The zymoni's broad toes abetted Lucetta's partner in the sand, allowing her to keep her swiftness as she sprinted over the dunes though the heat was hard on her thin skin, making her unusable in the day. At least Kara's eyes also saw well at night. Two nights after moving out from the oasis, Kara came up to her master and licked her hand. Lucetta waved me over. Without waiting for me to catch up, she followed Kara into the dusty darkness.

I jogged after them, going about three hundred yards before I caught up to Lucetta and Kara on top of a small dune. Sticking out from the bottom of the dune's base was a crumbled corner of a mudbrick wall. I threw down a dragon stone and its ignited light revealed cubed stones poking out the sandy ground for fifty yards in front of us. We went back and awoke Fardin to tell him the news. His ecstatic shout awakened all else who slumbered. The enchanter, who had lost twenty pounds in pure sweat so far, ambled impatiently toward the site, forcing those already up to gather around him.

A cry exactly like his first left his flabby throat when he saw the wall below him. He then practically rolled to the base thirty feet down and stared agape at the signs of ancient human life. One of his shaking hands caressed the lumpy brick as though it were the firm breast of a young woman. He then had to take his red handkerchief to wipe away sweat that had not come from an outward heat.

"How will we know whether this is Kitiri'mor or your mystery town?" I asked him.

"By digging, my boy!"

Camp was repositioned by the dune's base. A few casters, which included my father, used gusts of wind and earth-moving spells to start clearing away the sand around the wall and bigger stones. Others shed light with either spell or torch. I stayed part of the guard team.

When the sun came up, its light bared a wall that had collapsed in places before a more completed section was uncovered a few yards later. The base of the barricade was deeper than I first fathomed. The casters had to dig thirty-five feet before reaching the bedrock that supported the sand. For its height, it was surprising to see how thin the wall was. Of course, this might have followed the double-wall style, where the first barrier acted more as a slowing influence as opposed to the main army stopper farther in.

By the time the shadows became long again, the diggers had exposed several flat foundations of stone found mostly within the defensive wall. Their small size and consistent distance from one another implied an uncluttered settlement. The enchanter soon supported my conclusion.

"I suspect this isn't Kitiri'mor," said Fardin. "The capital would be densely populated with larger collections of buildings better suited for civilians. We must be in a fort town once occupied by a garrison of soldiers."

"Then where would Kitiri'mor be from here?" asked Lorcan.

"The Howling Dunes are a two days journey north from here. Most of my colleagues believe the lost capital can be found in the middle of this waterless wasteland, but I suspect it lies at its southern edge. If my estimations are anywhere close to being correct, then a two days journey northeast will have us stumbling upon the great ruins."

"Would you be okay with us moving out in the morning?" I asked him.

"There's only one objective that would get me to leave this priceless ruin, and that would be to find the very heart of Old Voreen herself. We leave as soon as the first sleeper awakens!"

207

Chapter Twenty-Two

The first sleeper awoke three hours before dawn. Just as the light made the area visible for more than twenty yards, we saw the Howling Dunes were closer than Fardin expected. They rose less than ten miles distant, looking more like a boundless mountain range than a dune field. Despite their name, the winds that were said to whistle between the tall dune peaks did not make themselves known to us. Rather than entering the loose hills of sand right away, Fardin suggested we head eastward along their relatively stable edge. He wanted to wait for some kind of sign that pointed us to a ruin or easier path through the merciless core of the Hadarii.

Half a day after we started the trek, the guides in the front of the convoy called up the enchanter with excited shouts in their language. Both Fardin and I happened to be on camels, so he spurred his stubborn creature forward while I dismounted mine and went on foot. On catching up with the front of the convoy, I saw what interested the tribesmen. At their feet was a stretch of mostly sand free ground about eighty feet wide. Its width varied as the fractured land meandered to the south and north in river-like fashion. The waterless stream cut through the massive dunes in the north, creating a deep gorge between two sand-mountains.

Fardin squeaked a mousy cry when his camel came up beside me. "Impossible," he said under his breath. "Kitiri should have dried up hundreds of years ago."

"Uh, it is dried up," said the presumptive leader of the mercenaries, a grizzled sell sword named Malu.

"Yes, obviously, but the keyword here is *hundreds*. If Kitiri had shriveled away a mere five years ago, then the desert would have swallowed up any hints of its existence by now, but here's the splintered ground and an enduring valley in plain sight. No, this river was flowing as recently as last year, perhaps sooner. Whatever keeps it trickling is of no concern to us at the moment. The gods have placed a path of luck and we must take it! Onward men!"

Going between the shadow of the dunes sunk the temperature by ten or fifteen degrees, though I found myself favoring the heat over the unnerving impediments of sand towering on either side of us. I felt as though the echo of a dropped pebble could cause a landslide and have it bury us for all eternity. The narrowness of the trench converted soft breezes into denser drafts, but it wasn't anything too bracing. Our caravan advanced steadily under these amended environmental conditions, rarely straying from a northeasterly direction over the next day and a half.

Some mercenaries discovered an item of note in their forward patrol— a five foot tall block of limestone sticking out from a dune to our right. A little digging exposed more blocks stacked together or laying nearby. Several more were uncovered on the other side of the desiccated riverbed. The scholars believed the blocks were once part of columns or arches lining the ancient river. I didn't have to tell him, but I still instructed Ghevont to begin paying close attention to our place on the map. Since it would be difficult to get lost in a trench, we continued navigating the empty river long into the night. There were sometimes branching river imprints we passed by, but they looked too small to lead anywhere of consequence.

After a short break and seeing a dozen more evidences of limestone structures, the river bended sharply northward. A large dune appeared to have supplanted the river, but the genesis of light showed that the waterway continued under a hundred foot wide by thirty foot high stone tunnel. Thinking the arched passageway couldn't have been too long, we elected to travel within it. Penetrating just ten feet inside it had us smelling the clammy residue of fresh water. The ground was even a tiny bit spongy. It was easy to guess that the ancient builders were attempting to stop the river from evaporating in the increasing heat they were experiencing. The fact Kitiri still sometimes flowed after all these centuries told that their efforts weren't wholly in vain.

The center of the tunnel had numerous intact pillars helping to support the roof, but time and the elements had eroded several to the point where they had fallen. These weak points in the walls and ceiling allowed dribbles of sand to pour in. I couldn't imagine the tunnel being able to take the weight of the dune for many more decades. Lining some sections of the walls were glowing blue mushrooms. These fungi normally grew in deep caves, something I was already familiar with. The fungi had the scholars theorizing that at least some of the water had emerged from an aquifer. The blushing mushrooms weren't the only organisms in the tunnel.

Kara had gone beyond the rim of light that came from the group's spells and torches, and one of her barks attracted Lucetta to her. Those of us who had joined the piratess saw Kara's ears pinned back and staring intently at a lump in the ground. When Ghevont gave it a little more light, the lump turned into the rippled body of a plump, worm-like creature. The light nor our presence jarred it from its spot, and the bugs crawling and buzzing around it confirmed its nonliving state.

Ghevont knelt beside the eight foot long beast, his little sphere of light giving everyone the visual details of the worm. The ripple effect its skin produced came from the groups of gill-like frills rounding much of its amber-colored body. Ghevont's fingers lifted one of the flexible gills to show more rough skin underneath, implying that they were used to aid its underground locomotion rather than breathing. Unlike an Orda worm, this creature had an obvious tail that narrowed significantly in the last two feet of its body.

Its other unique feature was its foot long beak, a brown mandible that felt much like a smooth human tooth. The dense material was thickest at its mouth and tapered into a blunted point at the end. The beak was ajar, revealing the three separate segments that made it up. Ghevont opened one of these segments to allow us to peer into a rounded mouth rimmed with hundreds of stringy feelers. The back of the deep entrance ended with heavy flaps of skin, presumably preventing anything it didn't want to eat from going down its throat, if it had one.

With the help of three other men, Ghevont rolled the beast over. He endeavored to find anything that might have been used for eyes, nostrils, or ears, but its mouth appeared to be the only orifice that allowed external stimulus to enter, at least when alive. Its current deadness permitted little insects to burrow into the worm's tough hide, creating hundreds of incisions for them to eat the tastier entrails and lay their eggs. It was through these cuts that I noted the worm's dark green blood.

"A chukurn," said Aranath. "They are not of this realm, though their home does look much like this desert. Also, they become much larger than this dead youth, big enough to swallow a mammoth. Try not to make so much noise or you'll attract an adult."

The scholars already knew something of this creature, so I didn't have to alert everyone of our potential enemies or how to lure them. Moreover, Fardin mentioned the many names the creatures went by, which included sand-eaters, desert whales, dune-dwellers, and twenty others. Ghevont was disappointed that the corpse was too big to bring with us and that he had no time to dissect it properly. He had to settle for cutting off thin samples of its body and putting the pieces in his little vials to test on later. With that done, the extra muted expedition trekked on.

I didn't count how many hours passed, but we knew the sun was still high in the sky when we finally detected a bright light at the end of the tunnel. Despite the light our eyes received from spell and torch, they still required a moment's adjustment when we stepped back into the sizzling desert rays. The first sight my squinted eyes saw were two rows of pillars extending out from the tunnel. They once supported a now collapsed limestone roof that had once

211

helped to continue the shielding shade over the river. These pillars went on for half a mile before another dune-covered tunnel began.

To my flanks were more lofty dunes, but they did not spread all the way in. I quickly saw why this place was not as heavily bombarded as everywhere else. The sand hills were stopped from a full incursion by a sixty foot wall encircling us. Some segments of this wall had fallen to allow fringes of a dune to infiltrate the city, but enough of it stayed intact to remain a semi-successful obstacle.

Airborne sand still clung to buildings and formed miniature sand dunes around them, but a closer inspection of the ruins didn't seem impossible once we implemented a few sand-clearing spells. The most intriguing desert-laden structure, however, appeared to be too entombed to have anything but a small army attempt to unearth it. Only a tilting tower could be seen sticking up at the top of this dune.

When Fardin consumed the breadth of this jarring sight, he fell on his stubby knees and thanked every god from every land in Orda. He even sacrificed precious water in the biggest single tear I had ever seen. His assistants shared in his joy by embracing each other and their enchanter master. Many of the mercenaries and pirates gave jubilant shouts that had to be reined in after a few loud moments by those who remembered a threat loomed.

The first item of business on my side of things was to join the scout team in climbing up a slope to examine the surrounding area. As expected, though no less disconcerting, an orange ocean with no break in it dominated the landscape. I could walk fifty yards away from the brink and never know an entire city lied at the bottom of the depression. The winds were picking as I made my way back down to find shade. These whistling breezes helped form little twisters of dust that sometimes crossed into the dead city.

The first item of business for the scholars was to learn the general layout of the ruins and find a good piece of it to begin a proper excavation.

Their main goal was to find anything with writing on it. Without a reliable supply of food for our animals, we had only two days to seek out this discovery before we had to move back to the oasis. If Fardin had not found something worthwhile to glean information from, then the plan was to return for another pair of days before taking the long road back to an unfallen civilization.

In the interest of finding something useful as quickly as possible, some in the group took a less academic approach in their search for artifacts. The enchanter didn't reprimand them too much, as long as they kept away from the spots he deemed most interesting. They also promised to let him inspect everything they found before claiming it for themselves. These untidier excavations helped to reveal the bark of dead trees hiding under the sand. There were even a handful still standing, but most of these looked ready to crumble away as soon as a scorpion sneezed too close to them.

While I too didn't want to add an extra two days to the expedition, my lack of wind and earth spells made me useless in the excavation process. I would have experimented using small explosive stones to clear away pockets of sand, but even if it weren't for the chukurn risk, that didn't strike me as the greatest of ideas. So when I wasn't on guard duty, I simply traversed the ruins and gathered any piece of dead wood that could keep a fire alive.

It was late evening when somebody uncovered lettering etched on the stone ground. This particular white stone was lining the river and the small amount of writing looked to be a short edict. I didn't need Fardin to tell me that the language was not in the Old Voreen *Summertide* was written in. The supposed language of Old Voreen was a dense mixture of condensed words that flowed into one another and which was used extensively in the current Voreen's early regime.

On the other hand, the carved words at our feet were spaced far apart and had a few images that looked to be hieroglyphic in nature. Fardin was especially excited about these little figures. He, his assistants, and Ghevont chatted nonsensically for several minutes, using technical words few sword-wielders would ever bother learning.

When Ghevont became free, which was after he acquired a rubbing of the words, I asked him, "Having fun?"

"Some form of it, yes. You're not experiencing any amount?"

"I wish I was. Might make it a bit more bearable out here."

"You know, in my previously sheltered life, I always imagined everyone had a natural inclination to seek out knowledge, but that doesn't appear to be the case."

"Most people are just concerned with getting by."

"Yes, but 'getting by' can be made easier with more knowledge, no?"

"Depends on the knowledge, but that's why civilizations have scholars. I don't know if 'fun' is the way I would describe it, but I do find it interesting that Fardin's theory could be true, at least as far as the Advent are concerned."

"Yes, it seems their *Summertide* map was written by somebody in Voreen and passed off as something that came from the lost nation. The original author must have only been concerned with making their secret map, not about preserving real history."

"Perhaps someone with interests in both a dead god and getting power through a fake bloodline."

"Possibly. The differing languages also don't exclude a connection between the old and new, it merely weakens the assumed one. It does bring to question why someone hid the map in this roundabout manner. If they knew the location of a dead god's grave and wanted power, then why not take the grave for themselves? The diverse locations in the poem infer a well-learned, well-traveled individual who certainly could have taken advantage of such information."

"Some people don't actually want to handle world changing forces, Ghevont, but I suspect the reasoning and circumstances of someone who died two thousand years ago might be forever lost to us."

With assured conviction, he said, "We'll see about that."

I wasn't sure if the location of the ruins had anything to do with it, but the desert night became bitter enough to force us to use a portion of the gathered wood to build a fair-sized campfire. As I sat on a half-buried tree trunk absorbing a little heat before taking my nap, Leo, Athan, and Menalcus sat down beside me. Of all the pirate subgroups that would form, this particular triad was the most commonly seen together.

"We've been wondering," began Leo, "when are you going to ask us about your father?"

"It's a long way back to Ecrin, but if you guys are feeling left out, I suppose we can get this out of the way now. Let's start with you, big guy."

"Well, truth be told, I'm more of a friend to Thoris than Lorcan," said Menalcus. "I respect your father, of course. I've rarely questioned his orders, and even the ones I don't agree with are explained well enough for me to understand why he does something. Still, I'm here because of Thoris."

Athan laughed. "Should I tell him your lust for him or do you want the moment to be special?"

"Shut up! You're the one here to protect Lucetta."

With an angry whisper, Athan said, "Keep your damn mouth shut! I was just joking around and you have to spread shit like that?"

"Then don't call me a queer!"

Facing me, a chuckling Leo said, "As you can see, our fat friend here actually has very thin skin. Poking him always provides a good hour of entertainment."

"I do not have thin skin," said Menalcus, slapping his swollen belly. "It's simply a sensitive subject for me. You see, it turns out that my brother

215

bends that way. I've even heard stories that my father might have been… Well, at any rate, the knowledge alarmed me. I know I shouldn't worry. I have plenty of proof that tells me I'm not, but I can't help but get touchy about it."

"This is way more information than I wanted," I said.

Leo shook his head. "Information I'm sure you'll find invaluable in the future."

"Returning to what I do want to know, why are you out here?"

"Nothing as complicated as loving my captain's woman or my sexuality." Athan stuck up his middle finger. Menalcus followed his example. Leo only smiled back at them. "I was once caught by slavers not long after I joined the crew. Didn't think he'd come back for me, but he did. I owe my life to your father, simple as that. I've yet to find an opportunity to repay the favor directly, but I think finding you and your brother will finally make us even."

"And what happens if his next kid gets kidnapped? He's on his own?"

"Then it's obvious the gods loathe Lorcan's children. I won't fight against that kind of sanctified persistence."

Chapter Twenty-Three

There were two discoveries as I slept. The first was a crypt beneath what Fardin assumed to be a place of worship. He determined the structure's purpose by evaluating the size of the wide structure and by the small spires that bookended the center of the otherwise flat roof. Most of the tombs below had writing etched onto them, giving the scholars more rubbings to work with. In addition, the temple's undercroft held some artifacts the mercenaries avidly snatched up. They included a few dull jewels, silver pots and urns, and clay dishes.

My father wisely let the mercenaries keep most of the discovered relics. He recognized the untested mercenaries would be more willing to fight if they believed they had a store of riches to protect. It was possible this decision disgruntled his inherently covetous crew, but they did not join him for the prospect of more coin. Still, I later caught Lucetta and Sophia admiring a little purple gem before they spotted me. Sophia put it in a pocket, pecked my cheek with her lips, and told me not to let Lorcan know what I had just seen.

The second discovery was actually a marriage of two finds in the same area. Of greater interest to the scholars, the side of a black watchtower revealed itself at the bottom of a small dune. Between this dune and another, a patch of wildflowers and grasses grew a mile from the city ruins. According to the spotters, a group of mercenaries led by Lorcan and Lucetta, there wasn't a great deal of plant life, but it was thought worthwhile enough to begin sending the weaker beasts of burden to replenish some of their energy. Soon after waking, I and others were sent to watch over the first herd of hungry animals.

Dawn had crawled over the tall horizon by the time my group arrived at the feeding ground. Fardin didn't want to leave the city, so he asked Ghevont to study the watchtower in his place. Both assistants wanted to leave their master and join their more open-minded colleague, but due to her longer rest, only Janna joined us. Knowing this would be an all-day objective, we set up the wall-lacking tents near the base of the watchtower. From there we regarded the animals, making sure they didn't eat too much of the scant plant life or stray too far.

I volunteered to look after the second group of animals as well, which switched with the first herd a couple of hours before noon. This started the chain reaction of the pirates deciding to stay where they were, meaning Thoris, Menalcus, Yang, Sophia, and Gerard stayed part of my group. One of the four mercs also didn't change venues.

About an hour later, Sophia stood up from her meditation pose, a stance she often used when she cast her prana-detecting spell. She stepped over to me and said, "I felt something to the west. It's faint, but I can definitely tell it's not human. It's way too big."

I waved over Thoris and the three of us climbed to the top of the dune's steep slope. It was hard to see anything in the horizon's hazy heat, but we could soon make out a moving dust cloud a thousand yards away. It hovered just above ground level and charged toward the ruined city.

"Is that one of those worm things?" asked Sophia. "It's moving pretty damn fast."

"No way we can intercept it before it hits the city," I said.

"We'll have to try," said Thoris.

Just before Thoris shouted at the others below, I said, "Wait, what if we attract the worm to us?"

Making sure he heard me correctly, he said, "You want to attract it to us?"

"Yes."

"Do you think that's wise? The city does have walls and more manpower."

"Sure, but I think I have a good way to kill it quickly. Once it's dead, we can start moving out of this godsforsaken place. That sound okay with you?"

"You're certain you can kill it?"

"If it behaves like I've been told it will, then yes. Bring up a mule with a pack for me. I'll get the worm to come to us."

The pirate nodded and ran back down. Sophia remained beside me, bow in hand. I summoned ten of my bigger explosive stones and chucked them as far as my arm strength allowed. I ignited them as they struck the ever-shifting ground. The first four explosions didn't bring any reaction from the sand cloud, but the fifth one had it finally turn in my direction. Under the billowing dust was an incoming groundswell of sand ten feet wide. Thoris came back up with a mule when the enemy was about three hundred yards away. Just about everyone else came up with him.

I told everyone to stay as still as possible and summoned a heavy pile of dragon stones, dropping them in the pack slung over the mule's back. With the worm less than a hundred yards away, I slapped its rear to compel it to move away from us. The mule sensed the groaning ground and started galloping away from the sand wave.

"Clever," said Gerard. "If a little cruel."

"I could strap stones on you next time, if you prefer."

"That will be unnecessary."

We watched as the sand wave rushed past us, chasing after the scampering bait. The speed of the underground enemy was easily faster than the mule's sprint over the malleable ground. While a part of me hoped the mule outran its otherworldly predator, a bigger part of me wanted my plan to work. Sixty yards later, my plan bore fruit. A few feet behind the mule, the stretched wave vanished a moment. The still running mule then disappeared in a splatter of sand. It stayed missing when the sandy splash settled.

219

Wanting to bring the worm back within my range, I heaved a few rocky explosives, set those off, and told everyone to move behind me. The ploy worked. The sand wave appeared again, twisting and shifting the sand near its latest feeding ground before heading our way. I focused and waited to sense my dragon stones enter my prana's influence.

My training said I could ignite the stones from thirty or so yards, but the chukurn's thick hide blocked an easy transfer of prana. I had to wait for it to get an uncomfortable forty feet away before I felt the glimmer of prana come within my extrasensory grasp. I poured enough spirit energy to trigger every last stone at the same time.

A geyser of sand blasted into the sky. Immediately succeeding that was a gurgling growl coming from a lofty shadow. The tubular shape writhed in the air a moment before its enormous girth crashed onto the dune's surface. The murky dust and blurry shadow transformed into the squirming body of a chukurn, fifty feet of which was above ground. All its frills were flared and it was trying very hard to screech out the seething agony raging in its stomach, but a chukurn did not have a well-developed voice. The best it could do was mutter its misery in warbling grumbles.

With strained effort the worm lifted its head and opened its three mandibles wide enough to almost unhinge off its face. It next fell forward and swallowed half a mountain of sand, looking for anything that could smother the internal flames. It was either not enough or too much. The beast spun its bulk to dig deeper into the dune, but it stopped tunneling a few moments later. A segment of its twisting body was still exposed, sluggishly stirring the sand around it. Whether it was dying or not mattered little. It was obviously incapacitated and that was enough for us to gather our animals and get them back to the ruins.

Fardin tried to convince everyone we were safe from chukurn attacks as long as we stayed within the debilitated city walls, but no one bought it. We gave him two hours to collect everything he wanted to bring before the expedition would begin to move through the Kitiri tunnel, with or without him.

The start of our trip back to Prusal did have the disgruntled enchanter uniting with us. The mules who had their sariff sold were now lugging precious artifacts and rubbings. To try and stifle the telling vibrations of our movements, we elected to keep the caravan as sparsely bundled as possible, placing the more lucrative animals at the center. This arrangement appeared to work. Sophia's spell and the vigilant guides didn't pick up any chukurn activity as we moved briskly through the Howling Dunes over the next two days. The strong winds also helped deaden any noise we produced.

There was some relief when we exited the Hadarii's heart, but the animal bones we found earlier told us we were still well within chukurn territory. In any event, without an oceanic amount sand to traverse, it was believed the chukurn couldn't move as speedily in the shallower sand and hardier dirt.

Our first real rest came on reaching the first settlement we had rediscovered. Two of the weaker animals we didn't get a chance to feed were getting too frail to carry anyone or much of anything. I chose these animals, a mule and a camel, to act as more sacrificial temptations for the worms. They would also be the first to go should our food supply get too low. The items they carried were conveyed to others and replaced by my dragon stones. A long rope tied to these unwilling martyrs kept their fates aligned. I put Ghevont in charge of them.

Waiting for the hottest part of the day to subside, a big group of us began playing cards, which included my father. I assumed I would be good at reading body language and calling bluffs, but it turned out that my people-reading skills failed me when I didn't much care about the outcome. However, the more I lost, the more I started caring. Just as I was going to show everyone

221

the hand that would win the latest round, the group turned to notice a sprinting Gerard coming up to us.

The Alslana knight said, "The guides picked up a crawling dust cloud to the east. It's not heading for us right now, but it's out there."

In the midst of the group getting up to see what Gerard spoke of, Lucetta was entering the west side of the camp in her own run. To her husband, she said, "Malu saw something. I got Sophia to double check, but she didn't have to use her spell before we saw the dirt cloud ourselves. She cast her spell anyway and picked up another worm a little farther out."

"Three of them?" said Thoris. "Shit, we'll have to split up."

Turning to Lucetta, my father said, "Gather anyone who can't fight and round them up by the wall over there. Stay with them."

She nodded, kissed him, and dashed off. Not waiting to hear whether my father assigned me anywhere, I left to get my baits. I cut the rope in the middle and handed the camel to Ghevont. I took my mule eastward. Hearing the success of my last plan, a few animals had their packs removed and their pirate or mercenary handler pulled them toward the margins of the expedition. I didn't have enough dragon stones to fill anymore packs, meaning they would have to use different strategies on their lures.

The protectors of the expedition encircled the ruin, watching as the dust clouds circled us like sharks at sea. The region did not have many large dunes, so I was glad to see the dust clouds were slowed down by the bumpier soil. Yet even their slowed speed looked faster than a narrow-footed human running across this unstable land. A few minutes later and word came that Sophia sensed another worm enter her range. Still, they kept their distance.

"Fascinating behavior," said Ghevont, who helped keep my camel-decoy near me. "I wonder if they know what happened with the last chukurn? Or does being in a group increase their intelligence? Aranath doesn't know if they often work together, does he?"

222

"He doesn't. He does know they won't stay wary for long. This desert doesn't have the food they need to sustain themselves. Even with the animal offerings, they must be starving."

The sand-sharks appeared to be circling closer to us, foot by foot. I was getting anxious and began inching my way toward them. The heavy dust trails they kicked up had me feeling as though we were in the eye of a sunny typhoon, and all we could do was wait for its tumultuous winds to break for us. An unseen cue finally had the storm rapidly contracting. The worms continued their circular pattern in their new haste, making it difficult to determine where a worm was going to end up.

As before, I tried being proactive. Towing my nervous mule behind me, I broke from the defensive line to approach our ravenous enemy. The continuous tunneling through the hard soil generated a steady thunderclap that grew louder and louder. The soles of my feet felt the dull rumble increase with it. Since I was certain releasing the mule prematurely would simply have it run deeper into the camp, I had to keep hold of it longer than I liked.

When one of the dirt waves crossed eighty feet in front of me, I let the rope go and insisted the mule go forward by jabbing its hindquarters with my sword. The animal whinnied away from me, too pained to notice it was heading straight for the sand wave. The worms on the opposite side must have attacked sooner than mine did, as the area behind me erupted with the crackling hums of spells being cast and launched. With no word from a nearby Thoris or human screams forcing a review of the battle, I reserved my focus on what was ahead of me.

The worm's wave turned toward the mule. To prevent the mule's wits from turning it back, I threw an explosive stone and ignited it over its head. The little blast actually seemed to confuse the damn thing and stopped it in its tracks. All the same, by the time it perceived the netherworld hunter, it could do little more than turn around before it was sucked below ground. I waited a

223

moment longer until releasing flames no known creature had yet learned to overcome.

Mimicking the first worm, this one surged upward, a shallow moan going up with it. Flames bared through its open beak. The chukurn hooked its head and then flung it sideways. A ball of fire catapulted out of its mouth. The cautious worm had evidently held its food in its beak longer than the first, giving it the chance to cough up its devitalizing indigestion before it inflicted the intended mutilation.

Flames and smoke still sprang from its feelers. To extinguish it, the worm dove back into the ground, twirling the sand and dirt around it in the miniature earthquake it induced in its thrashing. I didn't know what it would do next, but I knew I'd be too pissed off to care what I attacked next.

Walking backwards, I exclaimed, "Ghevont! Remove one of the packs!"

When I reached him, the scholar dropped the heavy pouch at his feet. I went behind the camel and jabbed the point of my sword in the same place as the last animal. The distressed beast kicked its way forward, heading for the still churning soil. The blending ground suddenly shot toward the camel and tripped it up. A fountain of sand exploded alongside the newest bait. The chukurn's fuming upper form, eight feet wide and thirty feet tall, slammed down on the struggling camel. I briefly thought about triggering the camel's remaining pouch, but since I didn't imagine it would do much damage, I picked up my pack of stones and ran toward the worm.

The chukurn was sliding back down its hole, but I wanted it to stay above ground. "Earth spell! Hold it!"

A pulse of sand tightened around the chukurn's powerful body. There was no way Ghevont and Thoris could prevent a determined worm from breaking the hold, but the resistance seemed to puzzle it. It then detected something approaching it and, despite me being out of its range, bashed its head down to either crush or antagonize. Neither one happened. I needed its beak to open again, but it stubbornly kept it sealed. Noticing some of its body had stayed over the compressed camel, I ignited the dragon stones scattered around it. The flames convulsed the worm's body, opening its jaws wide enough for me to toss in the pouch.

I knew I couldn't just ignite them as before and let it be. I needed to fan the flames. Focusing on my training, I stood as still as possible and linked my prana with every rune I sensed within the chukurn's mouth, who was now spinning to both douse the fire and break the spells' hold. When everything but its sixteen foot long beak slipped back down, I poured a good chunk of my refined prana into the stones. The dragon flames burst forth, but I didn't lose immediate control. As the chukurn rushed upward again, I sent a dense bubble of prana into the flames, turning it into an inferno that cracked the chukurn's beak. The taxing effort spun my brain and forced me to fall on my hands and knees.

The most pitiful bellow I ever heard left the worm's body, but I didn't have the energy yet to see what it was doing. I did feel Ghevont place a hand on my shoulder and cast a kind of healing spell that transferred part of his prana into me. It would take a master to actually refill my spirit reserve, but he helped stabilize the prana I still carried. With the aid of a firm hand offered by Thoris, I stood up to see where my next steps should take me.

From the worm's hole, something that sounded like a hollow belly grumbling for food throbbed below the sand. The chukurn was there, but with an enfeebled beak, I doubted I had to worry about it burrowing with dangerous speed anytime soon. Surpassing the weak whimpers of the chukurn was the shrill wind carrying the thumping effects of casting. A sweep of my eyes behind me showed that the other three worms had, either through human tactic or chukurn perseverance, closed tighter around the ruins. This had the effect of

225

limiting their hulking movements, but they were also closer to the noncombatants.

Much of the action transpired to the northwest. Two of the worms were close together there, with one getting its flogging head blasted by every element. I don't know who managed it, but a thin green gash extended several feet past its beak. The second had gone under and was trying to circle behind the defenders to get to the panicking animals, but swirling earth spells deterred its trajectory. Both were being engaged by most of the pirates, including my father, a few mercenaries, and the tribal men.

The majority of the mercs were in battle with the chukurn straight to the west. In its effort to sweep away the human annoyances, the worm used its long tail like a thick whip. One of these lashes of the tail sent somebody crashing against a corner of a ruined structure. Sophia stood on a pile of rubble at the center of the ruins and fired her arrows at any part of the worm that came inside her bow's scope.

Also aiding the sell swords was Gerard, his knightly code urging him to help those he believed needed it more, I'm sure. Imagining myself having to tell a freshly motherless Odet that someone else she cared for was dead urged my steps toward the young knight. I had the ability to summon a few more dragon stones, but not the prana to take possession of their flames again. I thus didn't have much of a strategy beyond supporting those who still carried the capacity to cast their spells.

Getting nearer a scene jumbled by the grimy wind had me seeing that Yang was part of the western group as well. He and Gerard were among a group of two other mercs retreating from the worm's latest floggings when I caught up with them.

With a glance, Gerard studied my face and said, "I suppose you don't have much of your special fire left."

"No, but I do know we can stop them if we can break their beaks."

"That won't be easy. This one won't even show us its pretty face."

"It will, and we all have to focus on its beak when it does."

The cagey chukurn persisted in implementing its rear appendage. It still tried eating us by sucking the sand we stood over, but as long as we paid attention to the swelling ground, we easily avoided its suction attacks. I didn't like us wasting valuable energy on its tail alone, but I couldn't think of a way to force its head to the surface.

After ducking out of the way, I rolled backward to analyze the battleground. Yang was running straight for the front end of the worm. He stopped midway across and splayed his hands on the ground. Using an earth spell, the ground around him began pulsating up and down, as though he were beating a drum. The wave of sand veered toward this enticing beat.

"You don't think…" I told Thoris.

"I've seen crazier tactics."

"Did they work?"

He ran faster toward his crewmate.

Yang didn't react to either Thoris' calling his name or to the sand wave going under him. The pirate was swallowed in a puff of sand. Everything on our end paused for a few seconds.

Nothing happened until the mist of earthen powder completely blew away, prompting the worm to head right for us. We didn't take a step back before its head broke out from its lightless underworld. Sticking out from the center of its beak arose three glistening spikes of ice. The great worm shook its head, trying to fling these barbs off its face. It then smashed the ground with its body, rolling itself right for us. More of its body emerged in the process.

We had to leap out of the way to dodge a flattened fate. Almost everyone else was located at the safer tail end, but Malu needed some quick thinking to avoid being squashed to a pulp. He decided to run *at* the rolling mass and used a burst of air to help him jump on top of the worm. Then, with a precarious balance, the mercenary made his way to the tail end and dove off.

The chukurn's body stopped rolling to contract and curl up. This constricted form next sprang outward. It was incredible to witness something longer than a small ship use such built-up energy to maneuver itself so suddenly. It whirled its head to the west, its tail snapping toward us. All of us ducked out of the tail's path. Some of the sand grains I kicked up went into my eyes, forcing me to stay down a few seconds longer to wipe them out. Those extra seconds on the ground turned out to be fortuitous. The tail had come swinging back.

Thoris saved Ghevont by tackling him to the ground. However, Gerard on my left and one of the mercenaries to my right were barely picking themselves off the ground. My instinct told me to swing my leg under Gerard, getting him quickly back on the ground. He probably could have dodged on his own, but I wasn't taking any chances. The inept sell sword did not react in time. He soared for a hundred feet before becoming one with the nameless sand particles I already associated the mercenaries with.

The beast stopped spinning and grumbled in deep rumination. It was beginning to roll again when the mercs near its head started hurling more spells, but knowing this would only serve to start another round of monolithic wriggling, a word from Malu stopped them.

"You still in there, Yang!?" Thoris asked the worm's still slowly rotating head.

A muffled "Yes" answered him.

"Just try not to get swallowed! We'll get you out in a minute!"

"Is that one of your men?" Malu asked Thoris when he met him near the head. "Crazy bastard."

"Get the others to help with the other two worms. Tell everyone to break their damn beaks."

228

Not long after the mercs left, taking Sophia with them, the chukurn's tail acted up again. It punched and twisted into the ground, making a hole it slinked backwards into.

"Crap," said Thoris. "Yang! It's trying to go back underground! Get out now!"

"No!" said Gerard. "Wait until it goes almost all the way in! We'll all then combine spells to break open its beak!" To us, he explained, "It'll just thrash around if we attack now, but we should be able to hold its head long enough for Master Hur to escape once the rest of it is confined within the hole."

Thoris reluctantly agreed with his assessment. It was a dawdling suspense watching the worm bury its seventy foot length in reverse, about a foot a second. Having no spell to contribute in the pirate's breakout, I started receding from this circumstance to have a head start on the others, but I keenly observed the proceedings unfold. Just as the beak pointed skyward, Thoris, Ghevont, and Gerard combined earth spells to squeeze the sand around the chukurn's head.

"Now, Yang!"

One of the ice spikes shot outward, creating a wider hole when the thicker back-end of the icicle burst through the beak. The worm quivered and was able to drop a few feet lower, but the earth spells held it tight a few seconds longer. A slash of Yang's curved sword made the hole broader still. The worm broke the casters' hold and rapidly descended. Yang himself jumped through the weakened section of the beak just before the cavity disappeared. I expected him to be slimed up with worm fluids, but the mouth of a living chukurn was apparently as dry as a dead one. The quiet pirate nodded when asked if he was all right.

We went to reinforce the already prevailing humans. It drained everyone's physical and spiritual energy, but one of the remaining worms had

229

its beak cracked. The other seemed to hear the abject moans of its wounded brethren and took them as a sign that it too would be suffering if it persisted in its attacks. The healthiest chukurn thus withdrew, though its dust trail could be seen roaming the distance. While the one with the cracked beak still had the ability to burrow, it was far too slow to become a threat. This debilitation, however, didn't manage to halt its attacks until ten minutes after its companion had left. It then slothfully excavated three hundred yards of ground before stopping entirely.

Not a single one of us stood on their feet after the immediate danger passed. Every chest heaved, not caring that we breathed in the sand the wind gusted at us. Lorcan quickly took stock of the situation, confirming that every pirate's head was still working. Menalcus suffered a broken arm and Aristos had drained his prana to the point he fainted as soon as the last menace turned around to leave. Despite the injury, it was Menalcus who carried Aristos back over his uninjured shoulder.

Both guides also survived, but Banering's left arm dangled at his side. As for the mercenaries, three had been killed by body or tail and another was swallowed whole. I sensed some animosity grow between pirate and sell sword, as I was certain the paid men had noted the pirate's tendency to aid one another over any merc.

Three facts prevented the strife from reaching a contentious level. Firstly, the mercenaries weren't unified or skilled enough to threaten a seasoned pirate crew. The second was knowing that the untimely deaths of their associates meant more coin for them in the end. Of course, it was still a long journey to reach that end, making it the final reason no one would get at each other's throats. If we wanted to survive the last march out of the Hadarii, then every able bodied warrior was going to be needed.

With at least one healthy worm still in the area, we couldn't spend any time resting or going over growing grudges. We assembled the animals that

230

had strayed from the ruin and forced our weary legs to slog through what remained of the unconquerable desert.

Chapter Twenty-Four

No one noticed we had lost a sariff pouch until a full three days after the chukurn attack. This was half our remaining supply. If we didn't want capricious barbarians to respond poorly to their share of missing sariff, then our only choice was to avoid them altogether when the plants ran out. All the energy we expended in the worm fight also compelled us to exhaust our dwindling food cache. A feeble mule had to be killed a week after noticing the lost sariff to provide meaty nutrients for a few days.

Four days after that and we met with a roving tribe. We ended up trading much of our sariff for a collection of hardy cactus fruits. As it turned out, less than three days later, we ran into a large trading caravan with a much more varied stock of grub, some of which included literal bugs. A handful of seeds and roots for each of us was all we obtained on trading the little sariff we had left. As soon as this transaction finished, we created scout teams to look out for any sign of barbarian activity, our goal being to elude them at all costs.

The scout teams, which almost always included the guides, were largely successful in steering us away from more of their ilk, but not always. One windy night suddenly had forty tribesmen warriors flanking one side of the main group. All had their bows or spellbound arms trained on us. Luckily, Fardin's rough understanding of their dialect allowed the enchanter to talk them down a little. The tribal warriors apparently believed we might have been sell swords hired by a rival tribe to fight them. Fardin convinced them that our goal was academic, but as a sign of "goodwill," we were obliged to give up six of our best animals.

The mercenary treasures had to be moved to the remaining beasts. Since the added weight meant they could no longer carry people, basically everyone had to travel on foot the rest of the way. Only Fardin and his assistants could get away with riding the less burdened camels more often than not. Our weary legs needed longer rest periods, but having fewer animals at least meant less food to feed them. In fact, with the constant threat of barbarians and our desire to see civilization again, we reduced the number of times we stopped to let the animals graze on whatever plant life we came across.

Encounters with barbarians still occurred, but we were good at sidestepping the bigger groups, so these minor happenstances never escalated into anything serious. It helped that a group of over two dozen tired, dirty, irritated warriors was not a group one wanted to piss off. My experience with long treks on foot and familiarity with teeth-splitting pain gave me the fortitude to endure the final leg of our journey. Indeed, I felt as though I could leave everyone behind if I upped the pace by another mile an hour. I resisted the urge to go at my own speed, however.

As for everyone else, their states varied between solid health and suffering severe bouts of heat stroke and malnutrition. A few mercs underwent the worst symptoms, but Menalcus also needed to be treated for exhaustion, which likely came about due to the extra energy his broken arm needed to heal itself. His comrades gave up rations of their food and water to keep the big guy from passing out, but it still required four days of diligent observation before he was really out of danger. These sicknesses slowed us down somewhat, but we weren't going that fast to begin with. All in all, the slowdown probably didn't add more than a couple of days to the journey.

The first sign we were finally nearing a place to bathe off all the damn sand was when the guides and two of the traders separated from us to enter a large oasis controlled by a friendly tribe. Days later and an actual town with intact buildings of stone and wood was reached. This sight uplifted everyone's spirits back to what they were when we found Kitiri'mor. We stopped by that afternoon and filled up a small tavern to the brim, wasting the few coins we carried to buy anything with alcohol in it. I didn't get drunk, but it was the closest I had ever been. Despite the day of good business, I was sure the owner did not enjoy the sweaty stench that seeped into every wooden plank in his building.

Two and a half months after leaving Behar-Dural, its torches lit the eastern horizon on the cool night we came upon it. Our cheerful curses awoke every comfortable bastard in their bed as we marched down the city streets. Only Yang Hur kept his joy within himself, though I had no doubt it stirred somewhere inside him.

Everyone inside the college was awake, so there was no worry about our shouts disturbing dreams. Of course, that wasn't to say some old men weren't disturbed when they learned Fardin had found the legendary city. The testimonies and artifacts were almost not enough to convince the other enchanters of our feat. It was at the college where the procedure to account for every relic began. This was particularly important for the mercenaries, as they would need official documents to make a clay pot as valuable as a small house to art dealers and other academic institutions.

I wanted to immediately find any body of water to wash off the sand and dirt chafing in every fleshy crevice, but one of Fardin's pile of letters was addressed to me. It was a small piece of paper with no identifying marks, except for a week old date. The start of its short message was "A Business Proposal II." Three lines followed. The first said, "Both fit the description. They're fairly close to one another, so I hope this doesn't cause the scholar much confusion. Clarissa sends her regards." Below this line was a row of numbers, town names, and geographic points.

I would have given it to Ghevont right then, but I wanted to give his drained body a chance to recuperate. I thus went ahead with my bathing plan first. Before I stopped over at a communal bath, I and many of the pirates dropped off most of our desert clothes at a washhouse. It was the middle of the night, but the unwalled building by the small river stayed open at all hours.

Given the lack of other customers, the women there said they'd be done with everything in a couple of hours. As planned convenience would have it, the communal bath was a short walk upriver. After a long soak, I realized I would need a week more of baths to wash all the grime out.

Ghevont awoke in the inn bedroom we shared near noon. Not wanting to discuss what we needed to in public, I showed him a tray of food I had brought up for him. Leaning against his cup of lemonade was my letter.

"What's this?" he asked on picking up the note.

"Look for yourself."

He unfolded it and read the minimal contents. "So they found two possibilities, then."

"Will that disrupt your calculations?"

"Yes, but these coordinates are no more than fifty miles apart, so my 'confusion' will only slightly expand the circle of error that was always going to exist."

"How long until you can get a location?"

"Assuming I find the map I need at the college, then I suspect my calculations will take half a day's time."

"It'll take that long to line up some points on a map?"

"Tell me, Mercer, what is the shape of Orda?"

"A ball?"

"And of a map?"

"A square or rectangle."

"A *flat* rectangle. For me to correctly line up points separated by thousands of miles, I'll have to take into account the curvature of Orda and of the ancient techniques used to account for it two thousand years ago. Not to mention I now need to examine two different coordinates."

"And someone did all that centuries ago?"

235

"Impressive, no? We are obviously dealing with a mind as brilliant as my father's. I can only pray my work lasts as long."

"Just do me a favor and don't become as obsessive about a dead god as they did."

After eating what would likely be his last meal of the day, Ghevont and I headed back to the college to find the appropriate map. With easy permission from Fardin, the scholar rifled through dozens of ancient maps before finding three he liked. Fardin also gave Ghevont an office one of his few enchanter allies wasn't using. I didn't have to stay with him, of course, but realizing we were so close to finally discovering the grave site had me fixed to Ghevont's side as he worked. Gods forbid I leave him a minute only return to find a lodged grape had killed him.

The benefit of being in a building with only old cranks was that everybody minded their own business as quietly as they could. Not many sounds rose above Ghevont's scratching quill. I couldn't blame Marcela in those times I saw her sleeping as her friend worked away. The scholar occasionally spoke out loud in five or ten minute bursts, but this was always in the hushed tone one used to speak with themselves. I told Lorcan beforehand that only he was allowed to bother Ghevont, so he used that consent to bring us a few fruits every three hours or so.

Riskel's son worked well after the sun went down, but neither he nor I showed any hints of drowsiness, not when his quickening quill stopped his random sessions of audible contemplation told me he was near a resolution. The scraping of his quill stopped seconds after the clock tower tolled eleven times. Ghevont pushed back his chair and stretched. The act triggered a big yawn.

I stood up from my chair by the door. "Ghevont? Did you find it?"

"Find? No, I've merely isolated a relatively narrow area the grave likely lies."

"How narrow?"

"A little less than six hundred square miles."

"That doesn't sound narrow."

"Neither does twelve hundred miles, but that would still be within my definition of success."

"I'll take your word on that. Where?"

"In Efios. It's officially within a strip of land owned by Uthosis, but no one really owns the jagged mountains the grave appears to be in. I couldn't have thought of a better place to hide a tomb… Well, maybe the bottom of an ocean, but the execution of such an act would require-"

"What do you know of Uthosis?"

"Only that it was much more important to history before all its port cities were seized by anyone with a boat. I'm implying they had a weak navy, you see. The mountain range begins at its eastern edges and twists and turns for two thousand miles more. Dotted throughout the range are several volcanoes that are regularly spewing ash and magma at one time or another."

"So within an area of sharp rocks, ashen skies, and angry mountains lies a grave fit for a god. Will you follow me here as well, scholar?"

Ghevont moved his lips to the side and cocked his head the opposite way. "Hmm, there's a high chance we'll meet with forces beyond our capabilities at the grave, isn't there?"

"Yes. I know you want to see what your father died for, what he was killed for, but is it worth adding yourself to the list? You can always study the aftermath of whatever happens, you know."

"All I've read are aftermaths, Mercer. In any event, our personal stakes are quite similar, are they not?"

"How so?"

"Well, the Advent have taken the memory of your family, no? This circumstance isn't much different from my own. The Advent have taken future memories of my family."

"Aye, I suppose that's true." I didn't point out the fact that I could at least make new memories with what remained of my family.

"In truth, ever since leaving Gwen I've had theoretical visions of my parents returning. How would that have changed things? What would Vey have been like? Or myself, for that matter."

Ghevont's logical monotone was the same as it always was, but I had a feeling the day I heard his emotions conveyed in his voice would be the day he became more like his sister. "I know how this sounds, but I'm not sure a complete Rathmore family is a pleasant prospect for the rest of us."

"There's no evidence to dispute the contrary. I'm only selfishly contemplating, don't mind me. So you have no arguments against my joining you?"

"I'd say you've earned the right for a thunderbolt to blow us all to bits."

"Why a thunderbolt?"

"I don't know. What do you see when you imagine a god rise from the dead?"

His eyes looked up for a moment as he imagined it. "Hmm, fascinating. The skies are in illumination in my vision as well. This can't be a coincidence, can it?"

"Ask a hundred other people and ninety of them… Forget it, this isn't important. I have to let Lorcan know what you found." Just before I closed the door, I said, "And good work, Ghevont."

"I thought so."

Made in the USA
Middletown, DE
20 May 2019